THE GOLDEN BIRD: TWO ORKNEY STORIES

George Mackay Brown (*1921–96*) was one of the twentieth century's most distinguished and original writers. His lifelong inspiration and birthplace, Stromness in Orkney, moulded his view of the world, though he studied in Edinburgh, and later under Edwin Muir at Newbattle Abbey College. From 1941 onwards he battled tuberculosis, and increasingly lived a reclusive life in Stromness, but despite his poor health he produced a regular stream of publications from 1954 onwards. These included *Loaves and Fishes* (1959), *A Calendar of Love* (1967), collections of short stories *A Time to Keep* (1969) and *Hawkfall* (1974), a widely read novel *Greenvoe* (1972), *Time in a Red Coat* (1984) and a steady output of prose and poetry, notably the novel *Beside the Ocean of Time* (1994), which was shortlisted for the Booker Prize and winner of the Saltire Book of the Year. His work is permeated by the layers of history in Scotland's past, by quirks of human nature and religious belief, and by a fascination with the world beyond the horizons of the known.

He was honoured by the Open University and by Dundee and Glasgow Universities. The enduringly successful St Magnus Festival of poetry, prose, music and drama held annually in Orkney keeps his memory alive and is his lasting memorial.

D0233826

GEORGE MACKAY BROWN

The Golden Bird:
Two Orkney Stories

Polygon

This edition published in Great Britain in 2008 by
Polygon, an imprint of Birlinn Ltd
West Newington House
10 Newington Road
Edinburgh
EH9 1QS

www.birlinn.co.uk

ISBN 978 1 84697 085 6

First published in 1987 by John Murray (Publishers) Ltd

British Library Cataloguing-in-Publication Data
A catalogue record for this book is
available on request from the British Library.

Typeset by Hewer Text UK Ltd, Edinburgh
Printed in Great Britain by Clays Ltd, St Ives plc

Contents

The Golden Bird   1

The Life and Death of John Voe   155

To Kenna Crawford

The Golden Bird

One

They had not spoken to each other, the crofts of Gorse and Feaquoy, for three generations.

And once Gorse and Feaquoy had shared the same boat, *Hopeful.* Together Amos of Gorse and Rob of Feaquoy had built *Hopeful* on the greensward above the shore stones, when they were young men.

Then they had married, Amos of Gorse to Tomina who came from Voes, 'district of bays', on the far side of the hill, after harvest. And the next spring Rob asked Mary Jean for his wife, who lived in the next croft, Aird.

They went fishing, Amos and Rob, day after day when it was weather to fish and work on the land didn't compel them too much. And they divided the catch on the shore – haddocks or lobsters – and Amos and Rob took their baskets of fish up to Gorse and Feaquoy.

One day the two wives Tomina of Gorse and Mary Jean of Feaquoy were at the shore when *Hopeful* came in to the noust. A westerly wind had gotten up when the men were at sea.

The waves fell in long broken thunders on the beach. Amos and Rob leapt ashore and dragged *Hopeful* up among the stones.

They had a score of lobsters in the baskets, with tied claws – a good catch.

At once they fell to dividing the catch, paying small attention to their wives, who came nearer and nearer, one from one side and one from the other, for Tomina and Mary Jean had never much to say to each other, and they had been standing well apart, waiting.

Now Tomina and Mary Jean watched while the men divided the catch of lobsters, each taking one after the other, a lobster of approximately the same size, for there were big lobsters and small lobsters and middle-sized lobsters.

Soon there were only two lobsters left, a medium one and a small one.

And Amos said to Rob, 'You take the bigger one, you did most of the hard work this morning.'

Rob said, 'I only rowed, you hauled the creels, I think you should have this one that is neither a grandfather nor a boy.'

The men pushed each other in the shoulder, and laughed. Then Rob picked up a small flat stone, and spat on one side of it, and said they should toss for the bigger lobster.

'No,' said Tomina from one side of the boat, 'but why is it, in every sharing of the two last lobsters, that Amos always gets the small one to take up to Gorse?'

'That isn't true, woman,' said Amos mildly.

'It seems to me,' said Mary Jean, 'that the lobster shells I see every time I pass the midden at Gorse, are bigger than the lobsters we eat up at Feaquoy. And, if I may say so, it's a filthy midden you keep up at Gorse.'

'Keep a sweet tongue in your head,' said Rob to his wife.

But Tomina stepped between them and took hold of a bunch of Mary Jean's hair and pulled it. Mary Jean cried out.

The two fishermen tried to come between them, but Mary Jean turned on Tomina and drew the five nails of her right hand down the side of Tomina's face, and the scratches quickly oozed blood.

Tomina screeched. She stamped her foot on the stone.

'You asked for that, woman,' said Amos to Tomina, 'when you pulled hair out of her head.'

Tomina picked up a large round stone, so heavy that neither of the fishermen could afterwards lift it by himself, and she flung it at the side of the boat. There was a sound of splintering wood. One of the planks was stove in.

'There will be no more unequal division of fish from this boat,' cried Tomina. She drew the back of her hand across her cheek, and the hand came away smutched with red.

'Well,' said Rob of Feaquoy, 'that's a pity, for it's good fishing weather, and we won't be able to fish again for maybe a week, till we get a new plank put into the boat.'

'That's true,' said Amos.

'That wife of yours, Tomina, she was the one that flung the big stone at the boat,' said Rob. 'So I think it's only fair that you, Amos, mend the boat. I have plenty to do with sheep and peats in the next day or two.'

'I have sheep and a peatbank too,' said Amos. 'Who began this fight? It was your wife, Mary Jean, who said that our midden of Gorse was filthy.'

No more words were spoken that day. They separated. Amos took Tomina, the one side of her face grid-ironed, up to Gorse, pushing her in front of him roughly.

And Rob took Mary Jean by the arm, gently, for she was crying (but silently), up to Feaquoy.

The two lobsters in dispute scrabbled on the hot stones and died before dark.

And neither Rob nor Amos moved to put a new plank into *Hopeful*. The six other fishing boats of the valley went west day after day and came back with good hauls.

If the men Amos and Rob met on the sheep-path or shore or on the road to the peatbanks, they swerved to avoid each other.

One night, late, Rob got out of his chair beside the fire, and laid his pipe on the hearth. He said he was going at once to speak to Amos of Gorse. 'We have been lifelong friends,' he said. 'This is not to be borne, that we should be enemies now, just because two women have had words. Besides, we must have lost a hundred lobsters this past week.'

As he was going out through the door into the sunset, Mary Jean cried out from the bed. 'I'm in great pain,' she whispered then, 'Go and get Frieda the midwife at once.'

Next morning there was a new child, a boy, lying in the new-made cradle at Feaquoy. It had long been settled that his name would be Peter.

Three weeks later the new cradle at Gorse received a wailing bundle too: a boy. They called him David.

All that summer the fishing boat *Hopeful* warped slowly among the huge round stones of the beach. By the end of harvest, men said, she would never be fit for sea again. 'And that's a pity,' said Andrew of Fleece farm in the smithy, 'because *Hopeful* was the best fishing boat in the valley.'

Mary Jean went to help in the harvest, on this croft and that, binding sheaves with the other women. Always Mary Jean worked on the other side of the line of sheave-binders from Tomina of Gorse. She laid her baby, Peter, in the shade of a stook, always with his back to the sea. Bronze shadows fell across the face of the child.

When the time came for the oat-field of Gorse to be cut, Mary Jean was not among the sheave-binding women.

And two days later, when scythes flamed among the Feaquoy barley, Tomina kept inside with her scarred face and her beautiful infant.

It is true, Rob had turned up at Gorse with his scythe. But Amos had said to him, 'We'll manage quite well without you.'

It's said, those were almost the last words that passed between Amos and Rob; before death, in the snow-time and daffodil-time of the same year, twenty years later, silenced them for ever.

Two

There lived in the sea valley at that time, at a croft called Don, a man called Magnus Fiord and his wife Willa. And in that same good harvest when the youngest children lay swaddled under the stooks, John Fiord, the child of Magnus and Willa Fiord, was set under a stook too while his parents helped in the barley harvest at the croft of Burnside.

While the scythes of the men flashed and crisped through the corn, rhythmically, one of the women looked up from her corn-gathering and saw an eagle in the sky, high up near the sun.

The corn sighed and fell. The corn was upgathered and bound and set in stooks.

At noon the barley field was half cut.

The woman who had seen the eagle looked up again, and there the eagle was, only now it had something white in its talons and it was going in a wide circle towards a high cliff in the hill beyond.

The woman's cry and her pointing finger caused all the harvesters to look up, shading their eyes with their hands.

Dod of Skeld said the eagle must have taken one of the lambs.

Soon after that the men put down their scythes and the women went to bring the baskets of bannocks and cheese, and the crocks of ale that were lying in a shadow of a wall.

Willa Fiord and Mary Jane Sinclair and Tomina Flett went to see to their babies.

Willa Fiord cried out!

'Bless us all,' said Magnus Fiord, 'I thought there was always peace in a harvest field. But no – screechings of women even here!'

Willa came running with the news that the child John was not under the stook where she had left him.

'The white thing that the eagle was carrying,' said Tom of Burnside, 'must have been Willa's bairn' . . .

Willa Fiord left the harvest field at once.

Magnus her man took a few steps after her, then returned. 'The child is dead,' he said. 'We may be sure of that. The living must have food next winter. I will go on with the scything.'

After the harvesters had eaten and emptied the stone jar, they all returned to their work. Magnus Fiord took no refreshment.

But the scything and binding went slower and more clumsily in the afternoon.

It was noticed that Tomina and Mary Jean crossed over from time to time to see that their children were safe.

'It will be a poor sad house that Magnus Fiord goes back to this night,' whispered one harvester to another.

But Magnus seemed to be working more steadily than any of the other men.

Just after sundown the last of the corn was cut.

Tom Spence of Burnside thanked all the valley people. Solemnly he invited the men inside for a glass of whisky.

The women went home, carrying the empty baskets and crocks. Tomina and Mary Jean lifted their babies from the bee-humming stooks and went their ways.

Solemnly the men raised their brimming glasses around and nodded and smiled. A good day's work had been done.

Magnus Fiord drank his whisky quickly and asked if he might have his glass filled again.

Tom of Burnside hastened to oblige him. The valley men looked at Magnus Fiord sadly as he drank the second glass of whisky at one gulp. 'He just threw the yellow stuff to the back of his throat,' said Amos Flett later, wonderingly.

'Now we will have to go home,' said Magnus Fiord. He walked out of Burnside while the others were still at the dregs of their whisky.

When Magnus crossed the burn towards Don, he saw that the lamp was burning in the window.

'My wife's more contented than I thought she would be,' said Magnus to himself.

When he opened the door, he saw that the fire was burning high and red.

'I thought she would not be caring about warmth or cold on such a day,' said Magnus.

And when he crossed the threshold he saw that Willa was knitting a white jacket for an infant.

'She's out of her wits with grief,' thought Magnus.

And when he stood uncertainly in the middle of the stone floor, he saw the cradle and the child lying blanketed in it with a little bubble at the corner of his mouth, that broke, silently. His mouth was fluttering with life.

Willa got up from her chair. She showed Magnus her scarred hands. 'What have I been doing?' she said. 'I climbed up the crag and took our bairn from the eagle. That's what I've been doing.'

And then Willa kissed her man, a thing that surprised Magnus even more than her climb up to the eagle's eyrie.

'I see you've been at the whisky,' said Willa. 'A fine way to carry on, seeing you were almost a widower and a childless man on the same day.'

'I'm sorry,' said Magnus.

'You shall have a third whisky seeing it has been a hard day for you,' said Willa. She went up to the cupboard and opened it and took out bottle and glass.

While Willa was pouring whisky into the glass, Magnus went over to the cradle once more to make quite sure he was not in a white dream.

Little tremblings of life came from the boy – breathings, a tremulous beat at the temples, a faint flush on the cheek.

Bending close above him Magnus could see the curl of an eagle-chick's feather in the boy's hair. There was a thin red criss-cross of lines high on the forehead.

He drank the third glass of whisky even faster than the second. Then he turned and ran out of the house and off under the stars – leavng the door to the clashings of the wind – to spread the news round all the crofts of the valley.

Three

Of the hundred or so folk who lived in the sea valley – as in nearly every small community everywhere on earth – it could be said that they lived in a kind of willed harmony. There were small disputes about this and that, a score of times a year; about a boundary stone, for example, or about who owned a piece of drift-wood, or two of the young men might fall out for a time about a girl – come to fisticuffs and swear-words, even – but in the end most things were settled amiably enough. If the disagreement went on for too long, the oldest man in the valley, Isaac Brims, would come down from his croft of Quoy, and bring the disputants together and reason with them, and more often than not there would be a shaking of hands, followed by an exchange of small gifts for the women of the disputants – a half-pound of tea, or a necklace bought years ago at Hamnavoe Fair.

In disputes over a girl, it was generally the girl herself who settled matters, after a month or so of teasing and playing the young men off against each other. And mostly the rejected one acquiesced, and turned away.

If there had not been this state of perpetual compromise, of 'mending of nets and fences', life in such a small community would have been impossible. Nobody in the sea valley thought matters out to such a conclusion, but each one knew it in his heart.

The April following the dispute at the shore between the crofts of Gorse and Feaquoy, Amos of Gorse said to his wife

Tomina, 'This won't do at all. I will put up with it no longer. I've made up my mind. Tomorrow I will walk across the valley to Feaquoy and I will offer Rob my hand. I know Rob will take my hand. It may not be too late, *Hopeful* our fishing boat isn't utterly beyond repair. It could be that by the beginning of June we'll be sailing to the haddocks and crabs once again, Rob and I, as in the old days.'

Next morning when Amos of Gorse, having breakfasted, went out of doors, he found that two of his lambs had been killed in the night. The creatures lay there with their throats torn.

'And I think we know well enough who is responsible for that,' said Tomina.

'No, I don't know who could have done it,' said Amos. 'It must have been a dog.' Tomina pointed across the valley at the croft of Feaquoy. 'Need you look further?' she said.

Then Amos walked slowly across to Feaquoy, and he met Rob of Feaquoy just where the burn, grown deep and dark and still here, washes the outfield of Feaquoy.

Rob waited peaceably for Amos to approach.

There was an awkward silence between them for half-a-minute.

'Can I do something for you, man?' said Rob at last.

'Two of my lambs were killed last night,' said Amos. 'I know that you did not do it. But I want you to tell me from your own mouth that you didn't cut their throats.'

Just then Mary Jean appeared at the door of Feaquoy.

'No, I did not do it,' said Rob. 'I don't kill animals except for food, or to put an end to their sufferings if there's no hope for them.'

Mary Jean cried from the door of Feaquoy. 'If it has entered your head that Rob had done this thing, let the evil take root! There was no need for you to come here.'

'Go indoors, woman,' said Rob. 'Keep your thoughts to yourself.'

Amos turned and walked back slowly to Gorse.

As he went in at the door, he heard Tomina saying to the child in the cradle, 'I want you to know this, buddo. There are wicked folk in this valley that would take your inheritance from you. You're the poorer by two lambs since yesterday. There are folk here that would like to see you end your days a pauper.'

'That's nonsense, woman,' said Amos. 'You will not fill the boy's head with such darkness.'

And later that night, after the lamp had been lit, Amos said to Tomina, 'Why is there blood on the blade of that fish-knife?'

'I found three rats in the trap in the barn,' said Tomina, 'and I took the knife to them.'

Four

Later that summer, in early August, Rob of Feaquoy went out of his house and found that his new wooden plough had been smashed to pieces. Rob had spent the previous week making the plough in his barn. It was a well-wrought plough and he was pleased with it.

As he was standing over the ruin, Mary Jean appeared at his shoulder. 'There,' said she, pointing, 'is the axe that did the damage.'

Under the wall of the barn lay an axe with a newly-ground edge to it. When Rob picked the axe up, he saw that the letters AF had been burned into the heft.

'Now even you must know,' said Mary Jean, 'who the destroyer was.'

'I think there may be more in it than appears.' said Rob.

He took the axe in his hand and walked across the valley to the croft of Gorse. Amos was putting a stone here and there in a low wall that divided Gorse from the neighbouring croft.

Rob stopped beside Amos, who was kneeling with a stone in his hands, trying to fit it into the wall.

'This axe,' said Rob, 'does it belong to you?'

'That's right,' said Amos. 'It does. There's my initials in the heft. I've been missing this axe for two days. Thank you for bringing it back to me, man.'

'My new plough,' said Rob, 'was broken with this axe sometime last night. I don't think that you did it. Nobody would be so foolish as to leave such evidence in the place of the crime.'

'I treat every plough with reverence,' said Amos. 'Without ploughs there would be no bread for the folk of the valley.'

There suddenly was Tomina, standing in the middle of the small field of Gorse. 'I know who broke your plough, man,' she cried. 'Didn't I see the shadow of that slut of a wife of yours going like a thief among our out-houses last night! I couldn't see her face, but I know the ill-favoured shape of her. When I went out to see her off, there she was three fields away, going to your ruckle of a croft. She has a long shape under her shawl. I saw something glittering in the moonlight.'

'Go back indoors, woman,' said Amos sharply. 'Most things you see under the sun are lies and darkness.'

Rob turned and walked quickly in the direction of Feaquoy.

Amos pondered for a while at the end of his croft, smoking his pipe. He did not go inside until he was sure his wife was in bed and the boy asleep in the cradle . . .

When Rob reached the threshold of Feaquoy, he heard Mary Jean crooning over the cradle, 'Yes, the plough is broken. There are people in this valley who won't be happy until the byre is broken, and the barn, and the beasts slaughtered and the thatch ablaze. Never forget that.'

Rob went inside. He said, 'It's a good thing the child is asleep and can't hear a word of the things you say.'

From that day there was no more talk exchanged between the crofts of Gorse and Feaquoy.

The fishing boat *Hopeful* was now a cluster of festering boards down at the shore.

Five

At the end of July, four years later, the two boys David of Gorse and Peter of Feaquoy went to the valley school, with a few other five-year-olds, including John Fiord of Don. From his infancy John Fiord had been known as Eagle John.

For three years now, in accordance with a government law, all valley children between the ages of five and twelve had been required to go to the newly-built school.

Mr MacFarlane the schoolmaster received the new pupils kindly, and gave each one a peppermint sweet to make them think well of school and books and lessons. He took care to seat David Flett of Gorse and Peter Sinclair of Feaquoy at opposite ends of the classroom. Tomina of Gorse had visited the schoolmaster at his house under the hill the previous night. 'I'd take it as a favour,' she said, 'if my boy David were kept well away from the boy of Feaquoy.'

'That can't be,' said Mr MacFarlane. 'Here all the pupils mix together freely. That is as it should be. It would be impossible, in such a small school, to hide two boys from each other.'

'I think,' said Tomina, 'I have been kind enough to you since you came to be the teacher here.'

'Yes, indeed,' said Mr MacFarlane. 'And I thank you.'

'Never a weekend but you don't get something or other out of Gorse – a cock chicken for your pot, or half a cheese, or a dozen duck eggs.'

'Thank you, thank you,' said Mr MacFarlane.

'All I ask,' said Tomina, 'is that my David doesn't sit at the same desk as that brat from Feaquoy.'

'They will sit at different desks,' said Mr MacFarlane.

'Good,' said Tomina. 'Here's half a dozen mackerel for your supper.'

Lessons went on tranquilly at the school. There was a break of two weeks in August, for the children to help in the harvest. Then it was back to school with them, every day, into autumn and winter.

There was a 'play-time' each morning, lasting a quarter of an hour, when the children (of all ages between five and twelve) ran wild in the school yard. The girls sang choruses as the skipping-rope sent the dust flying. The boys played rougher games, leap-frog or football, and sometimes the smaller boys got roughly handled. But Mr MacFarlane was always near at hand to sort out any trouble.

It happened one day that the ball flew high and David of Gorse ran to kick it as it came down. Other boys went helter-skelter for the ball, and there was a wild mix-up, and David fell out of the shouting tangle of boys with a bleeding gash on his knee. David cried out with the shock of it.

At once the boys stood still, and let the ball go bouncing away.

Mr MacFarlane was on the scene quickly, his reeking pipe between his teeth still.

David whimpered at sight of the blood welling down his leg.

'Who kicked this boy?' cried the teacher angrily.

The dozen boys looked at each other and shook their heads.

'Do you know who kicked you?' asked Mr MacFarlane to David.

David's finger pointed uncertainly round three or four big boys. Then it settled on Peter Sinclair. 'It must have been him. That boy kicked me when I wasn't looking.'

Peter shook his head. 'I don't think I kicked him,' he said. 'I might have kicked him, but I didn't mean to kick him.'

Mr MacFarlane took Peter by the scruff of the neck. 'You're a thug,' he said. 'Come inside. What you want is a good thrashing!'

At that Peter of Feaquoy began to yell and to resist the attempt of Mr MacFarlane to drag him into his room.

Eagle John stood between them. 'Sir,' he said, 'the ball was going this way and that, and there were so many boots flying who can say what boot it was that kicked David on the knee?' . . .

Mr MacFarlane looked at Eagle John, outraged, for a short time. Then he appeared to consider. Then he let Peter Sinclair go. 'If this hooliganism goes on,' he said, his voice echoing round the schoolyard, 'I will ban football at playtime from now on.'

The boys looked crestfallen.

'You, boy,' said Mr MacFarlane to David Flett. 'Go home, till your mother washes your knee and bandages it. There's nothing to make a song and dance about. Tell your mother you were kicked accidentally.'

But David didn't return to school for the rest of that day.

Instead his mother Tomina arrived at the school just after the end of classes.

'Well,' said she to Mr MacFarlane, 'and what do you intend to do about it? My boy might have lost his leg with blood-poisoning.'

'It was an accident,' said the teacher. 'Playing football, there's always the chance that a boy might be kicked.'

'Accident!' cried Tomina. 'It was that black-hearted boy from Feaquoy! And his mother put him up to it.'

'If you want to pursue the matter,' said Mr MacFarlane, 'you can take the boat to Hamnavoe and complain to the policeman there. But I think you'll have difficulty in proving your accusation, Mistress Flett.'

Tomina turned and went home.

From that day no more gifts arrived at the schoolhouse from the croft of Gorse – neither fish nor cheese, butter or eggs or fowls.

David of Gorse didn't have to have a pin-leg after all.

Six

And the years passed. And Peter Sinclair and David Flett sat in the same classroom, but apart from each other, learning words and numbers, turning the pages of history books and atlases, standing up to chant verses of Burns and Wordsworth and Mrs Hemans.

Never once did the two boys speak to each other.

Once of twice in the school yard when the school-children were eating their 'pieces', it was seen how wistfully Peter Sinclair looked over at David Flett, as if he longed to break the silence. One summer noon, as they squatted in the school yard with their cheese and bannocks, Peter suddenly got to his feet, and broke off a piece of bannock and cheese, and walked towards David, offering the fragments. (He had noticed that David had brought nothing from Gorse to eat.) And David rose too, his hand half out to accept.

Then this happened. One of the great skuas from the moor above descended with a wild flutter and seized the food from the two meeting hands, and swallowed it in one gulp, and away it circled and soared to the high moorland.

The two boys turned their backs on each other.

Word got round the valley about this incident.

That afternoon, late, it was Mary Jean of Feaquoy who turned up at MacFarlane's door. 'I always give Peter cheese and bread, or an oatcake, or an egg, to eat in the middle of the day. There are some women – one in particular – in this valley, that are too mean or too neglectful of their bairns to send them out to the school with a piece. I'm thinking of one slut in particular. If her boy is hungry, let him not beg food from Peter. I'm very glad the skua got it, not that trash of a boy from Gorse.'

'Mistress Sinclair,' said the teacher, 'I'm trying to correct some compositions. For that, I need silence. Good-day.'

It happened one day that winter, when snow lay thick in the valley, that nearly all the children ate their pieces on the way to school. When 'play-time' came, at noon, they sat round the school fire of peats, most of them empty-handed, though a few had a crust or two left. Outside, a half-blizzard was blowing. It was no weather for building a snowman or having a snow battle. Among the improvident ones, who had eaten their 'pieces' on the road to school – the snow having sharpened their appetite – were David Flett of Gorse and Peter Sinclair of Feaquoy.

It would be a long hungry time for them, between now and supper.

It happened that Eagle John Fiord had been wise enough to keep his mid-day 'piece' in his school bag, intact.

Eagle John unwrapped his paper poke. He broke the barley scone with cheese in the middle of it into three parts. He handed one fragment to David Flett, and another to Peter Sinclair. He did this as secretly as possible, but the other hungry children could not help but see it.

Eagle John turned his back on them and went quickly out into the snow-whirls with the third fragment. The children thought he must have gone to eat it there, alone among the drifts. But the boy Peter saw him scattering the pieces to the small birds.

Just before classes resumed, Mr MacFarlane appeared from the schoolhouse carrying a large bag of apples and oranges. How the twenty children cried out with joy! (Apples, oranges, and bananas were new luxuries in the valley.)

But Eagle John, out in the tumults of snow – the fruit was all eaten by the time he returned, with blue trembling hands, and snow-tangled hair.

Seven

Ever since they had stopped fishing together in *Hopeful*, Amos of Gorse and Rob of Feaquoy had fished with other crofter-fishermen. But one spring, ten years later, as if a single impulse had gone through them both, they began to build boats for themselves, each working near his croft; Amos at the gable-end, Rob in the yard.

Many generations of boat-building skill were in them, and the boats grew together, separated by the burn, on opposite sides of the valley, long lithe fluent shapes. As the boats were building, men would come in the evening, smoking their pipes, and examine the work in progress, and occasionally they would pass comments (but always in secret, muttering behind their hands, for in that valley it was unheard of either to praise or to blame openly.)

Having seen the progress of one boat, a few of the men would walk slowly across the fields to see how things were with the other boat. And they would meet, near the burn, a few other men going from Gorse (it might be) to Feaquoy.

They might, this evening or that, give it as their opinion that work on the two boats was going on 'all right', they were shaping up 'not bad' – they might catch a fish or two when the time came.

All the crofter-fishermen noted how well Amos and Rob were served by their two sons, who were always in attendance with hammers and clinkers and planes and saws.

At last, near mid-summer, the two boats were ready. The sails and the oars were stacked inside.

Amos was first to launch his boat – he called it *Daffodil*. It rode the swell beautifully. There, on the shore, after the trial, Amos opened a bottle of whisky and it went from mouth to mouth. But Rob was not there to drink to *Daffodil's* success.

The next week a dozen men dragged Rob's fishing boat through the fields, and then (carefully) over the big round stones of the beach to the little noust that had been prepared for it. 'She's to be called the *Skua*,' said Rob. Other men from the valley joined the group. They nodded. They thought *Skua* a good enough name for a fishing boat.

Peter came running down to the beach from the fields above. 'The whisky, daddo,' he shouted, carrying the bottle in both hands.

Solemnly the opened bottle went from mouth to mouth, sunwise, until it was empty. Old Isaac Brims of Quoy sprinkled the last few drops on the boat itself. 'May it come back as many times as it goes out,' he said.

Amos of Gorse watched from the headland a mile away. He shook his head, lit his pipe, turned, and walked slowly up to Gorse.

'May she get many a haul of jelly-fish, that *Skua*,' said Tomina as Amos came in at the door. 'May she have dealings soon with a big destructive whale.'

Eight

And the children up at the school – next morning, at play-time, for no reason at all, they fell to making mockery of the new fishing boats. It was *Daffodil* that they picked on first, going in a kind of ragged mocking ring about David. 'Ruckle of old boards,' they called *Daffodil* . . . 'The first big wave'll break her!' . . . 'Old Amos, he should have smashed her up for firewood' . . . They shrilled the insults all around David Flett. At first the boy's face reddened with rage, then he turned and swung his boot at the boy who seemed to be shouting loudest, and the boy – James Stromay of Fleece – seized his foot and sent him tumbling and rolling over the grass. David got to his feet. His face was distorted with rage. He did not pause to take breath before he flung himself at his tormentors, beating with his fists, clawing with his nails. The children broke and fled in all directions, laughing, but a few laughed uncertainly, as if great trouble could come of this.

At last David of Gorse acknowledged defeat. He crept back to the school and sat under the window, his down-tilted face in his fists.

That ought to have been enough fun and drama for one day. But no: a spirit of mischief had entered the valley children. They regrouped. Peter of Feaquoy had taken no part in the tormenting of David. He had been standing all the while turning the pages of a magazine called *Deadwood Dick*, devoted to stories of the pioneers of the American mid-west and the Red Indians. Now the school children, one after the other, sidled up to Peter. 'Your old father, he'd have been better building a hen-house than that *Skua*' . . . 'I wouldn't row across the bay in that tub, not me' . . . '*Skua* – she's more like a scarf – with a broken wing' . . .

Peter went on turning the pages of the magazine. It was plain to be seen he wasn't reading it. His lip quivered, the paper shook in his hand. At last he turned away from the chorus and looked out to sea. And now his face was as cold as stone.

Two or three of the bigger boys did not like this seeming indifference at all. What they wanted was to break their victim, as David had broken, all too soon, before they had had their fill of mockery. Sammy Anderson of Straith croft and James Stromay of Fleece – the latter with his fist clenched and raised – went right up to Peter. 'I want you to admit it, Sinclair', he said. 'Say, *the Skua is an old tub*, and then we'll leave you alone. If you don't admit she's an old tub, Sinclair, we'll rub your face in the gutter for you!'

No one can say how it might have ended. Mr MacFarlane was in his study smoking his mid-morning pipe: all he could hear from inside was bursts of laughter, a cry, a few low words.

Eagle John Fiord came up from the burn carrying two pails of water for the schoolmaster. (Mr MacFarlane must have his tea and soup; and he must have his bath and his clean shirts, more than ordinary folk.)

Eagle John set down the buckets hurriedly inside the school gate. Water sloshed out of one, the surface of the other was all blue trembling circles.

'Phew,' said Eagle John, 'water's heavier than you think, especially when you have to carry it up a steep brae' . . . He looked down towards the bay. 'It's my opinion,' said he, 'that the *Skua*, now, is a good fishing boat. I think it's a while since

I've seen a boat with such good lines to her. I think the *Skua* will do well out there in the west.'

There was a silence for a brief while in the school yard.

'Yes, indeed, she's a fine boat, the *Skua*,' said Sammy Anderson of Straith. 'She looks good down there in the noust.'

The children shouted their agreement.

'I think it's a lucky thing for this valley,' said Eagle John, 'that in one year – no, within a month – there should be two fine new fishing boats here. There isn't another district in Orkney that wouldn't be glad to have them. The other good boat is *Daffodil*. The man who built *Daffodil*, he knew what he was doing. A good man at the boat-building, Amos of Gorse.'

'None better,' said James Stromay of Fleece. '*Daffodil*, she's a fine boat too – she is that.'

'Hooray for the two new boats!' cried an eight-year-old girl, Ethel Laird of Flinders. At once the school yard was shrill with cheers and joy.

At that, Mr MacFarlane appeared at the school door, frowning, knocking the dottle out of his pipe. 'Less noise!' he cried. 'What's all the row about, eh? You're disturbing the whole valley. Come now, it's high time to resume lessons. Come in quietly, two by two.'

Eagle John Fiord came last, carrying the water-buckets.

'Dear me,' said Mr MacFarlane, 'How comes it, John, that there's a good bit less water in one pail than in the other?'

Nine

The weeks, the months, the seasons, the years passed, as the waves fell incessantly on the wide bay, as the grass in hayfield and kirkyard rose and flourished and fell before the scythes.

Never a winter but a few of the old folk died in this croft-house or that. And the bright children came crying into time, to be laid carefully in cradles that had served their great-grandparents.

And sometimes a young man or a young woman died. And that called for a special grief – but silent as stone – as the men followed the coffin to the kirk on the far side of the hill.

'Time goes quick as sand through the fingers,' said old Isaac Brims up at Quoy one winter, and before the snow had melted his light witty bones were laid under the hill too.

One winter a boat was lost at sea, in a storm, and though fragments of the boat came ashore, the bodies of the two young fishermen were never found. Early and late, for weeks on end, some of the women stood at the shore, waiting and watching.

It was considered a bad thing not to have a grave to lie in.

All the children who whirled about in mockery or rage or delight in the school yard, or who stood apart silent and lonely – all whom Mr MacFarlane instructed so strictly and so well – at least, according to the standards laid down by the school authorities – in arithmetic, history, poetry, geography, grammar: the time came, and soon, when they had all left school.

And most of them became crofters and fishermen, like their fathers, or the wives of crofter-fishermen. But some went to sea more than a few tentative oar-strokes, they broke wide horizons and became ordinary seamen, ships' carpenters, bo'suns. Two of Mr MacFarlane's brighter boys became in due course master mariners: Tommy Spence of Burnside was one. And one, James Brims of Quoy (old Isaac's son), started a draper shop in Hamnavoe, and flourished, and many considered him to be the boy who 'had got on in the world' best of all. (The slow magic of money was beginning to touch the folk of the valley.)

And a few remained bachelors all their days and a few remained spinsters.

The waves rose and fell. The grass flourished and withered.

The crofts of Gorse and Feaquoy still had no words to say to one another.

Full of instruction and discipline, the mature 'scholars' left school at the age of twelve, at July's beginning. Half-way through August, a new troop of wide-eyed innocents lingered about the school gate with new satchels under their arms, for Mr MacFarlane to shape into literate citizens.

The waves gathered. The grass and the corn bent to the winds.

Peter Sinclair of Feaquoy – an end-of-session day came when he flung his empty schoolbag into the bushes above the burn and went to join his father in the cornfield, the peat-bank, the fishing boat.

The very same day David of Gorse walked stolidly down the brae from the school to the croft. 'I'll fish with you tomorrow and always,' he said to his father. But Amos said it was blowing up for a southerly gale. 'We'll turn the peats instead,' he said. 'Your mother has rheumatics in her hands. She can't come to the peats this year.'

The old withered, here and there in the valley. Here and there, with bright cries, children drifted into time.

The schoolmaster, every summer, went away to Dunoon or North Berwick for a holiday. Once he took a young woman back with him, and lodged her at a farm on the far side of the hill. The young woman visited the valley twice. She looked at the people and the small fields and the boats. She spoke to no one, even though the men and women nodded courteously to her in passing. Then she turned her back on the valley and went away a few days later, taking the ferry-boat from Hamnavoe to Scotland: and down through the Highlands in a train, back to towns and civilization.

Mr MacFarlane went on living lonely in the schoolhouse.

One winter a child said, going home from school, 'Mr MacFarlane has white hairs in his beard.'

Ten

Fishing trawlers from ports on the east coast of Britain began, in increasing numbers, to fish with great trawls out in the bay; the nets came up, weighted and dripping; the trawler-men poured torrents of cod and haddock into their holds, and steamed away.

Then, when the valley boats went out to fish, they came back with only thin scatterings of fish in their boats.

There were one or two hungry winters in the valley.

The men from the valley complained to the authorities in Kirkwall and Edinburgh. Mr MacFarlane wrote the letters for them. He wrote to the Member of Parliament, a man who had never set foot in the valley nor ever seen a fish but garnished with herbs and wine on a silver platter: 'Dear Sir, we humbly and respectfully wish to place the following facts before you. We are inshore fishermen, and we fish from small boats in waters that our forebears have fished uninterruptedly for many generations. But lately our fishing grounds are being plundered and despoiled by those large steam vessels called trawlers . . .'

For a while the trawlers stopped fishing in the bay and in the firth beyond. But at night the valley folk could see drifting lights a mile or so off-shore. They could hear the muted throb of engines. Old Nell of Flinders declared she could hear the thousands of fish screaming in the nets.

One night in late summer two of the great trawling nets were slashed as they were slowly filling up with fish . . . An hour later there was one light less out in the bay. It was said in the valley next morning that *Skua* had been pushed out at sunset, and Peter Sinclair had then a new-sharpened knife in his belt. (Rob his father had stayed at home – that summer he had not been in the best of health.)

A week later, in the dark of the moon, three trawls were slashed before midnight, and what had been the beginning of three great catches flowed back into the sea.

Next morning it was well known that, just after sunset, Amos and David launched *Daffodil*, pushing her as quietly as they could over the stones into the brimming flood. Amos and David of Gorse got smiles wherever they went next day, though neither of them was particularly well liked in the valley. 'But,' said Amos, 'I can't understand it. We attended to two of the trawls, that's true. But three trawler lights left the Firth before sunrise.'

Then it was remarked that Peter of Feaquoy spent an hour after breakfast putting a new edge to his knife at the grind-stone. 'It's hard on the steel,' said Peter, 'cutting thick ropes' . . . And that same morning Peter yawned often, as if he had been up late.

For months, no more sea-wolves came by night to the fishing-grounds.

A child said, over the supper table one night. 'Mr Mac-Farlane is as bald as a stone on the top of his head. And some mornings he limps and groans about in the classroom. And he bites his lips sometimes.'

'Everybody gets rheumatics sooner or later in this valley,' said the old grandfather, smoking a clay pipe at the fireside. 'It's the dampness. MacFarlane was a bonny spry man when first he came to the valley.'

'And that's twenty-five years ago,' said the child's mother. 'He'd have been the better, poor man, of a wife to look after him.'

'He once had a sweetheart,' said the child, 'but she didn't stay.'

'If he'd married that creature,' said the old man, 'he'd have been in the kirkyard years ago. Better rheumatics and white hair than a niggler and a nagger at your elbow day and night.'

Soon Mr MacFarlane was walking here and there with a stick.

How he would rage at the children who were stupid at sums or parsing! The earlier generation had heard mostly sweetness and reasonableness from his mouth.

Old Nell of Flinders died. She got her death, they said, down at the shore, all one night peering out to sea, on the lookout for trawlers. They carried her round the hill to the kirkyard on the other side. Her son, Tom, made her coffin, as he made all the coffins in the valley.

The trawlers returned, but secretly and sporadically, and keeping somewhat further out in the firth; by the time the trawl-cutters had got to the place, the trawlers were up and away with their pirate-hoards, puffing black smoke into the sunrise.

There was not so much fish in the valley as there had been. Some of the younger folk hired themselves out to the big farms in the south part of the island. Some of the girls went to be servants in the big houses of Hamnavoe.

The snow melted from the ditches. There was only a large star of snow on the summit of the big hill. Daffodils came, singly or in ditch-side droves. A lark sang high and higher.

And that April David Flett, in his best dark suit, was seen leaving the valley night after night. The vigilant ones – mostly women – saw him returning before midnight. They nodded and winked and whispered to each other, getting buckets of water from the well next morning. That was an old story; its wonder never faded. Amos Flett had set his fancy on a lass on the other side of the hill.

One afternoon in the month of May David brought his sweetheart home. She was a sturdy red-cheeked girl, the youngest daughter of a farmer who lived five miles away. Maisie Spence got a poor welcome from Tomina. 'What are you seeking here?' she said. 'There's no room for two women in this house, let me tell you that. I can do all the work that's necessary. David is well looked after. All his needs are seen to. Good-day to you.'

Amos said, 'Once they're married, the lass can come here indeed. It won't take much trouble to build a little house out beyond the barn. The boy and I, we'll have it up before winter. Welcome to Gorse, lass.'

'Thank you,' said Maisie.

Tomina left the house and spent the rest of the day till dark walking about on the shore, backwards and forwards, 'the thundercloud on her brow,' as one old man said.

And she never spoke to either Amos or David for a week. But when she saw the first stones of the new cottage going up, she did say a few words.

The green corn grew in the twenty crofts of the valley. Small boys, free of school, ran here and there keeping the cows out of the oats and the barley. The sun climbed higher. The boats came in, one by one, laden with scuffling crabs. The yellow iris unfolded in the wet places, and the bees, heavy with plunder, stumbled here and there.

The four walls of Little Gorse were up, strongly built, Even Tomina had helped in the carrying of building stones from under the great cliffs in the north. Twice or thrice a day she scaled the crag with her basket of stone on her back, and walked over the moor and down the hill, and set the heavy basket at the gable end of the growing house. 'If she can work as well as your mother, boy,' she said to David, 'you won't lack for much.'

Every Sunday afternoon Maisie came to the valley to see how the work was going.

The young woman was forever whittling away at bits of driftwood with a knife – not just an idle nervous cutting, but she would shape the wood into useful things, clothes pegs or snibs for doors. She could cut the shape of a fish or an ox into a suitable piece of wood, too. 'That won't keep you in meat and clothes, a woman idling with wooden shapes,' said Tomina. 'Let her keep her knife sharp for the fish.'

Whenever old Tomina saw her and David standing there, she gave the girl a black look and went in at her own door and never appeared again until Maisie had gone home again in the evening.

One bright morning, Amos climbed the ladder to lay some stones for the chimney-head.

David had gone down to the shore to put tar on the boat *Daffodil.*

Tomina, going between the fire and the table indoors, baking oat-cakes, heard a thump and then a groan. 'The old fool's gone up the ladder with a wrong stone,' she said to herself. Then there was a long silence, when there should have been a creaking of the ladder and a chipping of chisel on stone.

When Tomina went outside, gloved to the elbows with oatmeal, she found old Amos lying dead at the foot of the ladder.

Every man in the valley went to Amos' funeral in the kirkyard on the far side of the hill, two days later. 'Rob of Feaquoy, he isn't here, of course,' the men said to each other, carrying the long plain wooden box along the road between the hills.

When they had lowered the coffin into the grave, one of the coffin-bearers saw, lingering at the kirkyard gate, his cap in his hand and his head bowed, Rob Sinclair of Feaquoy.

When the mourners trooped out of the kirkyard, Rob was nowhere to be seen. Nor did he come to Gorse when David Flett was pouring the funeral whisky into a score of glasses. The men stood around in their black Sunday suits.

A few of the crofters, with simpering sadness on their faces, went over with consoling words to the widow.

'Keep your mouths to drink your whisky,' said she.

Later she said to the men. 'Don't linger overlong. I have work to do, if you don't.'

When the last drop of whisky was drunk and the last mourner gone, she said to her son. 'In former days there were two men here and one woman, and things went well. In days to come, there's to be two women and one man. And I don't know how things will turn out then.'

David finished the building of Little Gorse before harvest.

One Saturday when she came visiting Maisie took a knife to the prow of the fishing-boat and she carved a daffodil deep into the wood. The valley folk didn't know what to think of that – such a thing had not been known before. Some shook their heads doubtfully. Others said it was 'pretty'. But they thought it wasn't woman's work, it served no purpose, the boat would have been as well without it. There were too many new things happening too quickly in the valley . . .

In October David married Maisie Spence in the manse, and there was a great wedding feast lasting three nights at Maisie's father's farm. But old Tomina, though of course she had been invited, was not among the guests.

After the wedding, David brought his new wife to the new cottage in the valley.

Tomina was standing in the door of Gorse. She had laid three stone jars in the yard between the old house and the new house. 'There's your wedding gift,' said Tomina to the bride. 'There's a jar for meal, and a jar to keep salted fish in, and a jar of oil to keep your lamp burning. See that they're always half-full, at least.

'Thank you,' said Maisie, 'I'll try.'

'Do more than try,' said Tomina. 'Work him like an ox till he drops. That's the only kind of life we know in this valley.'

'There's flowers and honey too,' said Maisie. 'There's bonny things to make and do.'

'It would be better,' said Tomina, 'if you and I, woman, were not to see too much of each other.'

'The sun shines on everybody,' said Maisie. 'We must see people whether we want to or not.'

'Well,' said Tomina, 'let there be as few words as possible.'

'That suits me well,' said Maisie.

'This man, your husband,' said Tomina, 'he can bring me a few fish if he has any to spare. If he grinds oats in winter, I could be doing with a handful or two.'

'You won't lack,' said David.

Then David and Maisie took Tomina's wedding gift – the three jars – and carried them into the new house.

Maisie cried out.

There was a fire burning in the hearth.

Next morning Maisie carved a pigeon – a dove – on the doorpost of the new house.

Eleven

The Hamnavoe Lammas Fair falls in early September. That year a few of the young men and girls of the valley sailed round in the big boat *Ruby Ann* to Hamnavoe. The young men wore their best dark suits, worn only for weddings and funerals and Sunday kirk-going. The valley girls looked like flowers in their bright dresses.

Peter Sinclair of Feaquoy sailed to Hamnavoe with them.

The younger valley people, those who hadn't been to the Hamnavoe Fair before, how they gaped at the coloured crowds of townsfolk and country folk, and the noise and bustle everywhere! The cries and cajolings of the fairground people amazed them. At the market green there were stalls everywhere, with bottles of sweeties, and piles of fruit and coconuts. And there was the fortune-teller's booth, and the booth of the strong man who tied pokers into knots, and cheap-jacks, and itinerant doctors who sold bottles of medicine to cure every ill for a shilling the bottle. A blind man wandered through the crowds playing his fiddle.

So much money! Silver coins flashed and rang everywhere. Young Paul Laird of Flinders could hardly believe there was so much money in the world.

And the open pub doors, reeking with beer and tobacco fumes! A man would walk in straight and smiling, and come out an hour later clawing at the walls for support. From this pub door and that came discordant choruses.

The young folk of the valley had been well warned not to enter such places, by their elders. Not only would they make fools of themselves with whisky and porter, but they would be robbed for sure, or they might be carried drunk into some whaling boat, and never be heard of again. (What misery, to be set ashore in Iceland or Newfoundland!)

So the young folk of the valley kept in a tight group all day, going here and there among the fairground booths, or along the jostling Hamnavoe street, looking into the grocers' windows and the drapers' windows and the bluebottle-buzzing butchers' windows.

Greatly daring, young Jean Brims of Quoy went into a draper's shop to buy six yards of blue ribbon and a packet of pins, and spools of cotton. 'Don't leave me! she whispered anxiously to the others.

How glad she was that they were still there when she came out of the shop with her little parcel. They might easily have been dispersed in that hithering-thithering noisy throng!

Sitting on a wall in the square was a line of young women. There was something extraordinary about those girls, over and above the other strange folk they had seen that day. They were chattering to one another like gulls, but in a strange language. Were they Frenchies, or Norskies? And their gesticulating arms were salt-bleached, and the hands had little cuts on them here and there.

'Fishing lasses from the Highlands,' they were told. 'They come ever year to gut the herrings. Yes, and they pack them in brine barrels to send to Russia' . . .

There was a notice in a lodging-house window,

TEA LEMONADE CAKES.

'Well,' said Lizzie of Whinstone, 'I would like a cup of tea. I'm sure I have blisters on my feet from the hard paving-stones' . . .

While they were sitting at a table waiting for the sour-faced lodging-house woman to bring in the pot of tea, they were aware all at once that one of their number was missing.

Peter Sinclair of Feaquoy – what had become of him?

At once they were uneasy, especially the girls. A dreadful thing might have happened to Peter. There were more than a few unsavoury-looking characters at the Hamnavoe Fair that day. Suppose he had been bludgeoned and smuggled aboard one of those whaling boats! In the fortune-teller's booth he might have been dissolved in magic coloured smoke – changed into a cat or a gull! Or he might be lying drunk behind a barrel in a pub, with a troop of mocking drinking red-faced farmers all about him!

So the valley girls went on, agitatedly, spilling drops of hot tea on table-cloth and flowery dress. The young men laughed at them, but even they looked uneasy, and young Ezra Scott of Flegs went to the door and looked up and down the street, to see if he could see the vagrant.

Nowhere.

They ate the cakes with chocolate icing on them. and emptied the big teapot, and hardly spoke a word to each other: they, who had been so excited since early morning when they set foot on the harbour steps.

Something bad must have happened to Peter of Feaquoy.

'We'll search through all the ale-houses, every one of them' . . .

'No, but we could ask one or two sailors' . . .

'The Provost, he's the chief man in Hamnavoe. We'll find out where he lives. We'll knock at his door' . . .

'He was there when we saw the Gaelic fishing girls sitting on the wall. He stopped to look at them' . . .

'Peter didn't look all that well in the boat this morning' . . .

'He might be looking everywhere for *us*' . . .

'The police station is the place to go. Long Rob the police-man, he knows where everybody is' . . .

And so, after the first silence, their talk went on, while a second tea-pot was brought to their table.

They tried to keep their voices down, because the big room in the lodging-house was full of festive folk coming and going. Always a little gull-edge or an ox-grumble seemed to startle or amuse the other patrons in the tea-room.

At last the lodging-house lady appeared. 'You've been sitting here all of an hour,' she said. 'Other people want refreshments as well as you. Don't you see them all staring at you? That'll be two shillings and two pence-hapenny. I see you've spilt tea on the cloth.'

It was well into the afternoon. The Lammas crowds, if anything, were thicker than ever. The country folk from Birsay and Orphir were coming in in carts, families and neighbours and friends. From the big pier, two hundred yards along the street, came the confused noise of music, cheap-jacks, evange-lists, gulls, drunks, children with balloons and coloured streamers.

In an hour – no later – they would have to be on their way home, carrying packets of toffee, bags of apples and oranges, and comic papers, for the old folk and the children of the valley.

They made their purchases half-heartedly, and always their eyes went here and there and everywhere, looking for the lost one.

Only John Fiord – Eagle John – seemed to be unconcerned. He went missing, but only for a minute, to buy a box of clay pipes for his father Magnus. How relieved the girls were, when Eagle John rejoined them on the far side of the street!

Ezra of Flegs and Willie of Skeld looked into five pubs, one after the other, but noise and smoke drove them back. They came out, coughing and watery-eyed. They could not say whether Peter of Feaquoy was inside or not; they hadn't had a chance to look properly.

Once Jean of Straith cried, 'Here he is!,' and smote a young dark-suited man on the shoulder. A strange angry face looked back at her.

Ezra Scott braced himself and knocked on the door of the police station. A woman with a kind face opened the door. 'We've lost our friend,' said Ezra. 'We're from the sea valley. Could Long Rob find him for us, please?'

'Bless you,' said the woman. 'And what way would my husband know your friend if he saw him? The town's full of strangers. That man of mine, Constable Stanger, his head's in a right whirl, ever since sun-up. (Constable Stanger, that's his name, not Long Rob.) Fights, drunks, window-breakings. He's got four men locked in the cells as it is. Do you want to have a look? Maybe your friend's sitting on the bench among them, holding his head.'

The girls turned away, covering their faces with their hands. Two of them cried softly, like pigeons. The very idea, that Peter of Feaquoy might be in jail! Better dead, almost, than that!

'I tell you what,' said Jean of Straith as they made their way to the pier, 'Peter's standing at the steps waiting for us! *What's keeping them?* he's saying to himself.'

But when they reached the steps where the *Ruby Ann* was tied up, there was no sign of Peter.

'We can't leave without him!' cried Sigurd of Burnside. 'What are we going to tell Rob and Mary Jean, when we get home?'

The *Ruby Ann* was afloat. Eagle John Fiord untied the rope and leapt aboard. A lurch. A splash of sea water. Shrieks from the girls. Salt drops had fallen on their 'fairings' and flowered skirts.

Half-way home, under the red cliffs, Eagle John said, 'Tell them – what will we tell them? We'll tell them exactly what happened. Stranger things have happened to the valley men, many a time. Always it turned out well in the end – or tolerable at least. What a miserable day you've had, worrying about Peter Sinclair. A ruined Fair! I think Peter Sinclair might be having the enjoyment all of us missed, seven-fold!'

As they rounded the crag and came within sight of the valley, Jean of Straith began to cry. And Lizzie of Whinstone began to snivel too, dabbing her eyes with a handkerchief she had bought at a stall. And little Bet of Flegs let on to weep too, but they all noticed that her eyes were dry.

Neary all the valley folk had come down to meet the *Ruby Ann.*

Ezra cried from the stern, 'We have fairings for everybody!'

The old woman Williamina of Burnside said, 'I don't see Peter. Is he lying drunk in the bottom of the boat?'

'I never saw such crowds at any Hamnavoe Fair!' cried Willie of Skeld from the bow of the boat, the rope in his hand, but seemingly not too eager to throw it to the waiting men.

As for the girls in the boat, their steadfast eyes were on the sea.

Mary Jean Sinclair said nothing.

One by one the young men leapt ashore. They lifted the quiet girls ashore. Many hands dragged the boat higher up the noust.

'So,' said Mary Jean, 'my hero hasn't come home.'

The young men, shame-faced, shook their heads.

'Well, said Mary Jean, 'if he wants to go to the Arctic whaling, who am I to stop him? It's a poor place, this valley, and it's like to be poorer. Was there a boat for Canada, or Australia maybe, in Hamnavoe? That's the place for a young man to go.'

Mr MacFarlane had come hobbling down on his stick. He was very short of breath now. 'No emigrant ships sail from Hamnavoe,' he said. 'They sail from Liverpool or Southampton.'

'Old Rob and I, we'll have to manage the best way we can,' said Mary Jean.

Then the fairings were distributed to the old and young. But there wasn't much joy about the giving or the receiving.

Mary Jean went back to Feaquoy.

As she crossed the burn, there were wild skirls of laughter from the other side of the valley. 'Oh,' cried Tomina of Gorse, 'I knew it would come to this! She's driven him away with that wicked tongue of hers. I never knew the boy had so much spunk in him. What misery from now on, in a certain croft in this place!' . . .

Tomina's mockery echoed and died among the hills.

But nobody else laughed.

When Mary Jean got to Feaquoy, Rob was standing in the door.

'Peter's gone away,' she said.

'Ah well,' said Rob, 'men go, and sometimes men come back, and that's always been the way of it.'

He began to fill his pipe.

The people of the valley began to disperse, in groups, to the crofts.

Next morning two people, a man and a woman, were seen walking along the road between the hills into the valley.

Old Jess Budge of Crag said, 'My eyes are not that good, but the man looks a bit like Peter of Feaquoy. But I don't know who the woman is.'

Soon there were faces at every door and window.

And Mary Jean came and stood in her door.

And Tomina of Gorse pressed her face against her window till her nose was flat and white.

Peter took the strange girl by the arm and led her through the ripe oatfield and up the potato-patch to the door of Feaquoy.

'This is my lass,' he said to his mother, 'and we're going to get married.'

'What's your name, girl?' said Mary Jean. 'Where do you come from?'

The girl looked at her, shyly, and said nothing.

Rob was sitting beside the fire, smoking his pipe and spitting every now and again into the flames.

'Who's this with Peter?' he called. 'Tell her to come in.'

'She doesn't speak English,' said Peter. 'Only Gaelic. Well, she has a few words of English. But she'll learn. She comes from a place in the west of Scotland called Ullapool. She came to Orkney for the herring fishing. I met her yesterday at the Hamnavoe Fair.'

'Come in, lass, till I see you,' cried Rob from the fireside.

Mary Jean stood in the door. She had grown stout over the years. A cat or a bird could hardly have squeezed in past her.

'And where will you both live?' said Mary Jean. 'There's no room for four people in this croft – and maybe five or six or seven in the years to come. Will you stay in the byre? There's a sheep-house on the side of the hill.'

Rob came and stood in the door, pushing his wife aside to give himself room.

'Her name's Lois,' said Peter.

'What kind of a name is that?' said Mary Jean. 'Lois!'

'I think it's a bonny enough name,' said Rob. 'And she's a very bonny lass, Lois. I didn't think, boy, such a bonny lass would give you a second look.'

The Highland girl looked at Rob, and if she didn't know what he was saying, she sensed a sympathy in the words. She raised her eyes from examining her fingernails to the old crofter's face. And she smiled.

'I think,' said Mary Jean, 'you'd be well advised, boy, to take her back to the herring boat where you found her. There's no place for the likes of her in this valley or this house.'

'She can't go back,' said Peter. 'She's broken her contract. The agent has sacked her.'

'Good,' said Rob. 'Here she is and here she'll bide. This croft could do with a bit of cheerfulness in it.'

'There's no room for her!' cried Mary Jean, and solidly blocked the door. 'Any bairns she had, what way would we understand them and their foreign words, when the time came for them to speak?'

'Peter,' said old Rob, 'I've been meaning for years to build a room or two on to the end of this house, on the sea side. But I never got down to it, what with this and that, and your mother grumbling at me to patch her hen-house or tar the boat. Do you think, if we put out minds to it, we could have two new rooms before winter sets in? It's been done before. We'll start work in the morning.'

At that Mary Jean left the door and went and stood at the gableend, looking at nothing. Her round face, said Samuel the neighbour man, was as tight as a fist that morning.

'Come in, lass. Come in and sit beside the fire,' said Rob. 'I welcome you to Feaquoy. And may you work well about this fire many a long day.'

And with that Rob Sinclair did what he had never done in the light of the sun before. As the girl stepped across the threshold he kissed her on the cheek.

Lois laughed, so happily that it brought smiles to the faces of Rob and Peter also.

(The neighbour man reported then that Mary Jean's face was as tight and streaming as a fist that had been plunged in the burn.)

That very afternoon Rob and Peter and a few helpers went down the cliff once more, to get stones for the building of the new extension to Feaquoy. By sunset there was a fair heap of stones at the end of the house, waiting to be dressed and shaped.

Next morning the stone-gatherers walked over the moor to the cliff, and men and women went down from ledge to ledge with their caisies.

Lois stood above, watching.

It was a fine morning in early September. The valley folk climbed up the rock-face, one after the other with loaded baskets.

At noon there was a sudden cry from half-way up the crag.

A man staggered on a ledge and fell, and his body hit the stony shore below, and the score of stones in his basket crashed and rasped and thundered all about him.

Rob of Feaquoy was dead when the stone-gatherers got to him.

There is always a muteness in the grief of the islanders. Nothing was said as they manoeuvred the broken body up the crag and laid it on the heather above.

But the girl Lois, when she looked down at the face of Rob, broke into such a torrent of lamentation as had not been heard in that island before.

She went down on her knees and kissed the cold hands. And the knuckles of the dead man were wet.

Lois lamented until it seemed she had no more sound to dredge up out of herself.

Then Peter helped her to her feet, and straightened the dark strands that had fallen all over her face.

And four men carried the body over the moor and down one side of the valley, and across the burn, and through the uncut cornfield to Feaquoy.

Mary Jean was sitting at the table beside the window, sewing black cloth diamonds on Peter's jacket and coat. Someone must have run on before with the news.

'Put him on the bed,' she said.

So the four men laid Rob out on the bed, and the oldest of them, Isaac of Quoy closed his eyes and folded his hands decently over his breast.

And again the girl Lois, glancing over towards the bed, gave a cry or two.

'Stop that noise!' said Mary Jean. 'You'll have to thole a death or two yet before your own comes.'

Tom Laird of Flinders made Rob Sinclair's coffin in the barn of Flinders. He left the coffin lid standing all night at the barn wall, outside, so that the wind could dry a little lingering damp out of the driftwood. When he came out in the morning with Paul and young Tom, his sons, to carry the coffin across to Feaquoy, someone had cut into the lid with a knife. 'What does it say?' said Tom, who couldn't read. 'It says, A GOOD MAN,' said Paul.

Mary Jean noticed the carving as soon as they set the coffin on the trestles. Nobody asked you to carve that,' she said. 'Who did it?'

Tom said he didn't know. It had been done when they were all asleep.

'I didn't order it, so I won't be paying for it,' said Mary Jean. 'If anybody had wanted to carve anything, his name and his dates would have done.'

'It's truth what they wrote, whatever,' said Peter.

*　　*　　*

Three days later Rob of Feaquoy was carried to the kirkyard on the other side of the hill. Every man in the valley who could walk was there, except David of Gorse. The coffin, with A GOOD MAN cut on the lid, was lowered into the grave.

The mourners returned to the valley in slow elegiac groups.

When Peter got back, with the black cloth diamond on the sleeve of his jacket, to Feaquoy, his mother had set out cups and a bottle of whisky. Presently the mourners would arrive.

Mary Jean pointed to Lois. 'I've been trying to tell this creature,' she said, 'that from now on she can live in this house with you, and I'll move into the bit of a pig-sty that's going to be built on to the end of Feaquoy. If I've said it once to her I've said it a score of times. But I might as well be speaking to a selkie.'

Just then the first of the mourners came drooping darkly in at the door. And then two more. Others could be seen through the window, crossing the burn.

'Pour the drink,' said Mary Jean to Peter. 'That's what they've come for.'

By now the little room was full of mourners. Every croft was represented except Gorse. 'Try to look a bit cheerful,' said Mary Jean to the lugubrious faces. 'In my opinion, when a good man dies there should be a fiddle and dancing! Fill up their cups, boy. There's two more bottles in the cupboard.'

Lois carried round the cups of whisky.

And that evening Tomina of Gorse said to three other women who were at the burn, like her, with buckets to draw water, 'If you ask me, there's a witch come to the valley. A strong man like Sinclair of Feaquoy, how would he have fallen from a wide ledge like that? He's been up and down that cliff a thousand times. There she stood, on the clifftop, looking down. And over he went, and all his stones on top of him. What'll happen next, I wonder?'

Twelve

The harvesters saw, that year again, the eagle up near the sun. The bird eyed the golden surging sea of corn below, then it swung in a great arc towards its crag among the hills.

'We don't worry about the eagle this year,' said one harvester to another. 'There's no infants for it to carry off.'

There were a few bairns, but they were old enough to run here and there. There were no swaddlings under the stooks that summer. Never had there been fewer children in the valley.

Across the valley, among the encroaching heather, a fissure had appeared in the long-deserted croft of Garth; now, it all but severed the gable-end from roof and wall. 'To think,' said Isaac Brims, 'that once Garth sent out ten folk, old and young, into the harvest fields' . . .

The Gaelic-speaking girl worked with the other women in the harvest-field. Lois was not used to this kind of work. She was quick to learn. The other young women were eager to instruct her, after those first few shy weeks. 'Corn,' she said, putting a strange music into the word that made the women laugh. 'Scythe,' she said, 'Stook,' she said. And 'bairn,' she said, and 'bread,' and 'fire' and 'winter'. And she bent her fluent waist to the fallen oats, and her sun-browned hands gathered the stalks and bound them.

'Eagle,' she said, shading her eyes to look at the loiterer round the sun.

Sad news came to the valley that harvest. Mr MacFarlane had gone to Dunoon on holiday, and he had died there, suddenly, in his sister's house. And they had buried him among his own people. The old men shook their heads. 'Mr MacFarlane,' they said, 'would have been much happier lying among the dead of the island' . . .

Word came from Kirkwall, from the education office there, that a new teacher had been appointed, a young woman just out of the teacher training college in Edinburgh, a Miss Yvonne Strachan. 'What kind of name is that?' said old Ben Smith of Skeld.

A few of the men went to meet Miss Strachan off the Hamnavoe steamer that called twice a week at the pier five miles away. They put her cases in an ox-drawn cart, and brought her to the schoolhouse. The woman Janet, from the highest house in the valley, Upland (perched near the cliff edge), had a meal of broth and fish ready for her.

Miss Strachan walked through the valley, right down to the shore, that same evening. From this door and that she was greeted, with a muted cry or a wave of the hand. She stood on the bench for a long time, watching the slow sea surges, till the lighthouse on the coast of Scotland began its silent pulsings, again and again.

Coming up through the fields, in the first darkness, Miss Strachan stumbled and half-fell into the burn. She rose, wet to the elbows and with her long skirt draggled; half-laughing, half-sobbing.

Willie Smith of Skeld had seen her plight. He came running, he helped to steady her. Then he walked with her all the way to the schoolhouse door.

Inside, the room was bright. Janet of Upland had lit her lamp, and also her fire, and the kettle was beginning to sing on its hook.

'I think I've come under a kind star,' said Miss Strachan. Wisps of steam rose from her wet skirt.

Then she bade Willie Smith goodnight at the door, and thanked him.

Thirteen

The children were eager for the harvest holiday to be over, so that they could get back to the school and study under this young bonny new teacher.

It was arranged that Peter Sinclair of Feaquoy and Lois MacIsaac would be married in the barn of Feaquoy in the middle of October. Peter worked hard at building the new extension where his mother was to live. A few of the other men helped him. Within six weeks they had the roof-beams on and the flagstones and thatch laid.

Mary Jean and Lois moved about inside Feaquoy, barely speaking to each other. 'Fire,' said Mary Jean occasionally to the girl. 'Water. Cow and milk and cheese. Sheep and spinning wheel. Hens and broth and eggs. Lamp and oil. And labour from morning to night, summer and winter, year in year out. – That's all the words you need, or any other woman if it comes to that. And pain.'

'Pain?' said Lois, wondering.

'Pain,' said Mary Jean. 'Pain and sorrow. And after the marriage, I'd rather you didn't come visiting me. I can manage fine by myself.'

The girl nodded, as if the tone and rhythm of the words carried well enough the burden of the meaning.

It was from Peter that she learned the new language best. In the evenings he led her all through the valley, and up the hills, and along the high crags, naming all the flowers and birds and plants to her. It was enchanting, how she gave him back, like echoes, his words. Often he had to stop and laugh with delight, throwing his head back. Once or twice, if he thought no one was looking, he would stoop and kiss her. He could not imagine there lay such beauty in the ordinary words and names the valley people used. 'Kestrel' she echoed him as the high shadow crossed, lingering, their upturned faces. The bird, clothed in the music of her voice, drifted and was lost in the gathering shadows of the hills.

'Stars' – 'lamp-light' – 'moth' – 'sheep-path' – 'ferns' . . . Such small lyrics accompanied their home-going in the darkness.

As they passed the high croft of Upland, they heard Ezra Scott playing his fiddle. Upland had always had music and musicians.

Inside Feaquoy, the old woman sat, saying nothing. The gray wool ran through her fingers from the turning wheel.

'For the bone and the blood to be warm in winter,' said Lois, pointing to the jersey and sea stockings and bonnets that Mary Jean had knitted that year. They lay in neat piles on the shelf above the box-bed.

'Yes,' said Mary Jean, 'the blood's warm for a winter or two, then it's cold for a long long time.'

Lois turned to Peter, to know better what the old woman had said.

Peter shook his head: It was nothing, he had heard the speech a hundred times.

'The kettle's boiling,' said Mary Jean. 'I can't do everything! Maybe the fish-gutter could make a pot of tea. I don't want anything. I'm going to bed.'

She gathered up her wool and went to her room without another word.

'Goodnight,' cried the girl happily, and the way she chanted it was enough to summon angels about the house, to guard it till morning. (Or so the new crofter of Feaquoy thought, fleetingly.)

The harvest, a good one, was gathered in.

Stone was laid upon stone at Feaquoy, and window and door fitted.

Eagerly, like a swarm of starlings, the children ran to school on the first morning that Miss Strachan rang, a bit erratically, the bell.

'Now,' said Peter to Lois one evening, 'you know the names of everything that lives and grows and moves in this valley. What I long to hear from you are the names of the shells and the different seaweeds. I never thought to hear such good sounds from the mouth of a woman. Good. This evening before the sun goes down I'm going to take you down to the shore.'

'No,' said Lois.

'But you must know the shore names,' said Peter. 'The shore is more important than the fields even. Without sea and shore there could be no people in this valley.'

'No,' said Lois.

'The shells,' said Peter. 'Seaweed. The names of the caves and the crags. Crabs and mussels and limpets. Starfish. I want to hear you say them.'

'No,' said Lois. And she stood before him, stubborn, her lip trembling.

'Lois,' said Peter, I have a boat down there on the beach, the *Skua*. She's the best fishing boat in the valley – no, in the whole island. She's mine, the *Skua*, since my father died. I love that boat, Lois. I want you to come down with me now and look at her. Put your hands on the curves of her. Then say her name,

Skua – no boat on this earth will be so lovely then, with that music about her.'

'No,' said Lois.

'You're a fisher lass,' cried Peter. 'You were brought up among boats and nets! Without *Skua* and the fish she'll catch, year after year, we couldn't live here at all. My father built her. Come down with me now.'

'No,' said Lois. He could see the tears on her cheek.

A shout came from the next room. 'She's had enough of the sea, that fish-gutter! I hope her ladyship'll boil the fish, once you take them home. A poor life for the both of you if you have to live on oatmeal and milk.'

But no: Lois had no objection to cleaning and cooking the fish that Peter brought up to Feaquoy from the *Skua*. Lois had, it seemed, spells for the black pot that hung on its hook over the peat-flames. Peter swore he had never tasted such good haddock and cod and lithe. (Her bannocks, to begin with, were a bit tough – but before the end of winter Lois could bake as well as any of the women.)

Mary Jean admitted that she could just stomach the fish-gutter's boiled fish, with or without butter.

Fourteen

The wedding took place in the little barn of Feaquoy in October. Everybody in the valley came, after the ring had been put on Lois' finger, and she had responded *I do* (in a way that made the ceremony more mysterious and beautiful than ever) and the minister had closed the book and pronounced the blessing.

Even the old fireside graybeard and the seven-day-old child were there, when the wedding cake was broken over the bride's head and the bride-cog was brimmed up with whisky and hot ale and honey, to make the first of its night-long sunwise circles.

The minister smiled and took his departure.

The fiddler, Ezra Scott from Upland, came. He tuned his fiddle. He drank from the cog till golden drops hung from his moustache. Then he sent his bow flashing and skirling across the strings.

The dancing began, in slow sunward circles to begin, but faster and faster, with ritual shouts and cries, as though the whole labour of the past year was gathered into this wild whirl of rejoicing.

Small girls went round with plates of cheese-and-oatcakes and sweets, and apples and oranges. The old men who were too cripple to dance told each other stories in a corner, over glasses of whisky. The old women – most of them – said derogatory things about the bridegroom, and about the groom's mother, the hostess. ('Poor food and fiddling and drink, compared to some of the weddings we've been at in our time' . . .)

The hostess herself, Mary Jean, made one brief appearance after the ceremony. 'Eat and drink till you burst,' she cried, – 'it's the last meat and ale you're like to get here at Feaquoy' . . . She set another two bottles of whisky on the table, and went off to sleep in her annex of new stone and timber.

No one from the croft of Gorse had been bidden to the wedding.

Miss Strachan the new teacher arrived, with a gift of cups and plates. She danced three times with Willie Smith of Skeld, and he swung her about so hard in the eightsome reel that she stumbled against the table and upset a platter of cold chicken. Willie lifted her to her feet at once; and she was reassured by the concerned faces all about her. She took the merest sip of the hot bride-cog as it made (replenished) yet another circle of the barn. Then, at the door, she buttoned up her coat and put on her bonnet and gave Peter and Lois a beautifully-articulated 'goodnight' and 'good-luck' . . . And she went alone in the darkness up to the schoolhouse – for now she knew most paths in the valley, and that night there were a few stars to light her way.

Just after midnight Ezra Scott took a last great gulp at the tilted bride-cog, and the fiddle fell out of his hand, and was a songless bird for the rest of the night.

Old Dod Budge of Crag was sent home for his melodeon; to its meeker music the dancing went on. A young man, half-drunk, cried, 'Oh, Dod, I would take an axe to that mimsy-mamsy thing, if I were thee!' . . . Dod, much offended, put his melodeon in its box and went home. (Dod was very proud of his melodeon. It was the first melodeon seen and heard in the valley. He had bought it in Hamnavoe for two pounds.)

A very old man, Frank of Whinstone, who had once fiddled when he was young, was lured and cajoled out of the circle of story-telling old men; and he picked up the fiddle and bow and did his best. So long as the fiddle had pulse and power and urgency in it, the dancers were pleased enough. The old fiddler seemed actually to play better as midnight approached: as if the music-bird had remembered ancient springs and leafage. He played with sweetness and power. 'And,' said old William-ina of Aird, 'I swear, Frank, you look as bonny tonight as you did fifty years ago.'

At the end of the sixth eightsome reel, in the early hours of the morning, an old woman looked up to see how things were with the bride – as she had done from time to time throughout the feast (for much can be told about the future happiness and prosperity of a household from the way the bride bears herself at her wedding) and then the old woman turned and whispered urgently to the women on either side of her.

The bride and bridegroom were no longer there!

Another schottische was called. Old Frank struck the strings as sturdily as ever he had done as a young man, and caressed the fiddle like a lost love. The feet rose and fell.

In the barns of the valley, high and low, the plough and the seed slumbered.

The sun was red in the east when the last of the revellers left the barn of Feaquoy.

Two men dragged old Frank home, half destroyed with music and reminiscence and drink. One carried the fiddle – it had broken a string.

The bride-cog lay on its side on the table, last drops oozing from it, among the crumbs of cake and cheese and the chicken bones, and the apple-cores.

Fifteen

That winter, after New Year, Maisie of Gorse gave birth to a child. The registrar on the other side of the hill wrote the name of the new child in his book: Matthew John Flett.

Sixteen

Now the story must concern itself briefly with the young man John Fiord of Don, who had been known as Eagle John since his infancy.

'I think,' Mr MacFarlane had said, after Eagle John had been at the valley school for two years, 'there has never been such a clever boy in this place' . . . Eagle John Fiord picked up all the offered branches of knowledge with effortless ease. It was extraordinary. By the age of six he could read fluently from whatever book was put before him – *From Log Cabin to White House, The Last of the Mohicans, Tales of a Grandfather, The Shorter Catechism, The Poems of Burns.*

And writing, that made the other children furrow their brows and curl their tongues to the corners of their mouths: John Fiord could do that too with ease and fluency. 'Now,' Mr MacFarlane would say, 'let's suppose you are grown up, you are working your crofts, you have surplus produce to sell, and you also require certain provisions from this merchant or that in Hamnavoe. Very well. I know that some of the older folk here know nothing about shops and cash. Times are changing. You will all have to engage in that kind of business some day, sooner or later. This morning you will write a letter to Mr James Tomison, merchant, Hamnavoe, telling him what you want. Sharpen pencils. Open jotters. Begin.'

The creatures, they were all at sea, they didn't know how to set about the task at all; they looked at each other, lost and wide-eyed; they whispered behind their hands. 'Silence!' roared Mr MacFarlane.

Never were such poor tatters and travesties of essays set before Mr MacFarlane, at the hour's end. 'It seems,' said Mr MacFarlane grimly, 'that this valley and the great world outside will have difficulties dealing with each other in a year or two. You might be Hottentots, or Eskimos, trying to communicate with Mr Tomison the merchant. Disgraceful!' . . .

Then, thumbing through the scratched and blotted sheets of paper, Mr MacFarlane's face brightened. 'Ah,' said he, 'at last, an oasis in the desert. This is more like the thing. John Fiord, come forward and read what you've written. Well done. Listen, you other dunderheads. Take this as a model.'

Seven-year-old John Fiord read in a high treble: 'To James Tomison, esquire, General Merchant, Hamnavoe, Orkney, Scotland. 12th June, 1887. Dear Sir, I take leave to inform you that I have now in the croft of Don here certain items that you may wish to purchase, namely, 6 dozen eggs, 3 large well-seasoned cheeses, one stone of best butter, 4 good quality fleeces, and several boxes of good quality home-smoked fish, mainly cod. You may also be interested in purchasing lobsters from me. I get anything from a dozen to a score of lobsters, most days, in the season. I would be much obliged if you could send over by the steamer the following items: one stone sugar, a can of paraffin for the lamp, a two-pounds jar raspberry jam and a one-pound jar of marmalade, two bakehouse loaves, three yards muslin to make curtains for the windows, and a pot of best white paint. Also fish-hooks, factory-made, in a variety of sizes. And I would like you to send weekly a copy of the *Orkney Herald* and the *Christian Herald* and *Fireside Words*. Next time that I chance to be in Hamnavoe we will balance our account. I would be much obliged if you could accommodate me in this matter. I am, Yours sincerely, John Fiord' . . .

'Precise, fluent, up-to-date, and to the point,' said Mr MacFarlane. 'But I hope that, in years to come, John doesn't have to write all your business letters for you.'

Eagle John, blushing, went back to his seat. Some of the pupils looked admiringly at him, a few sneered.

But the boy showed the same mastery in all the other subjects. How eagerly he pored over the little globe of the Earth that stood tilted on its axis on Mr MacFarlane's desk – at the mystery of seas and continents, islands and cities and mountain-masses! The characters who moved through the legends of Scotland in the history book fascinated him: Margaret the Maid, Wallace, Robert the Bruce, Mary Queen of Scots, Bonnie Prince Charlie, Montrose, Watt, Livingstone. With bated breath he listened while Mr MacFarlane described the great Battle of Bannockburn. His lips trembled at the first telling of the tragic Battle of Flodden.

And mathematics: Mr MacFarlane was already instructing him in algebra and Euclid while the others were blundering through the labyrinths of multiplication and long division. 'Next term, John,' said Mr MacFarlane, 'we'll try you with trigonometry. I think you might like that.'

Eagle John Fiord had access to Mr MacFarlane's private library. 'Now, John,' said the dominie, 'I never lend books, on principle. But I make an exception for you. Any book on the shelves there, anything you fancy, just take it home to Don for an evening to two. I know you'll treat my books with care.'

And John, once a week at least, bore home to Don a book from Mr MacFarlane's private collection. Once, when he was ten, he read in the lamplight a book called *The Orkneyinga Saga*, a new translation from the Icelandic. He was still turning the pages at midnight, when his mother was in bed and his father was putting on the hearth the large peat that would burn slowly all night long, and then be stirred into flames by the first thrust of the poker next morning. 'To your bed, boy,' said Magnus, but the boy sat and turned another page as though he had heard not a word.

Magnus Fiord was the kind of man who never shouted or used force. John was turning another page. Magnus walked across the stone floor and lifted the lamp glass and blew the light out. The boy, left darkling, let out a wail.

His father and mother heard him sobbing for ten minutes in the next room before he forgot the outrage in the gentle rhythms of sleep.

Next morning, after his porridge and milk, how eagerly he ran to school, *The Orkneyinga Saga* under his arm, to be there before the other pupils arrived. 'Oh,' he stammered as Mr MacFarlane emerged from the schoolhouse, shaved and brushed and breakfasted, and began his brief stately somewhat self-important little walk to the school. 'I didn't know . . . You never told me, sir' . . .

'Now, now, John,' said Mr MacFarlane, 'it's too early in the day for all this excitement. Calm yourself. Take a few deep breaths. Now, then, what's the matter?'

The matter was that a light had broken upon the boy, reading that thick book the night before. Orkney: surely Orkney was and always had been and always would be a backwater in the great ebb and flow of the ocean of world history. A few islands where yokels and fishermen, generation after generation, eeked out a living! Not a bit of it. Those humble people were descendants of jarls and vikings and sea-kings. In medieval times – and that wasn't so long ago, considering the vast span of human history – the earldom of Orkney was one of the chiefest centres, politically, in Europe. The lands of the earl of Orkney went deep into

Scotland, and influenced affairs in the Hebrides, Argyll and Man. His voice was listened to with respect, and sometimes fear, by the great and the little kings of Ireland. William the Conqueror, he was a near kinsman to the kings of Norway and the Orkney earls. The longships of the Orkneymen ruled the sea from horizon to horizon. The Earl Rognvald had gathered great poets into his court in Kirkwall. The same earl, a famous poet himself, had made an epic voyage through the Mediterranean to Jerusalem, Byzantium, and Rome. He had fallen in love with Ermengarde, countess of Narbonne in France, and composed a sequence of love-lyrics to her: a new thing entirely for the Norsemen at that time. A former earl, Magnus, had been martyred and made a Romish saint. That big red kirk in Kirkwall, it had been built to honour Saint Magnus. And just fancy, his own father had the same name! – It showed how the magnificence of history had seeped and sought down into the present, in a poor kind of way, admittedly, into the poor hard place they still lived in . . .

'Can I keep the book for another night or two?' said Eagle John.

'For as long as you like,' said the teacher. 'I'm glad the book has impressed you, John. And now stand out of the way. I must ring the bell.'

Along every path and track the children of the Vikings, ignorant of the glory that had once been theirs, trooped glumly for another day in the hard mill of learning.

Seventeen

One summer, early, John Fiord was twelve years old. He could leave the school at the session's end. There was nothing more that Mr MacFarlane could teach him in that small temple of learning.

'I'm glad of that,' said Magnus Fiord. 'I'm getting old. I need help with the ploughing and the fishing. Now I'll be able to take things a bit easier' . . . He had always been a rather lazy man, always behindhand with his croft work.

News of what old Magnus Fiord was saying got to Mr MacFarlane's ears. One evening he knocked at the door of Don, and was bidden to enter.

The Fiords were eating their supper of haddock, potatoes, and butter. No knives or forks. A hand sought the pots where fish and tatties smoked, and laid the food on a plate, and then poured on hot butter out of a jug.

Magnus Fiord invited Mr MacFarlane to sit down and share in the meal. Mr MacFarlane shook his head. He was rather fastidious. He remained standing over by the door.

'What's this I hear?' he said. 'When John leaves school, he is to help you with the croft and boat.'

'That's so,' said Magnus. 'That's what must happen. The sooner he puts his mind to it, the sooner I'll be able to sit at the fireside. The work's getting too much for me.'

'That's the way it must be indeed,' said Willa Fiord.

Young John carefully removed a large fish-bone from his lips.

'I wonder if you realize what you're saying,' said Mr

MacFarlane. 'That boy there has a mind. He is simply the cleverest boy I have ever taught in my whole career.'

'That's good,' said Magnus. 'But this is more to the point, will he be clever at baiting creels? Will he be clever controlling the ox and plough in the furrow?'

'Indeed,' said Willa. 'That's the only kind of cleverness that counts in this valley.'

'And to tell the truth,' said Magnus, 'he's been clumsy up to now with the boat and the ox. I blame myself. I've let him go his own gate. He might learn yet. Experience will teach him.'

Mr MacFarlane sought for words. His brow darkened a little. He cleared his throat. He sat down on the little stool under the window, but immediately rose again, to give more authority to what he had to say.

'Let me try to put the situation before you fairly and squarely,' he said. 'This boy has gifts, he has a questing mind, a whole realm of knowledge is waiting for him to enter. And you would let him waste those rare gifts on a barren acre or two.'

'What would you have him to do?' said Magnus Fiord.

'This croft has been in the one family for five generations,' said Willa Fiord.

'I'll tell you,' said Mr MacFarlane. 'At the end of August, when the new school session begins in Hamnavoe, John will enrol there.'

'And what good would that do?' said Magnus.

'He would learn things that can't be taught him here in the valley,' said Mr MacFarlane. 'Latin, French, Advanced English and mathematics. Navigation. Physics.'

'And what way,' said Willa, 'can we afford to lodge him in Hamnavoe?'

'There are grants, bursaries for poor students,' said Mr MacFarlane. 'I will make enquiries at the Education Office in Kirkwall. It will cost you nothing – not a penny.'

'The boy will be lonely, in a big place like Hamnavoe,' said the mother. 'All them shops and ships and horse-vans. He'd be frightened.'

'Pooh!' cried Mr MacFarlane. 'A little twopenny-ha'penny place like Hamnavoe! Two thousand people. John would meet and mix with his equals. No, I'm quite sure the boy's brain will prove more than a match for any of those town boys. He will be a credit to you and to the whole valley.'

'Well,' said Magnus Fiord, picking his teeth with large fish-bone, 'suppose he goes to the big school in Hamnavoe. How many years would that take?'

'Till he's sixteen or seventeen,' said the teacher. 'Until he sits and passes the higher certificate.'

'That's a long time to be without him,' said Willa Fiord. 'Five years. And us getting no younger.'

'After the higher certificate,' said Magnus, 'what then? Will he rise, maybe, to be the laird's factor?'

Mr MacFarlane drew himself erect. He sighed, twice. There were further struggles ahead.

'When John has gained the higher certificate,' he said, 'a wider horizon still opens for him. He must proceed to the university, either in Aberdeen or Edinburgh.'

Magnus Fiord shook his head gravely.

'That will not be possible,' he said. 'Say no more.'

'No,' said Willa. 'Here we have always been quiet humble simple folk. That's the way it will still be, with John and with his bairns after him.'

'Pride,' said Magnus. 'Pride must be avoided at all costs. This is the only kind of life we know. Your plans for the boy would be a ruination. For this croft, and for us, and maybe for John himself.'

John wiped his greasy mouth on the sleeve of his jersey. He rose from the table and went over to the open door of Don. On the other side of the valley men were shearing sheep. A shaggy ewe stumbled up the hillside from David of Gorse, who caught it at last by the fleece and threw it down. The boy shifted his gaze. Down at the shore, Peter of Feaquoy was gathering bait for tomorrow's fishing in the *Skua*.

Mr MacFarlane picked his words carefully. 'Many a hungry winter there has been in this croft. Many a year when your father and your grandfather were sold poor seed, and only a thin harvest was cut. Do I need to tell you? Or else some worm got into the root. Or there was not a drop of rain for the seven growing weeks of summer. Then the meal was low in the grinal, here at Don.'

'That's true,' said Magnus. 'I remember one or two years like that, when I was younger.'

'A few hard winters,' said Willa. 'I remember a hungry winter or two, and not so long ago either. I do that.'

'The fish,' said Magnus. 'They saw us through till the spring. The smoked fish and the salted fish. The lamps never lacked for fish oil.'

'But hard work,' said Willa. 'Hard dangerous work. The men's clothes never dry on their backs. Even then, there could be poor thin catches, week after week. There was that year the *Fulmar* was swamped. My own grandfather was in her that day. They never found his body.'

Mr MacFarlane sat down on the seat the boy had vacated. He leaned forward, smiling into the two grained and solemn faces. With his white hand, as he spoke, he made gentle persuasive gestures.

'One or two boys from this valley,' he said, 'have gone to sea and become master mariners. Has it corrupted them? Has it ruined them? No. Captain Tom Spence comes home to Burnside once a year at least to visit old Tammag and Williamina. You know it as well as I do, he sends them money orders through the post regularly. They won't fall into poverty in their old age.'

'Tom Spence's done well,' said Willa. 'He hasn't got above himself, that I can see.'

'He speaks a bit proper and perjink,' said Magnus. 'But forby that, I can smoke a pipe with him yet.'

'John will go to the university in Aberdeen,' said Mr MacFarlane. 'He will encounter no serious academic problems there, I can assure you of that. I went to the university of Glasgow myself. I may say, your John has far more promise than ever I had. That will take four years, or five years, or six years, depending on which faculty he embarks on.'

'Mercy!' cried Willa. 'But we'll be very old then.'

'We'll be in our graves,' said Magnus. 'Don will be in ruins!'

'You'll live to be proud of him,' said Mr MacFarlane. 'I don't know, as yet, what career he should follow. The law, medicine, divinity, the humanities – these are all possibilities. No doubt, once he gets settled into his studies at the senior school in Hamnavoe, he will begin to see his way clearly. The teachers there will know how to advise him. He'll come home summer after summer – mark my words – all our far-scattered children love to come back to the valley.'

Magnus Fiord lit his pipe and puffed in silence for a minute or two.

Willa went over to the fireside and took up her knitting.

'The fire on that hearth,' said Magnus, 'has never stopped burning for two hundred years.'

'Once the fire goes out, the roof begins to sag. And rain and snow and wind come in at the broken windows,' said Willa. 'That's a sad thing to see. There are two or three crofts in this valley like that now, and there are like to be more in the future.'

'I wouldn't like it to be said,' said Magnus, 'that I brought about the death of Don. "After old Magnus Fiord," they'll say, "only ghosts lived at Don"' . . .

'Progress,' said Mr MacFarlane earnestly, 'the slow onward and upward thrust of people – not only individuals, families, communities, but the whole of humanity. A sure steady enrichment of the human race, culturally and economically. This is the prime law of life. It works like a yeast, universally. It is seen most obviously in the great cities of Europe and especially in that marvellous young country, the United States of America. But our ways of trade and religion and learning are touching the most backward and primitive tribes on earth. All must share in the feast. There is a future of unimaginable prosperity for the whole human race. Do you think this valley is exempt from the universal trend?'

'Indeed,' said Magnus, 'I don't know what to think.'

'Such thoughts never entered my head till now,' said Willa. 'How could they? – I got poor learning at school.' In the firelight could be seen, as she turned the sock she was knitting, the eagle-scar on her wrist.

'This valley will be changed utterly in the course of the next few generations,' said Mr MacFarlane. 'We may be sure of that. A few farms only, instead of sixteen half-starving crofts. Agricultural machinery. Better crops, harvests far more abundant. A few boats only, but they'll venture further out into the Atlantic, and their nets will be full to bursting. The boatbuilders in Hamnavoe are laying bigger and bigger keels.'

'I can't imagine that time,' said Magnus, shaking his head.

'Happy the people who will live to see it,' said Mr MacFarlane. 'And another thing, medicine is improving all the time. Our children's children will live longer – they'll be spared the troubles of our wretched flesh.'

'Happy the man,' said Magnus, 'who knows nothing about this rheumatics I have in the shoulders.'

'And what,' said Willa, 'has all this to do with our John?'

'John,' said Mr MacFarlane earnestly, 'is destined to be a part of the new wave of enlightenment, prosperity, and progress that is breaking upon the world. If you deny John his chance of education, you are taking the boy's true inheritance away from him. You will choke a good seed before it has had time to root itself – yes, and to thrust itself up into the new sun and wind.'

Mr MacFarlane had become so enthusiastic over his vision of the future that he had taken his pince-nez from his nose and was sketching elaborate gestures with it over the table. His naked eyes seemed as big almost as an ox's.

Magnus went on smoking and shaking his head.

Willa – her knitting needles clacking – said at last, 'The boy will have to decide for himself.'

'John,' said Magnus from the deep straw chair. 'Come in. Mr MacFarlane and your mother and me, we have a thing to discuss with you.'

John was watching – what those inside could not see – the slow high hover of an eagle. It dropped in a slow descending spiral, it hung in the air above one of the lambs on the far side of the valley. Its shadow fell on the lamb. The lamb bleated and stumbled into the bracken. The eagle shifted, and dropped lower. And then the crofter of Gorse saw what was happening. He left off shearing the ewe and made for the bird, shouting and brandishing a stick. The eagle eased itself higher with a violent threshing of pinions. It swung off in a wide arc, out over the bay: it was mirrored in the waters. Amos of Gorse brought the lamb down to its shorn and shivering mother.

But the great bird drifted inland. It stooped and fell on a very small lamb grazing far from its mother in one of the fields of Feaquoy. The sudden thunder of its wing-beats drowned the fluttering cries of the lamb. Rob saw what was happening from the beach where he was gathering bait. He cried, he stumbled up the beach, knocking over his pail of limpets with a clang! The bird rose in a steep proud curve, and swung out over the bay towards the cliffs with the frail white burden in its talons.

John Fiord turned in the doorway. 'Yes,' said he, 'I'll go to the school in Hamnavoe at the end of summer.'

Eighteen

The years passed. In the sea valley were seedtime and harvest, birth and blossoming and death, sea-silver, sea-dearth.

In winter there were trudgings with the coffin of an old one or a child, in gales or in great white luminous winter calms, to the kirkyard on the other side of the hill.

And sometimes, if it chanced to be the last old man or old woman in a croft, the door was closed for ever. The hearth-fire that had never gone out for maybe a hundred years was gray peat-ash. Kettle and pot rusted. Rain dripped from the thatch. The curtain across the bed rotted. The wood of rafter and table began to warp slowly. A roofing stone might fall and smash in the narrow alley between house and byre.

The children of that croft, if any, had drifted away from the valley. They were farm-servants in the fertile south part of the island, or they had gone to Hamnavoe or Kirkwall to work as maid-servants or shop assistants or labourers. A few of the young men had gone to the colonies – Australia, New Zealand, Canada, South Africa – or were sailors on the far trade-routes of the world.

There were more deaths than births in the valley.

A year after her marriage, Lois of Feaquoy gave birth to a girl. All the women came, singly or in small groups, to look at the child in its cot and to lay gifts on the table for it. Most of the women thought they had never looked into such a beautiful child-face. But never a word of praise or rapture passed their lips. (It was thought to be an unlucky thing to say good things at the cradle of a new child. To do so would enrage the trows, the ugly misshapen earthspirits who moved through the valley about their secret ceremonies in winter and darkness. They thirst for music and for the comliness of human infants. Unless a mother kept constant vigil, the trows would seize the baby from its crib and substitute one of their own ugly twisted children. That is why there are so many unlucky-looking and sickly people in the world.)

'Bless the bairn,' said old Wiliamina of Burnside. The women standing here and there in the room murmured blessings too. They lingered awhile. They left, singly or in groups. The table was strewn with their little gifts – shawls, a sampler, cakes.

Mary Jean, though she rarely visited Lois, put her head round the door to see what gifts had been brought. 'What meanness! What misery!' she said. 'You would think they were poor as tinkers. Did Selina knit those mittens? She's made three bad mistakes – look! I know why Selina took them here. Because the shop in Voes refused them.'

Mary Jean came back the very next day. She put a coin on the table. 'For the bairn,' she said. It was a sovereign.

On the third day Mary Jean was there again, standing between the window and the crib. 'What name are you going to give the child?'

Lois turned from stirring the fish soup in the pot.

'Sunniva,' she said.

'What kind of a name is that? – I suppose it's one of them Gaelic names,' said Mary Jean; and went away shaking her head.

Someone had come early one morning and left a gift on the doorstep. It was a piece of driftwood, raw and torn as the waves had cast it on the shore, but someone had carved a cornstalk on it. The knife-marks were new and fresh. It had been well carved. It represented 'the full corn in the ear', a barley-stalk ripe and heavy for the scythe.

Who could have left such a gift?

Peter and his mother Mary Jean shook their heads, examining it. 'It is a good piece of carving,' said Peter, 'whoever did it.'

'It's a useless thing, if you ask me,' said Mary Jean.

A few mornings later, Lois went to the burn to wash some clothes. The other women had already done their washing and gone home. A shadow fell on the pool. Lois looked up. Maisie of Gorse was standing on the other side of the pool. She knelt and began to wash her own baby-clothes.

From this hollow the two young mothers could not be seen from any door or window in the valley.

They kneaded and wrung and shook out their washing in silence. The small music of the burn and the water-drops raining back into the pool were the only sounds.

Then Maisie straightened herself and threw back her long bronze hair from her face.

'Bless the child,' she whispered, not looking at Lois. Between the noise of the burn and a sudden outcry of gulls along the shore – for the fishing boats were in – it could have been a mere solemn beautiful movement of Maisie's lips; locked soon upon silence.

Maisie took up her basket of washing and turned to go.

Lois said, in the strange melancholy accent of her people, 'Someone in your house is good with knife and tree. I thank you for the cornstalk. Sunniva thanks you.'

Maisie put her finger to her lips. The two young women smiled to each other.

They went their separate ways.

Nineteen

The valley turned about the sun, in a slow year-long wheel of harvest burnish and brimming sea silver and hungry cats and gulls.

From plough to quernstone and fire, the time of corn is reckoned in days. And therewith men nourish themselves for the longer rhythms of childhood, labour, love, and the wisdom of age (but often enough it is babbling folly.) From cradle to coffin the time of a man or a woman is reckoned in a few years – seventy, according to the psalmist.

The time of a man is not very much longer than the time of cornstalks. For each, equally, a reaper waits with a scythe.

And sickness and death can come to a child as well as to a person weighed down with years. 'He's well by with it,' an old cripple man might mutter from his open door, looking at a small white coffin being carried along the road that winds to the kirkyard on the other side of the hill. 'Why is a bright bairn taken, and an old thing like me left lingering in misery?'

About this time there was more contact than before between the valley folk and outsiders. Some kind of sicknesses unknown in the valley up to then began to appear – fevers, infections, and especially the sickness they called 'decline' or 'wasting' or 'consumption'. That illness carried off many of the valley people, of all ages, in a few years. In one stricken house a whole family of five people perished in a twelvemonth: a grandmother, a father, three children. A son of Flinders croft, who had gone to sea, had come home the summer previously, wasted and bright eyed with fever.

Another croft began to waste and wither too, but stone is harder than cornstalks and the bright flesh about the bone. A roofing-stone slid, the thatch leaked, the spider plied its trade unhindered.

It had been known for men from the valley to die by drowning. But no such death had happened for two generations. The men were famed all over the islands as good boatmen. Sudden storms they encountered, but always the fishing boats came back, full or half-full or empty: and a steady hand kept the tiller.

To the women waiting at the shore on a stormy winter afternoon, it seemed that two or three boats might well be whelmed under the sudden great seas. They stood there, their faces cold as the stones around them.

But Lois, whenever the storms blew up suddenly and the fishing boats were out, never went down to the shore. She sat at home, and turned the spinning wheel, she set the cradle rocking from time to time.

And always, in the darkening, the door would burst open, and Peter would be there, 'a ghost with a red mouth'! He would squeeze spindrift out of his beard, and set down the basket of fish in a cold corner, and go over and look long into the face of the child. And, last, he would turn and put his cold mouth to the fire-flushed cheek of Lois.

Lois would light the lamp.

Through the window she would see, lamp after lamp, the crofts celebrating a dozen safe home-comings from the sea.

And then the old grandmother's cry from next door. 'Did you not see this storm coming, Peter? Your father had more sense. Do you want to leave three women to starve after you? You're a fool!'

And as the fish was boiling in the black pot, and Peter squatted beside the fire to dry the last of the sea out of his clothes, Lois went over to the cradle and brought the child to its father.

Gentle and firm he held it, while the roused fire threw over them its gold-and-dark net. And he sang to it, and kissed it, and uttered all kinds of nonsense to it.

And Sunniva laughed into his face; but she laughed without sound.

The child was deaf and dumb.

'I've known it since she was born,' said Lois. 'But I did not like to tell you, man. She'll never have music inside her head, or words on her tongue and that's a pity. She won't know the sounds of wind and sea either. It's maybe better, so.'

Twenty

It happened that those two old women, Tomina Flett of Gorse and Mary Jean Sinclair of Feaquoy tried to get in touch with each other before they died.

It was a hard winter, with much snow. One morning soon after sunrise old Tomina was seen wandering down to the shore in her nightgown, with bare feet. 'Tomina, you'll get your death,' said Charlie Budge of Crag who was going along the shore with fishing lines to his boat.

'I'm looking for that old fool Amos,' said Tomina. 'Have you seen him? I warrant he's off the Old Man by this time. I warned him well. "Amos," said I, "there's a bad storm coming, you'll be swamped if you go on the sea". I can't do anything with that old fool.'

'Amos is dead twelve years now,' said Charlie Budge.

'If you see him out there,' said Tomina, shading her eyes seaward, 'tell him to turn back. You'll be all right, but I see drowning, drowning, and a salted body carried through the fields, and I see salt pools on the flagstones of the floor.'

She shook her head and went back the way she had come, her feet leaving deep irregular marks in the snow.

Young Charlie of Crag was relieved to see Maisie running across the white field towards her mother-in-law.

That was only the beginning of the old one's winter wanderings.

Maisie kept an eye on her till the snow had gone. There Tomina sat beside the fire with the shawl about her head, muttering disconnected things out of her past. Food and drink were of small interest to her. She would consent, sometimes, to take a spoon or two of soup, or a piece of fish, if Maisie put them near her mouth. Often she sighed, and shook her head. 'Who's that man?' she said one afternoon when her son David stood in the open door, just in from ploughing. 'What is he wanting here?'

One morning she got up before dawn. The shepherd at the laird's big farm found her wandering along the road between the hills. 'Mistress Flett,' said he, 'and are you off to catch the Hamnavoe ferry at this time in the morning?' She had managed to get her Sunday coat on, but her thin white hair was loose in the wind, and she thumped and flapped her way along the road, for she had only one shoe on.

'What business is it of yours, where I'm going?' she said darkly. Then, having hobbled on a few steps, she turned and took the shepherd by the elbow. 'It's the debts,' she said. 'Amos and me, we're to be put in the prison, for fraud. You're a friend, don't tell anybody. There's been three of four lawyer's letters. I'm taking the boat to Hamnavoe. I'm going to settle up with the shopkeepers – it mightn't be too late. Now then, where did I put the purse?' Tomina fell to rummaging through her coat, into this pocket and that. 'The money's not here!' she cried. 'Whatever will we do?'

The shepherd was pleased to see David Flett running along the road from the valley. In a distant farmyard a cock crew.

'Mother,' said David, 'I'll take you home with me now. Here's your other shoe.' To the shepherd he said, 'She's a bit confused in her mind.'

'That man has just stolen all our savings!' Tomina yelled, with such energy that the strings of her throat stretched. 'The vagabond!'

In the end she went quietly back along the road with her son.

The shepherd watched them, shaking his head.

Tomina appeared at the school door one day when Miss Strachan, the tuning-fork in her hand, was taking the children through an English folk-song: 'Sweet less of Richmond hill, I'd crowns resign to call her mine, that lass of Richmond hill,' the shrill voices went, high and low. Miss Strachan paused, her conducting hand like a swan in the air. Tomina peered here and there, at the scholars. 'Margaret,' she whispered at the silence of twenty gaping mouths, 'are you there? You're to come home at once. The undertaker's coming this afternoon. I have the flowers for you, look. So come' . . . She had a ragged bunch of marsh marigolds and dandelions in her hand.

Miss Strachan rose from the music stool and said gently, 'There's no girl called Margaret in the school just now.'

The old woman sighed, 'Ah, well,' she said, 'maybe father's carried her to the doctor in Voes. Maybe it's not her time yet. But there's no hope for her. No hope.'

She threw the flowers on the floor and turned away.

Miss Strachan watched her as she went carefully across the burn on the stepping stones, as though each stone was a great delicate egg.

Matthew Flett of Gorse said, 'That's my grannie.'

'She's gone off her head,' said another child. 'She's daft.'

'Be quiet, you!' cried Miss Strachan, quite sharply. 'We will all be old some day. Old people get lost in their memories, that's all.'

'My grannie had a sister called Margaret,' whispered Matthew. 'She died when she was twelve' . . .

Old Tomina took to wandering all over the valley. Maisie no longer tried to restrain her. In her new world of fantasy her will was harder than ever. She would stop this one and that, whomever she met, and look deep into their faces. 'I don't know you,' she would say, 'but you have the face of Moll of Flinders' . . . Or she would take a crofter urgently by the elbow. 'I haven't been a good woman, but I haven't been a very bad woman either, have I?' . . . And she wouldn't let go until he had assured her that she'd been a good neighbour and a kind person in the valley.

'Thank you, thank you,' she would say . . . But after a few steps she would stop, and shake her head doubtfully.

For a whole week in early summer she sat quiet in her chair at the fire. She made several sensible remarks. 'The peats never properly dried after the wet summer last year' . . . 'Maisie – that's your name, I know – I'd like an oatcake and rhubarb jam to my supper' . . . 'What did old Amos have to climb up to the chimney-head for? Ah, well, he's at rest now' . . . 'My sister Margaret died too, a long while ago. She looked that bonny in her shroud' . . . 'I haven't been very well lately, but soon I'll be better' . . . 'I suppose David could have had a better wife than you, Maisie, but you'll do, you'll do' . . .

'The cloud's leaving her mind,' said Maisie to David when he came in from the sea. David said nothing. Maisie went down with the knife to gut the haddocks. (With that same knife she had put carvings everywhere about Gorse, on the bed and windows and doorpost. On the table she had cut a loaf and a bottle and a fish. There was an incised ox on the byre door. She was forever whittling bits of driftwood into flower-shapes, bird-shapes; there was a likeness of the laird, at which everyone laughed, if a bit uneasily.)

Two days later the old woman said to Maisie, 'There's one thing I must do yet: I would like to have a word with Mary Jean Sinclair over at Feaquoy. I'll go there tomorrow, if I'm able.'

But the next day Tomina couldn't rise from her chair. 'Who are you?' she said to Maisie. 'Leave me alone. Who asked you to cross this threshold? Go back where you came from.'

She sat muttering over the flames all that afternoon. Sometimes she would turn her head and give Maisie a dark look. She pressed her lips together like a trap when Maisie offered her a spoon of broth.

Young Matthew came in from the school and threw his school-bag in the corner.

The old woman screeched at him, 'You're not to go out in that boat! Do you hear me! Stay on the land. You are never to go to the fishing. I won't have any arguing about it. What I've said, I've said!'

The boy began to cry.

Half an hour later old Tomina slumped sideways in her chair. She was dead by the time Maisie had stretched her out on her bed.

Three days previously, old Mary Jean Sinclair had fallen on a wet stone crossing the burn, and broken her thigh-bone.

What she had been doing trying to cross the burn nobody asked. For ten years she had not been on the far side of the burn. The far side of the burn was enemy territory. Meantime her huge bulk half-dammed the water in the little burn.

The water rose about her, brimming. It happened in the hollow between the banks. Nobody had seen the great stumble and splash. She lay there for an hour.

'I'm not going to cry out,' Mary Jean remarked, half in and half out of the burn, to a starling who had been sole witness to the mishap. 'I never cried out for help in my life, and I'm too old to start now. Still, it's strange that it should happen on this particular day' . . .

It was the dumb child Sunniva that found her.

'It would be you' said her grandmother. 'You won't be able to tell a living soul. Don't distress yourself. I'm quite content to be where I am.'

The girl had surprising strength. She waded into the burn and raised the huge body out of the suck and drag and pulled it half on to the bank, and laid it among the clover and the bees. The starling had long since flown away.

The free burn water sang on its way to the sea.

Sunniva kissed her grandmother, then she turned and ran quickly back to Feaquoy.

Four hay-makers carried Mary Jean indoors.

'I'll dry myself,' shouted Mary Jean from her bed. 'Fetch the thick flannel nightgown from under the bed. I don't want the white weave on me for a day or two still. I'll be long enough in that shroud. Oh, a very long time.'

And she laughed.

'Soon you'll be as right as the rain and the sun and the wind itself,' said Lois, half singing the words. 'Your chickens and your goat will have a great longing for you, if you keep to your bed. But you'll soon be out among them. Yes, and down at the beach gutting the fish. Peter needs you for that. For I will be gutting no fish, today or any day to come. If that burn had been in spate, grandmother, you'd have drowned. Thank God our girl saw you in time. You look beautiful in your bed, with your wet combed hair.'

'I don't feel beautiful,' said the old woman. 'Anything but. Get the mothballs out of the winding sheet.'

The girl Sunniva stood in the door, looking gravely at her grandmother.

Peter said, 'I'll go to Voes now for the doctor. Your leg needs setting.'

'That'll be too much expense,' said Mary Jean. 'I'll be glad to be let die in peace. But it's funny this thing should have happened on this particular day.'

'How so?' said Peter.

'Never mind,' said his mother. 'You wouldn't be able to take it in. I was just going an errand to the far side of the burn. I wanted to see a certain person.'

'I'll make you some porridge,' said Lois. 'It will keep the strength in you.'

'I have to laugh when I think of it,' said Mary Jean from the bed. 'Stones have been the death of us both, Rob and me. Only Rob died in a great shower and clash and clatter of stones, they fell on him and broke him. And as for me, I slip on one wet stone, crossing the burn, on a certain peaceable errand. But it won't be so quick for me as for old Rob . . . Did you say porridge, woman?'

'Yes, to strengthen you,' said Lois.

'Strengthening's the last thing I want,' said Mary Jean. 'Let the oil burn up quickly. The lamp's nearly out. Leave me alone now, I feel tired.'

Sunniva waited at the bedside till her grandmother fell asleep.

When Sunniva came, with the first shadows, to light the lamp in her grandmother's room, she saw the sweat-silvered face.

A slow internal fire had been kindled – it was beginning to eat at the old huge woman.

'Yes, I have a little bit of pain,' she said to Peter and Lois at midnight, 'but nothing to make a song and dance about . . . Yes, I'm short in the breath. I've been more winded, many a time, trying to turn round the old ox at the end of the furrow . . . I've been on the go seventy-two years – it's little wonder – I'm short – in the wind . . . No, I want no whisky . . . and I want . . . no honey . . . I want . . . nothing . . .'

In the morning, though she blazed with fever, (and those flames seemed to have shrunk hers) she said distinctly, 'How is it with the old woman over at Gorse?'

'Will I tell her?' whispered Peter to Lois.

'Why not, whatever?' said Lois.

'Don't whisper like that' said Mary Jean. 'I'm not a bairn or a fool.'

'Tomina Flett of Gorse died on the night,' said Peter.

'I won't be long after her,' said Mary Jean. 'They can carry us through the hills to the kirkyard on the same day. It'll save a journey.'

'You'll be better soon,' said Peter.

'You were always a deceiver, boy,' she said. 'Leave me now. I was never so tired.'

The deaf and dumb child lingered. 'Come here, Sunniva,' said her grandmother.

Sunniva put out her cold hand into the burning hand on the counterpane. Mary Jean clung to Sunniva as though she was drowning in a sea of fire.

'I bless the day you were born,' said the old woman.

And those were her last words.

Twenty-One

'Well,' said the valley men when the news of those two deaths got around, 'it's good in this sense, there'll be a double funeral, and that'll save us half a day's tramping to the kirkyard and back in Sabbath suits' . . . 'Yes, and the hay's still to be cut' . . .

But when old Tom Laird the coffin-maker mentioned the possibility of a double funeral to David of Gorse, he was quickly put in his place. 'My mother that's away wouldn't have wanted that. Every person's entitled to her own funeral.'

So it came about that Tomina was carried to the kirkyard on the Tuesday. All the valley men were there, except Peter of Feaquoy. While the minister was reading the words of committal round the open grave, the gravedigger who (his work being half done) had retired behind a gravestone to light his pipe, saw Peter Sinclair passing on the road outside, in his fishing gansy and moleskins, as if he was going for twine and hooks to the shop in Voes. Peter stopped at the kirkyard gate, and raised his bonnet, and went back the way he had come, quickly, so that none of the mourners should know he had been there.

'No disrespect to your mother,' said old Tom Laird to David Spence, 'but we won't come to Gorse and drink the funeral whisky till the evening. There's a smell of rain in the wind. This hay must be carted.'

Mary Jean was buried the next morning, in another part of the kirkyard.

'I wonder,' said the gravedigger in the lee of a big head-stone, lighting his pipe, 'if David of Gorse is anywhere around' . . . But David of Gorse was nowhere to be seen.

If, on both mornings, the mourners had praised the good qualities of the two women, going home they grumbled low among themselves, but out of hearing of the sons, about the waste of two fine hay-making mornings.

They noticed, entering the valley, that David of Gorse was not out in his hayfield. For him, too, it had been an idle morning.

There were heavy rainclouds over the Atlantic. They told Peter to keep the funeral whisky till the evening. They got out of their Sabbath suits into their coarse sarks and breeks, and swarmed out into the hayfield. Only when they had begun did David Flett of Gorse take his own fork to the hay.

And the women came out in the middle of the afternoon with jars of ale and baskets of bread and cheese.

Maisie came out with a black shawl over her head . . .

It was noticed that those two young wives, Maisie Flett and Lois Sinclair, always washed their clothes on the same day, in the same part of the burn, where it broadened into a deep still pool. The two washer-women couldn't be seen from the croft houses. But on a still morning the hollow seemed to be brimming over with words and laughter. Always, when she was happy, Lois sang: they seemed to be melancholy songs, yet there was a blitheness in them too. The valley folk listened, and shook their heads and went on with their tasks.

One day David of Gorse said to his wife, 'You will do the washing of your clothes in the place where my mother did her washing, higher up the burn. She that's away would have wanted that.'

For the next three Mondays Lois carried her basket of washing to the pool, and Maisie wasn't there. She saw Maisie kneading her clothes, and wringing, at a part of the burn higher up. Lois gathered her wet washing to move upstream too, but Maisie held out the palm of her hand at full stretch, and slowly shook her head.

Lois went back to the hidden pool. There were no songs from the hollow that morning.

'I am a stranger in this place for ever,' she said to Peter, when he came up from the shore with his lobsters. Peter could see the strains of weeping on her face. 'It's hard to break an ancient quarrel,' he said. 'We must have patience. We will see what is to happen. I think it might be better, in the meantime, if you keep to the part of the burn my mother that's away used to do her washing at.'

It was soon the time for sheep-shearing. The crofters sorted out their own sheep from the communal herd that had been grazing together on the high moor all summer, and brought them in, each man to his own enclosure.

Peter Sinclair asked Willie Smith of Skeld, as a favour, to bring in the sheep of Feaquoy. Peter had discovered a warped board in the *Skua*. He would be most of the day putting in a new plank.

When he came up from the beach with his saw and plane and hammer and bag of nails, Peter saw a group of valley men discussing the sorting-out of the common flock and the condition of the sheep. A few had died on the moor – all that was left of them were shreds of filthy fleece and a few bones. One or two had gotten a kind of rot in the hoof. But on the whole they were in better shape than most summers. David of Gorse said he had rounded up all his sheep but one – very likely it had gone over the cliff.

Willie of Skeld noticed Peter Sinclair passing on with his tools. 'I got all your ewes, Peter,' he said. 'They're in good condition.'

After supper Peter went into the small field to look at his sheep. 'This is strange,' he said, 'there's one more than there should be.'

Peter examined the ear clippings one after the other. One of the ewes had the mark of Gorse on it.

Peter singled out the ewe and drove it slowly in front of him across the burn towards Gorse. David was smoking his pipe at the end of the house. He gripped the pipe so hard when he saw Peter approaching that his knuckles showed white.

Those men had never spoken to each other since they were children.

'This ewe is not mine,' said Peter. 'It has your mark in its ear. It was driven into my pen by mistake. I ought to have known better than to ask Willie of Skeld. He can't be entirely depended on. I have brought it back so that there should be no trouble about it.'

David behaved as though he saw no one and heard no one. But when he struck another match to light his pipe he burnt his finger. The clay pipe fell and smashed on the brigstones.

Peter lifted the struggling ewe over the low stone wall of Gorse and let it run.

'May tomorrow be a better day,' said Peter gravely, and turned his face homeward.

The deaf-and-dumb girl ran to meet her father, and threw her arms about him.

Lois stood at the door. She looked across the valley towards Gorse. Maisie was standing in her open door, alone. David had gone inside.

Maisie raised her hand in greeting. Lois raised her hand, then put her fingers to her mouth six or seven times and sent kisses over the burn. She gave a cry of joy and greeting in Gaelic.

'Behave yourself,' said Peter of Feaquoy. 'People will think you're out of your mind.'

Twenty-Two

Miss Yvonne Strachan, the teacher – more than a few islanders thought that, if she wasn't exactly out of her mind, she was a very strange person indeed. 'Her ways are not our ways,' they said.

They reasoned within themselves, for it never came to open discussion, that it was they who must seem uncouth and weird to her, an educated young woman from the city of Edinburgh. To her they must seem half-savages, sunk in ignorance and old ways. Miss Strachan existed in a place of light; they ought to be grateful that their children, in these days of free education, could have the eyes of their understanding touched with the radiance of true knowledge.

Perhaps Captain Thomas Spence, of the Ben Line, might have something in common with her, when he came home on leave. But, after being introduced formally to each other, Miss Strachan treated this far-travelled son of the valley, who had done so well for himself, and even spoke with an English accent, quite coldly.

Surely she would have interesting conversations with John Fiord, when he came back on holiday from the university in Aberdeen. They did drink tea together, once or twice, up at the schoolhouse. But after that it seemed they had nothing more to say to one another. Indeed, Miss Strachan seemed uneasy in John Fiord's presence. Perhaps it was the way Eagle John fixed her with his wide absent eye, half curious, half amused.

They had discussed, over tea, art and literature. Miss Strachan spoke warmly of Christina Rossetti and Mrs Henry Wood. The student didn't seem to know their works. He was immersed in the classics, Theocritus and Pindar. He quoted bits of *The Greek Anthology*.

When John Fiord came home next time at Christmas, there was no invitation to him to have tea at the schoolhouse.

No, but for Miss Strachan to have chosen Willie Smith of Skeld – the valley folk could not get over that! If there was a more useless young man in all Orkney than Willie Skeld, they would like to know who he was. His parents, old now, worked Skeld as well as they could, but whatever would happen to the croft and the fishing boat and Willie himself, when they were no longer there? It wasn't that he was utterly idle or useless. No: he was only too willing to do odd jobs here and there about the valley for other people – such as sorting out the hill sheep for fleecing, or painting a boat, or carrying home peats, or getting thatch for a roof. His face shone with eagerness to be asked. But let old Ben or Liza, his parents, tell him to do anything around Skeld, and Willie was up and off like a scalded cat!

After Miss Strachan had been appointed to the school, a kind of enchantment fell on the young man. He devoted himself to Miss Strachan utterly. 'He hangs about her like a dog.' the valley folk said to each other. No longer, after that first summer, was Willie Smith there to give the crofter-fisherman a hand with the boat-launching or the peat-stacking. Willie moved forever between the croft of Skeld and the schoolhouse. Willie's whole time and attention were given to the teacher. Ah! Miss Strachan was a nervous wreck one weekend – one night soon after she came she had heard a mouse scrabbling between the walls of the schoolhouse. She could not bear it! She would have to leave. While she was teaching geography on the Monday morning, a face appeared at the school window. It was Willie, holding up two dead *rats*. The children cheered. Miss Strachan screeched. Willie disappeared, to throw the rats to the gulls.

She would send Willie on errands to the shop in Voes, ten miles away. Off he would trot, like any obedient boy, with basket and purse, and return before nightfall: the basket brimming with things the valley folk never knew to exist: jars of health-giving malt extract, a whole pineapple, sheets of piano music, brushes and water-colour boxes and blocks of painting paper, packets of macaroni, jars of herbs and spices, cigarettes. Yes, cigarettes. Old Lizzie of Whinstones, seeing a light in the schoolhouse kitchen one evening, thought it no harm to take a look inside. There, at the upright piano that had been shipped from Edinburgh a fortnight before, sat Miss Strachan, 'a neck on her as long as a swan' (according to Lizzie), her long fingers going plink-plonk over the keyboard, while Willie watched and listened, entranced, from the rocking chair. The music ended with a loud triumphant chord. Slowly the dreamy other-world look passed from Miss Strachan's face. Didn't she then reach for a small packet from the mantelpiece, and open it, and offer one long white round thing to Willie, and put another into her own mouth? Then the little flame of the struck match wandered between them, and they gave out smoke as if their brains were on fire! Willie was often seen outside after that, lounging at a wall with a cigarette between his lips.

What must tobacco taste like, without the seasoning of briar or clay? . . . But soon, a few of the younger men threw away their pipes and took to cigarette-smoking too.

When Miss Strachan had first come, the croft-women would often leave fish, or a chicken or a lobster, or a dish of warm eggs, or a basket of potatoes at her door. Miss Strachan wrote a note to each of the crofts, which the children carried home. 'I am deeply grateful for the presents you have so kindly set on my doorstep. However, being a vegetarian, I do not eat the flesh of animal, fish, or fowl. I am sure you will respect my scruples. An occasional small fish for Beatrice would be most welcome' . . . Beatrice was Miss Strachan's cat, brought in a basket from Edinburgh, a white fluffed-up useless creature that fled in terror from the half-wild cats of the valley, and at last never ventured further than the window-sill.

The valley folk shook their heads more than ever. Without strong nourishing meat from sea and land, Miss Strachan wouldn't likely live much beyond the age of thirty . . .

Occasionally Willie was despatched to the pier, to see if the ferryboat had not yet brought the new novel by Marie Corelli that she had ordered, it must be a month since . . .

Came the next early summer, and Miss Strachan wandered through the valley in a dream. As the wild flowers came in their season, she plucked one or two and brought them home to press dry in a special book. She would set up her easel here and there in the valley and paint, swiftly and ecstatically, a water-colour. 'You live in a little heaven here,' she said to Lizzie of Whinstone who was trudging home with two full buckets of water on a yoke.

'Heaven!' cried old Lizzie to Steven her brother when she had set down her buckets. 'She's maybe clever, too clever for her own good. This heaven, as she calls it, has made a wreck of the two of us' . . .

One Saturday, Willie Smith appeared in the valley wheeling the queerest contraption they had ever seen. Crossing the burn, he had to hoist it on to his shoulders. They watched from near and far. A few advanced to the corner of their fields. But the children were all about Miss Strachan, open-mouthed, when Willie set the iron whirling thing against the school-house wall. 'This, children,' said Miss Strachan, 'is a *bicycle*. In the next few weeks it will, I hope, take me to many places in the island that I haven't been able to get to. There are so many birds and flowers to observe!' . . . Then Miss Strachan, to the general amazement, mounted the bicycle and rode round and round the school yard on it. 'Thank you, Willie dear' . . . The children danced with excitement.

Bird-watching: that was another of Miss Strachan's delights. Before the advent of the bicycle, she had walked everywhere in the valley and along the cliffs farther on with her binoculars and her bird-book. She scanned the skies over sea and hill. If she caught a bird in her lucent prisms, she would stalk it for a while, then let the binoculars hand down and thumb quickly through the bird-book in the pocket of her tweed jacket. 'A kestrel, Will!' she would cry in triumph. As like as not Willie was out of range, smoking a cigarette behind a rock: for even Willie saw little point in looking at birds flying. Still, summoned, he would come, he would stand beside her, he would raise the binoculars to his eyes. 'I can see the town of Thurso in Scotland,' Willie would say. 'Just imagine that! Every roof, near enough. There's the kirk steeple.'

Once Miss Strachan intruded, inadvertently and alone, on the nesting ground of the skuas. Bird by bird they came at her, full-spanned, cold-eyed, sharp-curved, hurtling down at her head till she felt the wind of their passing in her hair. She turned and fled. She fell among the heather and rose with torn stockings, bleeding fingers. Maisie Flett went out to meet her and brought her in to Gorse for a cup of tea; till she felt strong enough to go home.

That evening she raged at Willie, when he came on his visit, 'Why didn't you tell me, man? Those birds could have killed me!'

'They never actually touch you,' said Willie. 'They just want to scare you away from their nests.'

Before sunset Willie had to return to the high moor to retrieve the binoculars and bird-book she had abandoned in her flight.

Miss Strachan did not visit skua territory again.

Once they scrambled together up the scree hill. A bird, no bigger than a pulsing dot, hung high above, on the edge of a cloud. The binoculars caught it and held it. Miss Strachan adjusted the focus, and looked again. Then her fingers scurried through the pages of her bird-book: 'birds of prey' section. 'I can't see this one anywhere,' she said.

'It's an eagle,' said Willie idly, without even bothering to look throgh the binoculars.

'An eagle!' breathed Miss Strachan. 'Oh let me see! I must drink this in to the full! The king of the air.'

The eagle turned and veered off, flying high, and the great brown shoulder of the hill hid it.

On Monday morning the children all recited the poem Miss Strachan had written on the blackboard:

> He clasps the rock with crooked hands
> Close to the sun in lonely lands
> Ringed with the azure world he stands
>
> The wrinkled sea beneath him crawls.
> He watches from his mountain walls.
> And like a thunderbolt he falls.

'Now, boys and girls,' said Miss Strachan, 'what is the poet Alfred Lord Tennyson describing so wonderfully?'

The children looked blankly at Miss Strachan, at the blackboard, at the floor, at each other.

'A bird?' prompted Miss Strachan.

Still they had no idea.

'Why, it is the eagle, king of birds! By great good fortune I managed to see one, flying high over Coolag Hill, at the weekend' . . .

On one occasion that first winter the laird and his lady invited Miss Strachan to dinner at the big house. The other guests were the minister and his wife. Once only it had happened – never again . . . Jemima Ritch, who served at table that night, told how Miss Strachan had refused the broth, the trout and the grouse, and the wine, and made do with a potato and a spoon of cabbage. For dessert, she had eaten an apple.

Jemima Ritch had never known the laird's lady, or the minister, to be so upset. Nor had she seen the laird himself splash so much red wine from the decanter into his glass, again and again.

The table talk, according to Jemima, had been very dis-jointed – she had never known it that way before at the laird's table – usually it was the laird who dominated the meal with reminiscences of his days in the Indian Army: Lucknow and the Khyber Pass – and with observations on the present state of the nation, and what should be done with the Irish to pacify them for good and all. On this unique evening, Miss Strachan had broken into the monologue time and again, questioned his opinions, countered with opinions of her own, until the laird, who had been very gallant and avuncular towards her at the beginning of the meal, had gradually fallen silent, while his cheeks and nose (with the wine) became ever more crimson-engorged. Jemima did not rightly know what the talk had been about: all she could tell the awed country folk later was that Miss Strachan had declared herself to be 'a socialist' and 'a suffragette'. Somewhat later in the evening she had turned to the kindly old minister. 'No doubt, Mr Blackie,' she had said, 'you are wondering why you haven't seen me in church on Sunday. I will tell you. I am an agnostic. Not an atheist, mark you: an *agnostic*'. 'I see, I see, I see,' poor Mr Blackie had stammered, dabbing his whiskers with his napkin. 'Well, well, well.'

And it turned out that Miss Strachan was against blood sports of every kind. (This while the laird's whisker dripped with the juices of a roast grouse.) The laird paused. 'And what, pray, would my people in the island do if they couldn't fish and breed animals for food, eh?'

'That kind of flesh-eating is of necessity,' Miss Strachan replied. 'They do not slaughter for the fun of it. Hunting for sport is a vileness, especially when the birds and animals are often more beautiful than the hunters.'

As for the two ladies, Mrs Blackie did not seem to know what everyone but Miss Strachan was upset about; Mrs Blackie existed in a tranquil inner world of her own, defined by the flowers, herbs and birds in the huge Manse garden, the dew and the rain and the sundial; on the whole she did not like evenings such as this, when she had to eat too much and listen to the laird, and afterwards play whist. Something was wrong tonight; she would ten times rather have been back among the flowerbeds with her watering-can. It must be that strange young woman, the new teacher.

Nor had the laird's wife known anything like it before. Her mind wandered between secret glee at her husband's discomfiture and cold anger at this young ill-bred upstart of a woman. That such a creature should have the educating of the valley children! And yet a part of her exulted in the pummelling that was being handed out to the master of the house.

Jemima brought in the coffee and the brandy decanter. The laird offered the silver cigar box to Mr Blackie. The match-flame lingered between the two cigars. 'Wait one moment!' cried Miss Strachan. Out of her bag she brought a cigarette holder, and fitted a black Russian-type cigarette into it. 'Before the match goes out!'

The laird burned his fingers and shouted 'Damn!' . . . 'I see, I see,' murmured the minister, shawling his face in cigar smoke. 'Well, well, well.' . . .

The laird's wife got to her feet. 'I'm sorry,' she said. 'I think we'll have to dispense with whist tonight. One of my severer migraines is coming on – I feel it' . . .

'It has been such a lovely evening, thank you,' murmured Mrs Blackie, getting to her feet. 'I hope you feel better soon. Miss Strachan, it has been so nice to meet an original person like yourself. You must come and visit me at the Manse sometime. I'd love to show you the garden. Would that not be nice, James?'

'Perhaps, perhaps,' said Mr Blackie. 'It could well be so.'

'Migraine,' said Miss Strachan, searching in her bag for matches. 'You are eating the wrong food – all that meat and blood – that's what's giving you migraines. The dramatist George Bernard Shaw, a man of very great intellect, equates vegetarianism with good health and clear thinking.'

'Goodnight to you,' said the laird without getting up. Instead he swilled his jowls with brandy, and glared at the most impudent young woman he had ever set eyes on. So this was what education did to the lower orders. Those fools in Parliament might have known!

'Vegetables and water,' said Miss Strachan to the small company, rising from her place. 'It would add years to your life – it would intensify very greatly your delight in nature and the world of thought.'

The laird choked on brandy and cigar smoke.

'Jemima, bring Miss Strachan's coat,' cried the lady of the house, in a voice that mingled glee and disapproval.

'We have brought the pony and trap,' said Mrs Blackie. 'James will drive you back to the schoolhouse. It will be no trouble.'

'That won't be necessary,' said Miss Strachan. 'I enjoy a ride on my bicycle before bedtime. I have left it at the gate.'

She was never invited back to the big house.

Mrs Blackie would have loved to show the strange young woman her late roses, the beehives, the sundial. But she was persuaded that it would be inadvisable.

'Something will have to be done about that person,' said the laird, whose voice carried a certain weight on the Education Board . . . 'I will see to it, and that very soon.'

But that same winter he died, 'helped on his way by sclerosis of the brain, red meat, and brandy,' declared Miss Strachan.

The laird's son arrived from an office in Birmingham to manage the estate. He sat on the Education Board too, of course, but the name of Miss Strachan meant nothing to him (though his mother had told him more than once the story of the ruined evening that had had, nevertheless, she confessed, a certain strangeness and excitement in it.) And so Miss Strachan's stay in the valley was longer by eleven or twelve years than it might otherwise have been.

The new laird brought the first motor-car to the island.

The car stank and rattled and snorted into the valley one March morning when the crofters were out ploughing. The oxen stood stock-still in the furrows. The ploughmen gazed in wonderment at this metal machine that they had heard about but never seen; it came to a halt in a roar and a cloud of dust and fumes near the school.

The scholars had never known such a sound in their lives. 'You may drop your pencils for a moment,' cried Miss Strachan. 'Come to the window to look. What you are seeing is *a motor-car*. A motor-car. It is one of the marvels of the new age. I have, of course, seen them in the city of Edinburgh and in other places many times. In Orkney too, some day, they will be quite common.'

The new laird, having surveyed the valley with his eye – another part of his inheritance – whirled the starter till the engine coughed into life, got into his motor-car again, backed, turned, and drove off in a cloud of dust and fumes. He did not talk to anyone; he paid a factor to do his necessary business with the islanders.

At that time the only horse in the valley belonged to the croft of Quoy. It had been grazing peaceably under the hill. It rolled its eye round on the departing motor-car, then it gave a great whinny and reared up, whirling its hooves.

Ox by ox, smouldering, was prodded down the next unbroken furrow.

Twenty-Three

The valley folk had long gotten used to the sight of Miss Strachan bathing in the sea on summer mornings, early. She would frolic along the sand, clad in a black knitted bathing costume that reached from neck to elbows and knees, and throw herself with a cry into the breakers. Further out, her head would bob like a seal in the water. She would swim a few strokes this way and that, and then stumble ashore, shuddering, her mouth aflutter with little cold cries. Then she draped a scarlet-and-white striped gown about her, and passed quickly up through the fields to the schoolhouse.

To begin with, the valley folk had shaken their heads in unbelief.

The sea was for boats, kelp, ships, whales, nets, and the getting of fish. None of the fishermen could swim, nor their fathers before them. The sea was the bounteous mother, that even more than the earth had fed their people for a thousand years. If the sea chose, now and again, to take one of the fishermen to herself, that was her due, that was in the nature of things: a sorrowful but fair exchange. If a fisherman managed to scramble on to a rock, and so save himself, that was well and good – the sea had only touched him lightly on the shoulder, so to speak, as if to remind him of an ancient unbreakable bond. Next time, he might find himself entangled in deeper water, and slip into her keeping between two waves. To learn to swim might be an affront of the great mother; she, in revenge, might turn the great shoals away from their fishing-grounds.

And here was Miss Strachan, who didn't even eat fish, teasing the ocean, morning after bright morning. The sea, for the moment, chose to ignore her. But the sea, the great mother, was certain to resent this empty frolicking and flirting. That she should not hold it against the fishermen of the valley! So the old men murmured. But the younger men said that was all nonsense. In the south, thousands of people bathed in the sea in summer.

One afternoon, near the end of a summer term, Miss Strachan said to the scholars, in a very solemn voice, 'Dear children, I have something that I must tell you. It is this. I am leaving this island and this school. I have been with you for twelve years now, and the time has come for me to go elsewhere. I have, in fact, applied for and accepted a post in the town of Galashiels. Galashiels is an important market-town in the Borders. I have come to love this valley very much, and the people who live in it, and you, my dear pupils, most of all. It seems that my beliefs and way of life have not recommended themselves to certain wielders of power in Orkney – those who sit in high places. However, that does not concern you. Suffice it to say that I shall not change my beliefs or habits for any man or committee whatsoever. In order to forestall them, I have applied for this new post – alas, far from here – and my application, as I said, has been successful. Therefore, as from the fourth of July – the last day of term – I shall no longer be your teacher' . . .

By this time a few of the children were crying. Young Dora Budge of Crag set up a piercing wail.

'I am taking with me a certain person from this valley. In due course, in Galashiels, Will Smith of Skeld and I will be married. So you see, dear children, every day I shall have a piece of this valley with me, till one or other of us shall in the course of nature be no more' . . .

Loud sobs came from this desk and that in the classroom.

'This valley bore and shaped and made the man who is to by my husband. I shall see the blue of your lovely sky in his eyes, always, and his dear breath shall be the wind that moves among the grass and the corn, and his bone the rock, and his flesh the earth, yes, and his blood the burn and the breakers. I am sure you will not deny me this dearly loved part of yourselves, now that I am leaving you forever.'

By now the whole school, except for a few dunderheads, was convulsed with grief.

Down Miss Strachan's face, too, the tears streamed, unchecked.

'And so, my very dear children, I bid you a long and last farewell.'

The silent girl, Sunniva Sinclair, did not know what tragic spell had been cast this morning over the school. She looked in wonderment from face to face. A wave of grief had broken upon the scholars and all but drowned them. She rose from her desk and ran towards Miss Strachan, and clung to her, long and fiercely.

Miss Strachan's tears splashed down on Sunniva's upturned face . . .

Of course Miss Strachan would not be leaving them for a full month yet.

Casually, over supper one evening, Willie mentioned to his parents that when the teacher left for Galashiels, he would be going with her – and there, in a registry office, they would be married.

'The Lord help her, poor lass,' said Willie's mother.

Ben, Willie's father, said, 'I never thought, from the first time I laid eyes on her, that that teacher was quite right in the head.'

Twenty-Four

Time passed in the valley. The years gathered and fell, like waves, like cut corn.

The dark figure, that nobody can see but a few 'sighted' ones – and, this generation, there were few of them – entered the valley from time to time; would seem to linger and hesitate briefly; then would go to this croft door or that, and knock. Then, a few days later, there would be the funeral procession to the kirkyard on the far side of the hill. Usually it was to a house with an old person in it that the dark one came. But sometimes a child was taken, and sometimes a young man with 'a knot in the bowels' or a ruptured appendix. Once or twice a family of four or five people would be touched by the flames and ash of consumption; not all were taken, usually one, the mother, was left to see winter of coffins, procession after black procession leaving the one door for the kirkyard.

The sound of fiddle music on a summer evening was heard no more from the high croft of Flegs: only, from a bare rafter, a blackbird sang sometimes.

The brightness of birth came to this croft and that.

But the older ones, who kept in their minds family trees, and kinship, and exact reckonings of death and birth, would remark how of late years the dark one was a more frequent visitor to the valley than the bright one, the life-giver with breath of daffodils and new grass on his lips.

The year after Willie of Skeld left for Galashiels in the Borders with Miss Strachan, his parents died one after the other. Once old Liza of Skeld was dead, her man lost all interest in life.

Slowly the croft of Skeld began to wither: once a hearth fire goes out, rot and rat and dampness begin their work. Heather and rushes take over from the ploughlands.

Lizzie of Whinstone died, coming with water from the burn. She staggered under the weight of the water buckets. There was a silver splash and a clatter. The old woman fell; when they came to her, she was dead, and the brown cow gazed wonderingly at all the outcry and commotion.

Magnus Fiord of Don died, suddenly, like a lamp going out. He was sitting on the bench outside his door, watching the fishing boats returning. He remarked, 'Look at all the gulls – that's a fine catch they have, especially the *Skua*' . . . Then the dark one tapped him on the shoulder, and he acquiesced at once. 'Well,' said old Willa, 'he won't be eating any of that fish. But I think I'll maybe eat a few haddocks and herrings yet, before my time comes' . . .

The old minister died; and Mrs Blackie walked through her garden alone for a few summer months. A new young minister was appointed. 'This is a beautiful garden, I love it dearly, you'll look after it well, won't you?' . . . But the new minister was a bachelor, and not at all interested in rose bushes and mint and blackbirds . . . So poor Mrs Blackie, shorn of her husband and her garden, departed to stay with her sister in Inverness.

The new minister had a motor-car with a canvas hood on it, and brass head-lamps. Soon a new young wife came from Aberfeldy to the manse; she was interested in the garden too, but to a lesser extent than Mrs Blackie.

The new teacher was already installed in the schoolhouse: John Fiord, who in his youth had been known as 'Eagle'. The valley people could hardly get over that – one of their own people come to be the teacher! There was something not quite right about it – a teacher, like a minister, ought to be a stranger of whose origins they knew nothing. And yet they were proud of him: here was one of their own folk who would never have to toil with earth and sea, until at last earth and sea broke him. He would sit in peace and security for the rest of his days, imparting knowledge to the children, and his wages would come regularly every month, a cheque in the post.

And yet perhaps he should have stayed in the south and taught there. The women, washing their clothes in the burn, couldn't help but remember things: such as, that his grand-mother had been fond of the bottle: the home-brewed ale was no good to old Margit Fiord. Once a week she would be up and over the hill for a flask of whisky from the shop in Voes, though she always let it be known that she had run out of pins, or knitting needles, or paraffin . . . And on the other side there had been a great-grandfather, a Corston, who had left the valley suddenly and signed on for a whaler in Hamnavoe. The very next day two policemen arrived on the island – the laird's house had been broken into and a silver plate and two silver candlesticks stolen, and they were making enquiries. The policemen went so far as to search in a few barns and outhouses. They never found the silver. But it was remarked on that the morning the young man Jack Corston had left the valley so suddenly, he had a clanging sack over his shoulder . . . If there is ever the slightest tendency to 'uppishness', the long memories of country women are there to redress the balance.

He should never have come back! There was something strange in that family. Imagine, old Willa fighting with the eagle – sometimes, when she did her washing at the burn, they could see the eagle scars on her arms. It was uncanny. Perhaps the child should have been left in the eyrie, the way a drowning man is taken by the sea: for they too, for many generations, had taken birds and eggs from the crags, and there must have been, then, a long account to settle.

And yet John Fiord had been a decent good-tempered boy, and his comings and goings had offended no one, old or young.

But what would he do for a wife? He should by rights have taken a wife from the city of Aberdeen. If he chose one of the valley lasses – not that there were many to choose from nowadays – it would cause ill-speaking in some of the other crofts. That bride's pedigree would be gone over, too, with a small-tooth-comb; such peccadilloes as penny-pinching, or the pride of long golden hair that lingered all one summer by a rockpool.

On the whole, it was better for the teacher to be a stranger. Mr MacFarlane, for example, could deal out punishment to this child or that, and nobody questioned it; not even the weeping culprit with the beaten hand. Whereas if Eagle John dealt out chastisement, there might be murmurings.

Thus the women speculated, beside the burn, about the new teacher.

John Fiord arrived in a horse-and-cart driven by the farmer of the Bu five miles away. The cart was piled with boxes and a few bits of furniture.

The valley folk recognized him, of course: yet he was a stranger too, perhaps because of his golden whiskers and his new tweed suit. It was noticed, though, that one sock was gray and the other blue. He supervised the shifting of his belongings into the schoolhouse. The three young crofters who had come to give him a hand were his contemporaries. They spoke familiarly to each other. And yet, on the crofters' part, there was a certain reserve. This man was no longer one of them-

selves. They muted their voice in the schoolhouse. The new
teacher unbound a box and a chest: they were full of books.
Ah, he seemed glad to know that his books had arrived safely!
He held a thick book in his hands – *The Republic of Plato* –
smiling. He opened another case and unwrapped a bottle of
whisky from an overcoat. 'Let's be merry, my masters,' he said.
It turned out, there were no glasses or cups in the schoolhouse.
They drank, passing the bottle from mouth to mouth . . .

'The dutiful son will now visit his aged parents,' said John
Fiord. 'Old Magnus will drink what's left.' (Magnus, his father,
was still alive at that time.)

There were no effusive greetings at Don. 'It's you,' said old
Willa. 'What's that in your hand? A whisky bottle? In the
middle of the day! What will the folk think?'

Mansie took one dram, then put the bottle in the cupboard,
to drink before he went to bed. Then he thought better of it,
and had another dram.

His mother seemed displeased. 'I hear Mr Scott the minister
wanted to drive you from Voes in his motor-car. That would
have been something like it. What for did you have to come to
the valley in a horse-and-cart, like a vagabond?'

Mansie said there had been a lot of rain. It wouldn't do the
hay any good.

'A disgrace!' said old Willa. 'My two men, both reeking of
whisky in the middle of the afternoon. That old thing won't be
able to cart a peat for the rest of the day.'

She seemed to be pleased though when John said that he
didn't intend to cook – couldn't boil an egg or a tattie – and
wouldn't have any woman cluttering his kitchen; or disorder-
ing his books either, when it came to the house cleaning. 'If
you'll allow me,' he said, 'I'll come here, to Don, for my dinner
and tea. And yes, it would be fine if you could wash my
clothes' . . .

Willa Fiord had only one more criticism. 'That beard,' she said. 'A man in your position should shave every day. Only poor men have beards!' (The young laird and the young minister and Captain Thomas Spence, whenever he came home on leave, were now clean-shaven.)

The new teacher wandered back to the schoolhouse. Here and there a crofter or a croft-wife would quietly turn away when they saw him coming. They were still uncertain as to the proper ceremony that ought to be between them. It had been easy with Mr MacFarlane and Miss Strachan, a slight bow, a lifting of the bonnet.

After an hour he heard a slow knock at the door. A twelve-year-old girl was standing there with a jar of blue iris; she offered the flowers without a word. Mr Fiord wrinkled his brow; he could not place her.

'Come in, come in, Proserpine,' he said. But she lingered at the door.

'I will set the flowers in my window,' he said. 'I thank you. Now then, where can I find a jar?'

Still she said nothing.

'I have been too long out of the valley,' said the new teacher. 'Tell me your name.'

Gravely she looked at him. Then she turned and walked down the garden path, closing the gate behind her. Then she ran down the valley, following the burn.

It was only then that John Fiord remembered Sunniva, the deaf-and-dumb girl from the croft of Feaquoy. She had grown out of recognition. She was now a beautiful girl.

Twenty-Five

Now the crofters no longer stopped working at sound and sight of an approaching car.

The merchant in Voes got rid of his pony-and-gig and had a motor-car too, that he drove here and there about the island with his young wife from Hamnavoe in it.

A doctor from Dundee had 'put up his plate' – that is to say, started in practice in the south part of the island, where the village was, ten years before. He had a large powerful motor-car. Occasionally he visited the valley, in some emergency or other – a difficult childbed, for example, or a badly broken limb – but for ordinary ailments the crofters depended on herbs, or whisky, or tar, or the slow cures of nature.

One day the island postman delivered to every croft a circular with a ha'penny stamp on it.

TAKE NOTICE

MR JAMES HALCRO, MERCHANT IN VOES, BEGS LEAVE TO AN-
NOUNCE THAT AS FROM AUGUST 3RD HE WILL OFFER SERVICE
FROM HIS EXTENSIVE STORE OF GOODS, VIZ. GROCERIES, HARD-
WARE, GARMENTS IN LINEN COTTON AND WOOL FOR LADIES,
GENTLEMEN, and CHILDREN IN A VARIETY OF STYLES (BOTH
OUTER AND UNDER GARMENTS), ALSO SPIRITS WINES AND ALES
AND TOBACCO, COFFEE CHOCOLATE AND TEA, STRONG ROPE AND
TWINE OF GREAT UTILITY TO CROFTERS AND FISHERMEN, and
INNUMERABLE OTHER GOODS AT KEENEST PRICES, FOR IMMEDI-
ATE AND REGULAR DELIVERY AT YOUR DOORSTEP.

ALSO ALARM CLOCKS, ORNAMENTS, FLOWER VASES WITH
PRETTY DESIGNS UPON THEM, MUSICAL BOXES, AND WREATHS
OF EVERLASTING FLOWERS FOR FUNERARY TRIBUTES.

ALSO A NICE RANGE OF IMPROVING BOOKS.

MR HALCRO HAS NOW ACQUIRED A TRAVELLING SHOP,
MOTOR DRIVEN, WHICH WILL CALL AT EVERY ROAD-END
THROUGHOUT THIS ISLAND UPON EVERY SATURDAY, LEAVING
THE STORE AT VOES AT NOON, AND ARRIVING FINALLY AT THE
SEA VALLEY BETWEEN THE HOURS OF 4 and 6 p m

MR HALCRO IS WILLING TO TRADE IN TERMS OF BARTER, as
HITHERTO, ie CHICKENS, EGGS, BUTTER, SALT AND SMOKED
FISH, CHEESE, LOBSTERS, BUT HE WISHES NOW EARNESTLY TO
ADVISE THAT THIS METHOD OF TRADE IS RAPIDLY DECLINING
THROUGHOUT THE CIVILIZED WORLD, AND CASH (IF POSSI-
BLE) IS GREATLY TO BE PREFERRED.

WITH MANY THANKS FOR YOUR PAST ESTEEMED CUSTOM,
AND IN HOPES OF MERITING YOUR CONTINUED SUPPORT . . .

Every Saturday afternoon after that a troop of women and
children waited at the road-end for the motor van to come from
Voes. No longer did the women have to trudge over the hill for
their supplies, with laden baskets each way. To the valley
children the interior of the travelling shop was a cave of utter
enchantment, with the mingled smells of brown sugar, coffee,
apples, tobacco, cotton, cloves, On one small shelf was a heap of
sweets in white rustling paper bags, one ha'penny each. They ran,
shouting with delight all over the valley with their treasure.

One by one the spinning wheels in the valley fell silent.

The tailor at the north end of the island put up his shutters.

Ready-made clothes could be bought much more cheaply
from the shops.

The makers of straw ropes lost their skill.

The old woman, Madge Brims of Quoy, declared that the
best thing that had come to the valley in her time was the new

footwear, rubber boots, that the fishermen had been so reluctant to put on, to begin. Hitherto, their breeches and stockings had never had time to dry out properly, but now they could launch their boats and fish dry-shod, even when spindrift slashed in from a stormy sea. When the feet are warm, the whole body is comfortable. (Once salted, their trousers had never dried properly, in the old days, not even after a week of sea-sparkling days.)

It happened that young Matthew Flett of Gorse left school. He helped his father David with the croft and fishing-boat. But always he liked the sea work better than ploughing and shepherding. His father was content with this division of work. He had never greatly cared for the sea. But young Matthew, how eagerly, even in his schooldays, he tended the boat *Daffodil*, scraping her, painting and puttying, planing the oars till they were supple and pliant. And the lobster creels: he was adept at making them, almost from child-hood, of drift-wood bases, and black-tarred nets woven over bent wire frames, the whole creel weighted with a flat heavy beach-stone. There was a cunning circular door into which lobster or crab scuttled after the bait inside, and once there it was a prisoner; unless a storm rose from the west and smashed the creel against rock or crag. 'The boy makes better creels than yourself, man,' said Maisie over the supper-table when Matthew was in bed asleep.

'He does well enough,' said David. 'This place will never want for fish. Over at Feaquoy it's another story. There's no boy to fish there, once Sinclair himself is by with the sea, only a lass as dumb as a stone. That'll be a poor place, Feaquoy, in time.' And he laughed, rather as his mother had laughed in her time.

'Things don't always turn out the way you expect,' said Maisie.

One day, when Matthew Flett was sixteen, he came up from the shore with a bunch of haddocks. He was quiet at the dinner table: an unusual thing, for he was generally eager to tell his parents how things had gone with him and *Daffodil* at sea. If he had a fault, it was that he was inclined to boast overmuch. Oh, the things he would do, once he had his gear in proper order! . . . Yet the boasting came mostly out of recklessness and enjoyment. 'The years,' said the old folk, 'will quiet him' . . .

'What are you so dumb about?' said Maisie. 'Have you got your eye on some lass?'

He shook his head. He gave a snicker of contempt. Lasses were the last thing on his mind. (Yet there was a lass, young Dora Budge of Crag, who was always at the seabank whenever *Daffodil* beached.)

'Tell me again,' he said. 'How much did old ma leave me in her will?'

'A hundred pounds,' said his mother.

'There's no need,' said his father sharply, 'for you to bother your head about that for a long time. You won't lay your fingers on a penny of that till you're twenty-one. That money is for you to set up house for yourself, once you're married.'

'I would like to have it now,' muttered Matthew.

'Why?' said David Flett. 'For what? Tell me.'

'That boat,' said Matthew, 'she serves her purpose well enough. But her day is done. I need a new boat, a bigger one. I want to fish further out.'

'A bigger boat!' said his father. 'The boats here have been of roughly the same size for hundreds of years.'

'Hear him out,' said Maisie.

'A bigger boat,' cried the man. 'Nothing but ill-luck will come of it.'

'Let the boy speak,' said Maisie.

'A hundred pounds! When your grandfather built *Daffodil*, the planks cost no more than two pounds.'

'I won't be able to build this boat myself,' said the boy. 'They will build it in the boatyard at Hamnavoe for me. It is to have an engine in it.'

Maisie nodded.

David Flett looked from wife to son as if they were both insane.

Then he rose from the table and made for the door. He turned once to shout 'Never!' Then Maisie and Matthew were left alone. The boy's hand was trembling. Maisie laid her hand on his and nodded at him.

That same night, when David stood outside the door smoking his pipe, Maisie laid a bundle of ancient notes on the table in front of her son. 'Here is the money for the boat. Tomorrow you'll take it to the bank agent in Hamnavoe. There's no hurry to pay the boat-builder till the boat is built and you're satisfied with her. What do you think of calling her?'

Matthew said he hadn't thought about that.

'You could call her *Tomina*, after your grandmother.'

'I might give her this name – *Golden Bird*,' said Matthew.

'It'll be a great splendour on the shore,' said Maisie. 'The other boats will be poor things in comparison. I will carve a bird on her prow. Go to bed now. You'll have to be up betimes, to take this money to the bank in Hamnavoe'.

Outside, the sinking sun was turning the cliffs on the far side of the bay to pillars of fire. Under the red crags, Peter Sinclair was doing some small repair to his boat *Skua*. The dumb girl Sunniva stood watching him.

David Flett looked at them. He puffed steadily at his pipe. Still looking at them, the man of Gorse spat on the wall.

He laughed.

Twenty-Six

John Fiord, Master of Arts (honours in Classics) of the University of Aberdeen, commenced his duties in the month of August. The scholars didn't know what to make of him. The spell that Miss Strachan had cast on the school was no longer there. Instead, they were confronted morning after morning by a strict school-master who insisted on the importance of correct spelling and grammar; the multiplication tables were chanted over and over, until they were incised beyond chance of erosion in the children's minds; they knew the chief imports and exports of every nation in Europe; and all the kings of Scotland and the battles they fought, and their troubles with the great Border chiefs and the Highland clans to the north and west . . . The droning and the chanting drifted down the valley from the school on a quiet day. The older folk listened – this was how it had been ordained; it was best so; they themselves had never had the opportunity to read and write and count. In the year 1875 the school had been built. The middle and the younger generation of crofters remembered Mr MacFarlane and Miss Strachan, mostly with affection and wonderment. Apart from helping two sea-captains to make a start, and a draper in Hamnavoe, the Education Act had not so far touched them greatly. In every croft, in the window recess, reposed the Bible and, in some, *The Pilgrim's Progress*; the crofter-fishermen had no other literature, apart from the occasional magazines and newspapers brought back from

Hamnavoe. Arithmetic had helped them a little in their dealings with the general merchant; for, increasingly, barter was being discarded in favour of ready-money transactions. But still they preferred to keep their money in chests under the box-beds than to trust it to the banks in Hamnavoe.

Little anxious faces crossed the burn or hurried up from the shore crofts when John Fiord rang the school bell at the gate.

What sorrow, to be compelled from the freedom of shore and hill to this prison, smelling of ink and chalk and cold slates!

'Boys and girls,' John Fiord would say to them solemnly, 'I know it, you would rather be out in the sun and the wind. I know, because I have sat at the same desks as yourselves, in the time of Mr MacFarlane of good memory. And like you, I resented it. Listen. Let me tell you something. Life in this valley and in every country community in the land, has been stagnant for centuries, and rooted in superstition. I see it as my duty to put a new richness into your lives. Beyond this little stagnant pool lie the wonders and delights of Western Civilization, which is our heritage as well as the heritage of those who dwell in cities. I will lead you – it is my duty – into this marvellous region. But first of all we have to prepare ourselves – we have to yoke ourselves to the disciplines of word and number – we have to recognize that we are not isolated here in a little backwater, but that we too have a part in time and in place: which is to say, I have to teach you first of all the rudiments of history and geography. It is true that you live in a beautiful island, but you will never realize it – no, you will go to your graves dull and ignorant – until you acquire the facility of making voyages of the mind, into unexplored seas and isles, and then return, like the French poet Joachim du Bellay, to find that his dull rustic home was in fact a jewel beyond price.'

The children understood nothing of all this.

Instead, one pupil noticed that Mr Fiord must somehow, over his breakfast, have got a nugget of old Willa's butter tangled in his beard. Now, as he stood in the sun lecturing them in this incomprehensible way, the butter was slowly melting. Child whispered to child round the class-room. Fingers pointed, there were sniggers here and there, as drop by golden drop the butter fell on his serge lapel.

Mr Fiord suddenly shouted, 'What's all this snickering about? I am trying to talk seriously to you! I see that it is I that will have the hard job, breaking down the barriers of ancient superstition. You, Tom Laird, take that idiotic grin off your face, or I will deal with you severely, sir . . . Now, to work. Open your geography books at page 87: the mountains and rivers of Spain' . . .

Chastened, they turned the hated pages.

Twenty-Seven

John Fiord occupied an equivocal position in the valley: he was a part of the community, and he was apart from it; he found himself in a lonely situation.

It embarrassed the crofters to have someone so superior to them in education and social status coming about their doors. He did call at this house and that, in his first year, and was met with a wall of shyness and silence. If he tried to jog them with some old cherished half-forgotten memory, they might nod and laugh a little awkwardly – never venturing to make any observation themselves – and the schoolmaster, having drunk his cup of tea, would retire to the sanctuary of the schoolhouse.

The only one not awed by him was his mother.

Every morning – a widow now – she trudged up from Don to the schoolhouse to prepare his breakfast; and again at noon to serve up his dinner; and at five o'clock to set the table for tea. Also she washed his clothes and scrubbed his floor. When she tucked up her sleeve to put scrubbing-brush into bucket, the silver scars could be seen on her forearm. 'I don't know what'll become of you when I'm in the kirkyard,' she said to him often. 'You'll be a poor body. You will indeed. That Dora Budge, now, she's a fine well-handed lass. You could do worse. Only, I doubt, she has eyes for nobody but that Flett boy of Gorse. And he's taken up entirely with his boat and his creels.'

But it seemed there might well be a lady in the schoolhouse, and that before long. It was noticed that the schoolmaster –

the folk were at a loss what to call him, 'John Fiord' or 'Mister Fiord'; in the end they called him 'the schoolmaster' – ever Saturday morning, having called at the Manse for a bunch of fresh flowers from the minister's lovely wife, he took the ferry to Hamnavoe, and did not return till late on Saturday evening. It could not remain a secret for long: the schoolmaster was visiting a lady friend in the town. No Orkney woman either, it transpired, but a young person from the Mearns who was teaching in the primary school at Hamnavoe. They had met – John Fiord let this much be known – at the teacher training college in Aberdeen. One or two of the valley men, in Hamnavoe to sell their lobsters, had seen them on the street together, 'and', they declared, 'a right bonny lass she is.'

But John Fiord did not take his 'intended' to the valley; not once.

Slowly, in school, John Fiord broke the children into the disciplines they must acquire before they entered 'the realms of gold'.

'I am under no illusion,' he assured them on another day. 'This school has been built, and I have been sent to labour in it, so that you may rise a little above yourselves, both materially and mentally, and even spiritually, if that were possible. That is to say, some of you boys might go to sea, and study navigation, and become a skipper, like our own Capt Thomas Spence of Burnside. Such a dizzy height! No, but it is possible that you might go to Hamnavoe and work in a shop there, and by dint of prudence and hard work have a business of your own, like William Brims the draper. Another one "who has got on". What is it, this "getting on"? "Getting on" is part of the wave of progress into which we are all meant to be caught up. By that they mean that you, Mary, and you, Eliza, will not be content to be croft wives. By no means, you will want to become servants in some big house in Hamnavoe or Kirkwall, the banker's houses perhaps or the minister's. And you, Tom, and you, Ernest, and you, Willie, will turn away from your crofts and fishing boats and ascend – oh, dizzy thought! – to a stool in a lawyer's office, or a bank, writing in a ledger; and wear a collar and tie every single day in the year, and go to the occasional musical soirée or meeting of the Mutual Improvement Society. Boys and girls, I say to you, avoid this heresy of Progress. Be content with the station you have been called to, which is one immortalized by the pastoral poets of antique times: it was in the mouths of shepherds and shepherdesses, of simple country folk, that Bion and Virgil put all the delight that may be known to human-kind. For in their condition, joy is unadulterated by riches, pomp, ambition. I tell you, you are more precious in the scale of things than any pen-pusher or any shopkeeper with sweat-of-silver on their palms . . . And this I take to be my calling, to make you vividly aware of yours' . . .

What could their dominie be on about this morning? What their attention centred on, as the voice went on and on, was the diagonal crack in the left lens of the schoolmaster's spectacles. Sometime, either last night or this morning, the steel spectacles had fallen on the schoolhouse floor; behind the fracture his eye twitched and flickered.

Robertina of Whinstone put up her hand. He looked at her, frowning a little (and still his eye twitched and watered). 'What is it, girl?'

'Please, sir, you've broke your glasses!'

'What? What's that?' . . . He took off his spectacles and seemed to be genuinely surprised at the fracture. 'I see,' he said. 'Dear me . . . Well, to business. Arithmetic. I think, today, the seven times table.'

Morning after morning, still, he put on his cracked spectacles, to check the register. His left eye continued to flick and water; until, after a month or so, his lady friend the Hamnavoe teacher must have persuaded him to go one Saturday to the optician. He entered the class-room on the Monday morning with a smart pince-nez hanging by a cord round his neck.

Often the teacher would break off in the middle of a sentence, leaving it hanging in the air. He would go and lean against a wall, his eyes fixed on nothing, his fingers gently kneading his golden beard. He was pursuing some lonely train of thought. Sometimes, after a few minutes, he would take a notebook and pencil out of his jacket and jot down a few words. Sometimes he would snap out of his dream, or trance, as suddenly as he had entered on it; he would stride to desk or blackboard, and resume precisely where he had left off.

The children accepted those eccentricities as part of the pattern of their days. But while Mr Fiord was 'following his thought', they dared not whisper or fidget, lest they break the spell. If that happened, he would rage at the culprit terribly.

They waited upon the lonely flight and hover and stoop of his mind: until the quarry was seized, with a few words written in his notebook.

One morning, when John Fiord went through to the schoolhouse kitchen for his breakfast, his mother wasn't there. It did not occur to him to walk over to Don. He ate a piece of dry oatcake and drank a cup of water; then went outside to the schoolyard gate and rang the bell. The children who were not already in the yard came running from all directions.

John Fiord, before following the scholars inside, looked over towards Don. There was no smoke from the chimney. He set down the trembling bell on the window-sill, and lessons began.

Half way through the grammar lesson – analysis – there was a low tap at the school door. Mr Fiord frowned; he crossed over and opened. Old Lizzie of Whinstone shrilled like a gull, 'Your poor mother! Poor Willa Fiord! She's by with it, she's by with it! Have I not just found her lying cold on the floor.'

'Don't howl like that!' said John Fiord sternly. 'It comes to all of us. You'll frighten the children. Go and get some of the other women. Do what has to be done.'

The news-bearer gaped at him as though he was some kind of monster, then she gathered her shawl about her and turned away.

John Fiord stood once more at the blackboard. 'How many times do I have to tell you? Preparatory to analyse a complex sentence, first and foremost you must seek out the principal clause' . . .

At one o'clock he put on his hat and crossed the fields to Don. The house was full of shadowy women (for the curtains were drawn) going here and there, attending to fire and cupboard, or lingering among chaste whispers. They fell silent when he entered. Maisie Flett led him over to the box-bed where his mother lay in her shroud. John Fiord removed his hat, then he kissed the dead woman on the forehead.

'Do what has to be done,' he said earnestly to the women.

Then he returned to the schoolhouse kitchen and buttered an oatcake and drank a cup of milk.

The children in the school yard knew what had happened. When he appeared at the door, none of them would look at him. They turned their backs. 'Boys and girls,' he said, 'you can go home now. There will be no more lessons today. There will be no more lessons till after the funeral on Wednesday. So you will be back here on Thursday morning' . . .

The children drifted silently towards the gate of the yard.

He called after them, 'To make up for the time lost – for some of the time lost – we will study for two extra hours on Thursday and Friday.

Alone, he murmured, '*Sunt lachrymae rerum et mentem mortalia tangunt*' . . .

It was adversely remarked upon when John Fiord attended his own mother's funeral dressed in a gray suit, without even a black diamond sewn on the sleeve.

When the mourners returned from the kirkyard, the women had seen to it that all the formalities were observed: the whisky bottle on the table, the glasses set out, and the great platters of bread and cheese and cold chicken. The usual compliments were paid to the dead woman: her courage, her kindliness, her gaiety. They never referred to her by name; it was 'her that's away' or 'her that was' . . . The only one who couldn't keep back her tears was Lois Sinclair.

One by one they took their leave.

Maisie Flett was the last to leave. 'I'll tidy everything away,' she said to the schoolmaster. 'I'll keep what should be kept, and I'll burn what's of no further use. Then I'll lock the door and bring the key up to the schoolhouse . . . I expect this croft will go the way of so many other crofts. Once the fire's out, the rat and the spider take over.'

'Do what you will, Maisie,' he said.

When he got back to the schoolhouse, he found the deaf-and-dumb girl Sunniva pouring hot broth into a bowl. From the stove came a smell of baked fish. He was hungry; he had hardly eaten since his mother's death.

Sunniva set out the fish on a warm plate, beside a plate of buttered bread. Then, silently, she went away.

*   *   *

He went to Hamnavoe on the ferry, as always, every weekend. But now he went on the Friday evening instead of the Saturday morning, carrying a bunch of flowers from the Manse garden; and he did not return till late on the Sunday evening. He came back looking trimmer by far than he had set out, and sometimes it was noticed that he wore a new neck-tie, or long knee-stockings in the latest fashion. Always his shoes, so dingy when he left, gleamed like black mirrors when he came back. He looked pleased with himself, he would rub his hands, or twirl his golden moustache through his fingers as he walked up the beach.

'It won't be long now,' said the women to each other. 'There'll be the wedding before the winter. Then we'll see this fine wife, whatever she is' . . .

Indeed she could hardly come soon enough, this bride-to-be. He was neglecting himself in the schoolhouse, that was for certain. No one cleaned and cooked for him. After the lonely funeral dinner, Sunniva came back no more. He could neither cook nor bake; it would have been unseemly for a man, especially one in his position, to do such things. Sometimes a woman would leave a few fish inside his door, or bannocks. The fish lay there till they rotted, the bannocks till the mice had eaten them or they were hard as wood. Perhaps he boiled an egg occasionally. Always he brought back from Hamnavoe a basket of tinned food, corned beef or peas or sliced pears. 'What kind of nourishment is that?' cried the women washing their clothes in the burn. 'He'll poison himself.'

'For sure,' said another, 'the education authorities in Kirkwall won't like it when they see what a disorder his house has fallen into. The tinker's tent is cleaner.'

'He's getting thinner too,' said another. 'It's high time the marriage banns were called in the kirk' . . .

The schoolmaster arrived from his courtship in Hamnavoe one Sunday evening with his bag of tinned food, his shoes shining like black mirrors, and his beard neatly trimmed. It even gave off a faint perfume, that golden beard.

Next morning it was noticed in the school that his hair had been cut too, so that the thin silver scar on his forehead was plain to be seen.

'Oh sir,' cried little Georgie Laird of Flinders, 'there's where the eagle scratched you.'

At once Mr Fiord became stiff and severe. 'Eagle!' he said. 'What are you talking about, eagle?'

He was so annoyed that the children looked down, and Georgie Laird hid his head in the sleeves of his gansey.

'Eagles, seals, mermaids, trows,' said Mr Fiord. 'I am here to rid your heads of such nonsense! I have been trying to do so ever since I came to teach in this school. It is precisely that kind of superstition that keeps us sunk in our brutishness and ignorance. I have been hoping that, bit by bit, gently, I could wean you away from such darkness, such crude insular superstition, and lead you into the "sweetness and light" that the poet Matthew Arnold speaks of. It is yours by right – it is yours freely to partake of, the wide serene culture of this western civilization. Oh, I grew up on stories of seal-girls taken home to be the wife of some crofter – yes, and of the trows who stole human children out of their cradles and left their own misshapen offspring behind – yes, and of fiddlers enchanted away inside a green mound for fifty summers and coming out again, thinking they had played a ten-minute reel to the fairies. Yes, and Nuckleavee the terrible sea-horse – and the Stoorworm whose teeth became the Orkneys, the Shetlands, and the Faroes – and the giants petrified by the risen sun as round and round they went in their midsummer dance at Brodgar. This, and other crude trash, has been our nourishment here in this valley for a thousand years and more. No wonder if we are little more than oxen. Oh, and some child was taken by an eagle, carried up to his eyrie, till the mother came and fought off the eagle and brought the bairn home again to crib and fire. *It is not true* – not a word or a syllable of it is true. I am assured that there is no eagle capable of lifting a child up to its nest. Nor is there any woman who could match her strength against the power and ferocity of such a bird. It is utterly impossible. I will tell you what happened. I found a young falcon when I was very young, I brought it close to my face – as children in their innocence will do – and then the bird flashed a claw at me and flew away. That is what happened – that is all – I had it from the mouth of my mother. Oh, but that incident was too trifling and commonsensical to satisfy the fireside talk next winter. A truly wonderful story must be made to account for the bird-wound on John Fiord's brow. Some old toothless mouth in a corner began then to mumble about an eagle. Willa Fiord, the mother, she had scars too, on her arm. So the ignorant tale began to be stitched together . . . I may say that my mother's wound was caused by her stumbling on a harvest scythe . . . Listen seriously to me, children. I will not be able to raise you into that "sweetness and light"' I spoke of, until you discard the brutish stories out of our past. Besides, I can tell you for a fact that there are no eagles in this island, not one' . . . (Indeed, no eagle had been seen in the valley for twelve years.)

Even the children could not fail to notice how shabby their teacher had become of late, increasingly as each week wore to its close. Not only did he frequently have two stockings of different colours, but the cuffs and collars of his shirt, half way through the week, were dirty and crumpled. His jacket had a dark stain – soup or coffee – on the lapel. Sometimes he appeared in the classroom without a tie. But every Monday morning he was neat and polished again, and a slight perfume wafted from his newly-trimmed beard.

Meantime the croft of Don remained locked and shuttered. The heart of the house – the hearth-stone – had stopped beating. (To be strictly accurate, the hearth-stone had been replaced, two winters before Magnus Fiord's death, by a black 'Enchantress' stove, a black iron cube that stood a few feet further out on the floor; and, once set alight, could keep a pot and kettle simmering on top at the same time, besides baking a pie or a cake in the oven.) Now the winter rain found a fissure in the thatch; it dripped on one flagstone of the floor, in a small cold infrequent rhythm, and made a little pool that soon dried again. The mice scurried unhindered under the box-bed and in the cupboard. The February snow that lasted a week, a bright thick dazzlement, was washed away overnight by drenches of thaw. Then the pool of water inside Don was broader – it was longer in drying out. The cold iron of the stove began to rust.

In the deserted croft of Skeld next door two or three flagstones had shifted. It was beaten upon by all weathers. Even the sun through the roof and broken windows warped the woodwork inside. The framed picture of Queen Victoria had a large stain under the glass and it hung crooked at the wall. A few stone jars stood here and there, with an inch or two of dirty gray water in them. The interior, that had been so bright and fragrant five years before, had a sour decayed smell. The iron plough at the end of the barn had splotches of red.

Twenty-Eight

There was great excitement in the valley, the day that the *Golden Bird* arrived from the boatyard in Hamnavoe. The wingless fishing-boat, stuttering its oil-and-steel syllables, was guided round the crags and into the bay by Matthew Flett. It shuddered into silence beside the big rock.

Nearly all the valley folk were down at the shore that morning. They touched the marvellous boat, the wind-scorner, that now seemed to come to them out of the future; that would surely bring increase and plenty to the people of Gorse, and to all the crofts in time, no doubt, when the last sail had been stowed away.

A few of the older folk shook their heads. They stood well back. It might be that a boat like this, that had no need of wind or tide, was an affront to heaven. Yet, standing on the sea-banks, they had looks of wonderment on their faces.

The steady 'chug-chug-chug' of the boat rounding the headland had reached the children in the school. A rustle of excitement went through them. They knew that the *Golden Bird* was coming that day. One or two of the boys stood up, their faces yearned towards the window.

'Very well,' said Mr Fiord. 'You may go outside and look. But no further than the wall of the yard. And no longer than ten minutes. There is nothing to get excited about. Indeed, it may prove to be an ill day for the valley.'

The scholars were out through the door, all twenty-three of them, like a flock of starlings, climbing on to the yard wall and the pillars at the gate. Two of the older boys didn't stop till they stood, panting, beside the *Golden Bird*, in the circle of the young admiring men.

Matthew stood beside the new boat, knee-deep in the sea, quiet with pride. His mother and father stood on the rock, looking down on the *Golden Bird* and the new skipper. Maisie, a new-sharpened knife in her hand – how the sun-bright sea flashed from the blade – pointed out exactly where she meant to carve the eagle on the prow.

The girl Dora of Crag stood as close to the boat as she could get. She put on her hand to the white-painted hull. 'Don't touch it,' cried Matthew.

The girl drew back, almost in tears. But there is no weeping in public in the valley. Dora went and stood on the verge of the crowd, cold-faced.

It was noticed that Peter and Lois Sinclair were among the crowd that day, standing well back. But the girl Sunniva was among the younger folk clustered along the shore. Sunniva had bare feet and had taken up a station in the thin wash, not far from Matthew.

'Come on, lass,' said Matthew to Sunniva. 'Take one more step. I'll lift you on board.'

She was not looking at him. She stretched out her long arm and touched the curve of the hull lightly.

'I don't like that,' said David Flett. 'An enemy laying a hand on a new boat.'

Maisie whispered that that was all nonsense. A lass like Sunniva could mean nothing but good . . . David went on muttering and puffing at his pipe. He spat into the sea on the far side of the rock.

Sunniva turned – she hadn't looked at Matthew – and went up to join her parents on the sea-bank.

Meantime two cars had stopped at the mouth of the valley, above. The young laird and the young minister and his wife were seen walking down through the fields.

'Well,' said Maisie, 'that we should live to see the day that laird and minister came to wonder at something belonging to us! . . . They should have waited till I had carved the bird on the prow, though.'

A thin distant angry voice drifted from the school. 'John Spence and Charlie Laird, come back at once! Who gave you permission to go down to the shore!'

The guilty schoolboys hid behind a rock.

The men laughed. 'You'd better not go back. I hear he has a hard tawse. He'll make your hands burn like fire! . . . You'd better live in the caves for a few days.'

The two mothers turned Johnny and Charlie in the direction of the school. Very slowly the truants went along the burn, up to the school . . .

Matthew vaulted into the Golden Bird. He held up the large can of petrol. 'I'll start the engine now,' he said. 'You can come on board, but not all at once, only two or three at a time' . . . He whirled a handle and the engines shattered into life. In small groups the young men approached the rock.

Dora Budge went home to Crag, unnoticed.

The noise of the engine set the teeth of the older folk on edge. But the faces of the young men shone with delight. They were ashamed of their own hand-built sailing boats, lying here and there on the beach. But this new boat, built by craftsmen in Hamnavoe, powered by an engine that drank oil – that filled them on this morning with a reckless joy.

Soon there would be only motor fishing boats in the sea valley.

The laird and the couple from the Manse were standing now on the sea-banks, apart, discussing the new boat. 'Changed days,' the laird was saying. 'In my grandfather's time they did nothing without asking permission first. In fact, all the fishing boats belonged to him – they rented them, and the gear, along with their crofts.'

Peter and Lois Sinclair turned to go home. Sunniva had gone on before them, to milk the cows . . .

Mr Fiord did not, of course, punish the truants. But he had a few words to say to all the scholars. 'All this idle curiosity – all this striving towards whatsoever is new . . . It is vanity and vexation of spirit. What the spirit of man longs for, truly, is the wisdom and the enlightenment that is neither new nor old, being outwith the bounds of time. All that we see and hear and touch are but shadows, not entirely without meaning, for they are shadows of the eternal truth. A boat – a new boat in the bay – a boat of a kind never seen before in this place. But there have been boats in this bay since the first settlers came, a thousand years ago. And, so long as people live in the valley, there will be boats – there will be boats so strange in generations to come that we cannot imagine them. But all the boats that ever were in this bay, or ever will be, are but shadows of the one ideal boat . . .'

Mr Fiord had left the desk and taken up his position against the wall. He went on speaking, no longer to the children (who in any case understood not one iota) but to himself alone, out of a kind of dream.

. . . 'the one boat, that sets out in quest of the ultimate wisdom, the beauty that is truth and the truth that is beauty. What, Fiord, what do you say? Be sensible, man. Only the philosophers and the artists know such a launching, such a quest. Here there is only the seeking for fish, for the slime and the silver blood of fish, and always has been and ever will be. It may be so it is so, I grant you that, Fiord. Yet the ultimate urge of all men is to seek for truth. All men are seers and seekers and philosophers, in their heart of hearts: even those children seated here before you, sons and daughters of humble sea-folk. The time will come when those boys will fish too, and the girls will cut open and salt the fish at the rockpool. It is a great mystery. Forever in the quest we are beset with shadows and images. Yet, John Fiord, you must be forever striving to set their minds on the way that is destined for them and for all mankind, as the stars move in their courses . . .'

The children were whispering and laughing and scuffling with each other between the desks. One boy had even wandered out to Mr Fiord's desk and was idly turning over the pages of the register.

'I am tormented by those images, the fish and the rose,' Mr Fiord cried out suddenly, and his ringing words startled the children back behind their desks; and tolled him back to his diurnal self.

The children saw, with terror, that tears were streaming down the schoolmaster's face.

Twenty-Nine

One Friday evening John Fiord put on his overcoat, walked through the hills to the Manse where the minister's lovely wife had his bunch of flowers ready for him, and went on board the ferry-boat to visit his lady-friend in Hamnavoe.

Normally John Fiord stayed two nights in Mrs Magnusson's lodging-house, then returned to the island on the Sunday evening.

But this weekend he came back quite early on Saturday forenoon, on a Hamnavoe fishing boat, and he stepped ashore still carrying his bunch of flowers. His hair was unkempt and his shoes were dull and stained as if he had walked through ditches.

The laird's car was on the road above the landing-stage. 'Hop in,' said the laird. 'You're back early. I'll run you to the valley.'

John Fiord gave him a brusque dismissal with his hand. He walked half-a-mile westwards to the graveyard and laid the roses on his mother's grave.

Then he returned on foot to the valley.

He noticed that there was smoke coming from the chimney of Don. 'Some tramp has settled in for the weekend,' he murmured. 'I'll go and have a word with the man presently.'

When, an hour or so later, he opened the door of Don, the girl Sunniva was moving about inside. Not only had she lit the fire. She had taken his mother's crockery from the chest and arranged the cups and plates along the dresser. She had polished the rusty stove black again, and she had set the table in the middle of the room, with the four chairs on each side. Rabbit stew was simmering on the flushed stove-top.

Sunniva had not heard him come in. She was bent over another chest she had dragged from under the bed, lifting out blankets. She smelt them, one by one – ugh, the dampness! – then, filling her arms with them she turned and saw John Fiord standing at the window. She gestured for him to sit in the rocking-chair beside the fire – old Magnus Fiord's chair – then, burdened with blankets, she went outside to spread them in the sun and wind.

John Fiord sat down. The girl had been busy with mop and brush. She must have opened the door early, soon after dawn; sweet airs were everywhere in the room. He heard a small screeching of glass behind him; her fist with a damp cloth was going in circles at the window outside, scouring the dust and stains of two years and more.

She came back inside. She dipped a horn spoon into the stew and tasted it. Ah, there wasn't enough salt! She added a pinch of damp salt from the plate on the mantelpiece.

There ought to be flowers! The great blue vase was set down in the middle of the table and half filled with fresh water from one of the two brimming buckets. Then it was out with her and back in ten minutes, panting, her apron full of blue iris and thrift and clover. A bee buzzed somewhere in the rich coloured confusion. The shorter flowers were put in a cracked cup on the mantelpiece.

And now the rabbit stew was ready. She arranged chair and knife and fork for him at the table; looked doubtfully at the tarnished steel and breathed on them and polished them with her apron. Come – he was to come now and eat . . . She ladled stew into a clean plate.

John Fiord did as he was bidden.

Sunniva paused; then she took a second plate from the dresser, wiped it in her apron and ladled in stew. She sat down opposite him. No knife and fork – she would sup her stew from the horn spoon, as her grandparents had done.

After a few mouthfuls he could eat no more. After the strange home-coming, he remembered the pain of last night. He covered his eyes briefly with his hand.

Sunniva admonished him, silently. She went so far as to prise, gently, his fingers from his wet eyes. There were things that had to be endured, she seemed to be telling him, but there were good things also. So, he must eat.

John Fiord ate, and cleaned the last of the gravy from his plate with a slice of bread.

Now, at noon, there was a freshening wind outside.

Sunniva carried the used plates over to the board with the big basin on it. Then she went outside to turn the blankets on the line.

The schoolmaster visited Hamnavoe no more at weekends.

So it happened that the schoolmaster, John Fiord, moved his abode from the schoolhouse back to Don. There was no room in the little croft-house for all his books and papers; he carried them down as he needed them.

Sunniva Sinclair did almost everything for him. He had, it's true, to scrape a bit of butter on to an oatcake for his breakfast; but always at 5 o'clock his dinner was ready for him. The silent girl saw to the cleaning of the house, and also that he was respectably turned out for school and for the church on Sunday. (John Fiord was a lay-reader – he took the services whenever the minister was ill, or on holiday. The country folk thought the sermons 'above their heads', but they never lasted more than ten minutes; whereas the minister thundered and whispered dramatically for half-an-hour or so.)

Sunniva waited till a good peat fire was burning in the stove, and John Fiord was in his rocking chair, in a circle of lamp-light, with an open book on his knee.

Then she would smile, and give a little bow, and close the door gently behind her.

The education office in Kirkwall was not well pleased that John Fiord had vacated the schoolhouse. A sharp letter was sent to him . . . 'My committee considers it advisable, from every point of view, that a parish teacher should inhabit the schoolhouse provided for him. The teacher is a part of the community, certainly, but the dignity of his position necessitates a certain friendly distancing. Besides, buildings uninhabited and unfired are bound to deteriorate. You will therefore oblige us by returning at your earliest convenience to the house provided for you' . . . John Fiord put the letter in the fire. No more was said about it. The education committee in Kirkwall knew that they had a first-rate teacher; the annual inspector's report verged on the enthusiastic.

Thirty

It happened one evening that John Fiord was reading aloud out of a book: he did this frequently.

> . . . *Those beauteous forms*
> *Through a long absence, have not been to me*
> *As is a landscape to a blind man's eyes*
> *But I have owed to them, in hours of weariness,*
> *Sensations sweet, felt in the blood, and felt*
>   *along the heart,*
> *And passing even into my purer mind*
> *With tranquil restoration . . .*

He looked up from the page. Sunniva had not gone home. She was sitting on the stool, looking at him with grave intent eyes, her brows slightly gathered in concentration.

'Are you still here, Sunniva?' was all he could say.

It was impossible that the girl should understand, yet it seemed almost as if she did understand the poet's words. How could this be? The great spirit of Nature rolls through all things, it is true, clouds and rocks and trees and animals; though they seem not to be aware of it. The meaning and the movement of the verse seemed to have passed into her face.

He thumbed back through the pages of the anthology. He read aloud:

Tak any brid, and put it in a cage
And do all thyn entente and thy corage
To fostre it tendrely with mete and drinke,
Of alle deyntees that thou canst bithinke,
And keep it al so clenly as thou may;
Although his cage of gold be never so gay,
Yet hath this brid, by twenty thousand fold,
Lever in a forest, that is rude and cold,
Gon ete wormes and swich wreechednesse . . .

He closed the book. She was looking at him still, her lips slightly apart and moving, as if she was echoing silently those mysteries of freedom and bondage.

She got to her feet. Ah, her parents would be wondering what kept her! She took her shawl about her. Tonight, instead of the little bow, she pressed his hand. Then she passed through the door into the luminous summer evening.

After that, every night he read aloud, and Sunniva sat on the stool, in attendance.

It had long been plain to John Fiord that she could lip-read. The lovely Celtic mouth of her mother had, by its subtle tremblings, curves, dimplings, lingerings, closes, taught her the names of everything in the valley, and what it was 'to milk', 'to spin', 'to bake', 'to wash', 'to clean fish', 'to thatch', 'to stook', 'to knit'. The greater mysteries – birth, love, death – their meanings would have broken upon her simply and naturally, in the course of time. But the intricacies of poetry and philosophy – those delicate-spun webs that are yet more enduring than the hills and the sea – a girl born deaf and dumb could not possibly be expected to understand them. Not even if she had the seeds of poetry and philosophy in her, from before time: as, indeed, all men and women have. Without language any potentialities must wither surely.

Yet here she sat, night after night, following the movement of his lips, patiently, wonderingly, as if she could not have enough of the world's wisdom and beauty.

> *Heard melodies are sweet, but those unheard*
> *Are sweeter. Therefore, ye soft pipes, play on*
> *Not to the sensual ear, but more endeared*
> *Pipe, to the spirit, ditties of no tone.*

Often enough she was puzzled, and frowned a little, winding a coil of hair round her finger and turning her eyes from his face to the gulping flames in the stove, and back again.

Now for my life, it is a miracle of thirty years, which to relate, were not a History, but a piece of Poetry, and would sound to common ears like a Fable. For the World, I count it not an Inn, but an Hospital; and a place not to live, but to die in. The world that I regard is my self; it is the Microcosm of mine own frame that I cast mine eye on; for the other, I use it but like my Globe, and turn it round sometimes for my recreation. Men that look upon my outside, perusing only my condition and Fortunes, do err in my Altitude; for I am above Atlas his shoulders. The earth is a point not only in respect of the Heavens above us, but of that heavenly and celestial part within us . . .

At other passages, on other evenings, when John Fiord read aloud, her eyes would fill with a slow amazement, and her lips would tremble with delight, as if she was recognizing some truth or beauty she had known all her life, but uncertainly.

Your enjoyment of the world is never right, till every morning you awake in Heaven; see yourself in your Father's Palace; and look upon the skies, the earth, and the air as Celestial joys: having such a reverend esteem of all, as if you were among the Angels.

The bride of a monarch, in her husband's chamber, hath no such causes of delight as you.

You never enjoy the world aright, till the Sea itself floweth in your veins, till you are clothed with the heavens, and crowned with the stars: and perceive yourself to be the sole heir of the whole world, and more than so, because men are in it who are every one sole heirs as well as you. Till you can sing and rejoice and delight in God, as misers do in gold, and Kings in sceptres, you never enjoy the world . . .

She got to her feet, and kissed John Fiord on the cheek, and took her shawl about her shoulders, and went out under the stars.

Was it conceivable, John Fiord wondered, that she could be taught to speak? All that native intelligence locked up inside her, incapable of utterance – that must be cause of grief and secret suffering to her, in ways that not even he could understand.

Patiently, as the long winter passed, he tried to teach her. Patiently she struggled to loosen the knot of tongue, larynx, palate, teeth. They were like two people seated on either side of a trembling harp: waves of lucent lovely sound on one side; and on the other, blankness. Sunniva tried out words, again and again, she wrestled desperately with her dumbness; it was hopeless. Sometime, after a long labour, a sound or two would issue – a shrillness, a wail, a low gutteral – but nothing resembling the words on John Fiord's lips. In fact, her syllables were so weird and unnerving, like nothing heard on earth before, that John Fiord thought it best, after a few sessions, to bring the experiment to a close.

And Sunniva was glad to return to the quiet evenings beside the fire; watching the beat of his mouth over the turning pages with wonder, or delight, or incomprehension (a gentle gathering of the brows.)

Sometimes, between readings, she would darn his stockings. Sometimes she would boil the kettle for tea. Sometimes she would iron his shirts, having covered the bare table with a blanket and a sheet that bore, here and there, scorch-marks from Willa's overhot irons in the past.

John Fiord never turned up at school now with hose of different colours, or a soap sud in his ear, or spectacles dim with dust.

He even began to look a little plump round the jowls and across the middle, like a Hamnavoe merchant.

He walked among the hills on the fine spring evenings. Sometimes he would take the little notebook from his waist-coat pocket, and sketch or write in it with a pencil: he noted a cloud formation, or the shape of a great vessel going through the Pentland Firth, between Europe and America, or some plant he could not identify; or a thought, a pensée, that had drifted into his mind.

If he chanced to meet a crofter on the hill going to see to the sheep, or a courting couple, they always swerved on to another path to avoid him. So it was to be the schoolmaster: he was a part of the valley, and yet he was apart from it; even though he had been born and bred among these people.

Sometimes in the twilight, John Fiord would see two women whispering to each other across the burn, high up, near the stone bridge, beyond the reach of the croft windows. Once he came on them so unexpectedly, under the first stars, that both the women stepped back; one of them covered her mouth with her shawl and the other gave a little cry.

'Good evening to you, ladies,' said John Fiord, and raised his hat.

The conspirators were Mrs Lois Sinclair of Feaquoy and Mrs Maisie Flett of Gorse.

'And a kind prosperous night to yourself, sir,' sang Lois Sinclair, 'with good dreams.'

John Fiord passed on. The lamp was in the window of Don. Sunniva would have his supper ready for him. His slippers would be warming on the fender.

Afterwards he would read to them both, for an hour.

He read to her one night.

> *The fountains mingle with the river*
> *And the rivers with the ocean –*
> *The winds of heaven mix forever*
> *With a sweet emotion.*
> *Nothing in the world is single,*
> *All things by a law divine*
> *In one another's being mingle.*
> *Why not I in thine?*

Sunniva hung upon his lips anxiously, as if the mystery and the meaning were beyond her comprehension. Let him but have a little patience. Presently she might understand.

John Fiord sighed. The first gray thread was shuttled into him, firmly. The white thread and the black thread were to come. So long as this beautiful creature remained near him, 'the blind fury with the abhorrèd shears' had little terror. No, but death itself might be a kind of ecstasy.

He opened his copy of *The Greek Anthology*. He translated hesitantly, and his voice trembled from time to time:

Not any more . . . you girls with honeyed throats . . . with voices of yearning . . . are my limbs . . . able to bear me up. Ah, if only I were a kerulos winging over the flower of the wave, careless-hearted . . . the sea-blue bird of spring time.

He saw, closing the book, that she had tears in her eyes. Why had he been so stupid as to put the peerless lyric into English? The Greek, he felt sure, would have moved her even more.

Thirty-One

It was a dull oppressively warm June day in the valley. A stir of wind went across the bay from time to time, then died, and the sea was molten pewter again.

A few of the younger fishermen put to sea; the sails stirred and flapped and fell idle. They took to their oars, rowing out into the Pentland Firth.

Peter Sinclair of Feaquoy advised the younger men against going to sea. 'I've seen mornings like this before, two or three times. It's holding its breath for a storm' . . .

The young men pushed out their boats, one by one. A rustle of warm wind, a stir in the sail, no more. Then they set oars in rowlocks and rowed westward with their baited lines.

The fish on this day were torpid and sullen, too; as the first comers to the fishing grounds soon discovered.

In the croft of Gorse, Matthew Flett ate his dinner at leisure with his parents. Through the open door they could see the fishing boats idly scattered on the horizon. 'I don't need to worry about wind,' he said. 'I won't be straining my shoulders rowing.'

'Stay ashore,' said old David.

'Now,' said Matthew, 'you can see how wise a thing it was to have the *Golden Bird* built. A hundred pounds – but it was money well spent. I'll go down and start up the engine as soon as I judge the fish are ready to bite. I think the fish will be under the horizon, beyond the reach of their sails and oars. When the tide turns, I think, in the afternoon.'

A few spots of rain fell. Dry thunder rolled among the hills, like cart-loads of stone.

'Bide at home,' said the father. 'The only sensible man in this valley today is him over across the burn.' (He would not let the name of the man or the croft cross his lips.)

'I think I'll put some oil in the engine,' said Matthew. 'Where's the oil? Oh, I must have left it in the barn.'

The *Golden Bird* was moored out in the bay. She was too heavy to be pushed up and down the beach like the other boats. Matthew had always to row out to her in his flattie.

Matthew put on his thick sea gansy and rubber boots. He went to the door of Gorse and looked at the brimming pewter-coloured windless bay. A few more drops of rain fell. There was a mutter of thunder far away, among the Coolags. He saw Sunniva leaving Feaquoy with a basket over her arm. She would be going up to Don to light Mr Fiord's fire and put on his dinner to cook.

Matthew waved to her; he even shouted her name, though she was deaf. The young woman saw him. She paused, but gave no answering wave, and passed up along the burnside to the door of Don.

Matthew walked down to the flattie, carrying the black coiled baited lines in a fish-box. In an hour, perhaps, the tide would turn. Then he would start the engine, and steer out into the Atlantic, spreading a wake from the bow. Of the valley boats there was no sign at all. They had rowed under the horizon; they were hidden by the red cliffs to the south.

Another random gust lifted the sluggish sea. But it settled on the shore stones at once, like a tired dog, with a low growl in the throat.

Inside Gorse, Maisie said to David, 'Wind? I'm sure there'll be wind after a sultry day like this. There'll be far too much wind for the sail fishermen. But the *Golden Bird*, what's a gust or two to her? Matthew could bring her home through the worst storm.'

Maisie watched from the door as Matthew set his gear aboard the *Golden Bird*, and vaulted lithely in after. He whirled the starter; the engine stuttered into life. The sound possessed the whole valley.

Dora Budge watched from the open door of Crag. 'A fool of a lass,' muttered Maisie.

Then Matthew took the tiller and headed the *Golden Bird* into the open ocean.

The high gray weave of sky had shredded a little. The sun, a worn silver coin, put fleeting gleams on the bay.

Maisie saw a woman standing on the beach, half way between the horns of the bay. She saw with surprise that it was Lois. Lois had never been known to visit the shore; she rarely crossed the burn. Lois was intent on the *Golden Bird*, that was now disappearing round the crag. The boat left one thin wash over a rock, far out. The pulse of her engine died away.

Maisie hoped that Lois would turn and see her. She did not. She climbed up the sea-bank and crossed over the stepping stones of the burn to Feaquoy.

Her cows were lowing to be milked.

As Maisie stood there, the zinc bucket she used for the milking of her own cow toppled on to the brig-stones between barn and byre and trundled along like a madly clanging bell, until it lay in the ferns, muted and trembling. The ferns themselves swayed and shook. Maisie's long skirt whipped her ankles. A gull was whirled down about the chimney and thatch, and rose, shrieking.

Then all was quiet again. The wind had given one solitary blast.

A dark fan spread across the sea.

Up at the school this was an easy day. The term was drawing to a close. The exams were over; the school work was winding down.

'I am happy to say,' intoned Mr Fiord, 'that with one or two exceptions you have acquitted yourselves creditably this session. Once more His Majesty's inspector has been pleased with our work. I received his favourable report this morning through the post. Two days more and it will be the start of the summer holidays. Shall we keep our noses to the grindstone to the bitter end? Should I make a start on teaching you logarithms, at this late hour, Eddie? Shall I outline the simple framework of Latin grammar?'

'I don't know, sir,' said Eddie Brims.

'I think not,' said Mr Fiord. 'Those stern duties will confront the senior pupils when classes are resumed in August. So, what shall we do today?'

A random shaking of heads.

'Why not combine study with delight?' said Mr Fiord. 'While I attend to the register, you will go down to the shore and collect shells. Whoever collects the greatest variety of shells will receive a prize of. . .' He rummaged in his trousers pocket and came up with two dark coins. 'This prize, twopence.'

The children clapped their hands.

'No skylarking, remember,' said Mr Fiord. He beckoned two of the senior pupils. 'Tomasina and Albert, you will be in charge of the shell-hunt. You will report to me if there's any misbehaviour.'

While Mr Fiord, alone in the schoolroom, attended to the winding-up of the register for another session, he found that he was sweating slightly. He unfolded the handkerchief that Sunniva had ironed for him, and mopped his face and the inside of his collar.

It was one of those muggy unhealthy days.

Down at the shore, the school children darted here and there like birds. They poked among stones and pools, filling their pockets with shells. When their pockets bulged, they put the shells in the loops of their jerseys.

The skirls of the children, deadened a little in that oppressive air, trembled through the valley.

'What are they doing?' said David Flett. 'They should be in the school. That's what Fiord gets paid for.'

The heavy plate of the sea seemed to lift, once. It fell back, shattering on the stones. One small boy found himself up to his thighs in a cold swirl and surge. Tomasina caught him by the wrist and dragged him, yelling, ashore.

Soon, on the horizon, they could see two dark triangles, then three. The fishing boats were returning. Out there there must be a wind, for the sails to be up.

In the valley the green corn hardly stirred.

A few more heavy drops fell. Low thunder stammered among the hills southward.

The children, singly, and in troops, went with their treasury of shells back to the school. Tomasina took the wave-washed boy by the hand; bright spots of sea water still clung to his jersey. As for the shells this child had gathered, the sea had taken them all back.

One after another the fishing boats returned, each trailing a swirl of flashing chiding gulls.

'Ah, well,' said the first old woman on the shore, her basin under her arm, her knife in her fist, 'they've caught something.'

They returned, one by one: *Tern, Dawn, Dunter, Watchful, Selkie, Teeack*. Some had caught more than others. A few of the women complained, seeing a small hoard of fish in their men's baskets.

'We could have caught more,' said Thomas and Paul of Flinders, 'but we didn't like what we saw and heard out there. It'll come to coarse weather.'

The women flashed their knives. They swilled the headless silver-gray fish in the warm pools.

Gulls screamed over the flung guts. Cats probed, delicately, the severed heads.

David Flett of Gorse came down to the shore, 'Did you see the *Golden Bird* at all?' he asked the fishermen. They shook their heads.

'The best fish'll be further out,' said David. 'I expect our boy will be back in an hour or so' . . .

The fishermen turned their backs on him. David Flett was not a popular man in the valley.

Then David noticed Peter Sinclair of Feaquoy standing a bit further back. He raised his voice. 'Some men here,' he said, 'were either too lazy or too frightened to fish today.'

'I don't see fish-scales on your own arms,' said old Jemima of Aird to him, tartly.

Dick Spence of Burnside gave Peter Sinclair a few fish to take home with him.

'Don't stand there gaping out to sea!' cried Charlie Budge to his sister Dora. 'There's a dozen haddocks to gut.' Dora paid no attention. Her meagre cold face was intent on the one narrow sleeve of water between the horizon and the high cliff called the Too. She tilted her head, enlarged her ear with a cupped hand. Nothing could be heard for the fighting gulls.

Suddenly the heavens opened. Sheets of rain moved across the valley from the gap between the Ward and the Coolag. The

rain plucked little harps, rang little preliminary bells all across
the valley. The cats scattered. Old Jemima turned up her face
until it surged. 'Oh, that's good,' she said . . . None of the other
women thought so. With drops falling from noses and chins
they turned for home, carrying their basins of fish. The men
couldn't come till they had secured the boats and gear. The rain
came in great throbbing curtains, veil after veil. The hills and
the cliffs were indistinct ghosts. From the water-barrel under
the eave of the nearest croft, Aird, came the steady 'drip-drop-
drop' song of rain. The sedate burn was suddenly a roisterer
and a ranter, rushing peat-brown from the high moss to the
shore-stones. Still old Jemima Beaton stood, offering her face
to the onset. Lightning – one stroke – split the valley like a
sword-flash. The thunder spoke, terrifyingly, right overhead.
The old rain-worshipper covered her head with her shawl and
gathered her skirts and felt her way blindly up to the shore-
path, moaning. The deluge fell perpendicularly, each drop
bouncing from the round heavy shore stones. After the brief
preliminary harps and bells, there was now only the long
'hush-hush-hushing' of the downpour, going on and on as if
the rain would never stop: broken by grumblings of the
thunder moving here and there among the hills.

The sodden fishermen went, one by one, up to the crofts,
carrying their lines.

At last there was only one woman enduring the rain on the
sea banks.

Then, when all but Dora were indoors, the wind began from
the west.

The westerly gale soughed in the chimney of Don, and rattled
doors and windows, that Friday evening. John Fiord had eaten
his supper of cod and potatoes and ale; Sunniva was washing
plate and mug and cutlery in the aluminium basin.

The gale shouted, lurched and rebounded between the walls of the valley. From time to time Sunniva paused, feeling the croft straining at its foundations. Even after she had washed the dishes, the water in the basin was unquiet.

John Fiord had moved over to the rocking chair and opened his book. Sunniva made haste to light the paraffin lamp; she crammed another broken peat into the flushed stove.

Then she went over and stood at the window, looking out.

'Sunniva,' said John Fiord, 'by the look of it this storm will last all night. There's nothing you can do to about it, standing there at the window. Come over, sit on the rug, I'll read to you.'

The girl stood at the window, looking out.

The rain had stopped now. The wind had swept the last rag of cloud from the sky. The valley had a drenched exhausted look. The cows and the sheep had sought shelter from the weather at lee walls here and there. The scarecrow of Flinders had broken under the first knock of the storm; gusts threw an occasional drop from its sleeve over the young wind-beaten corn.

'Sunniva,' said John Fiord, 'I have something very particular to say to you tonight. Come over here to the fire. I want you to listen carefully.'

Through the window Sunniva could see Jock Beaton of Aird leaving his house and, having turned his face to the shore, struggling with the gale. It blew him hither and thither like a drunken man.

Other doors across the valley, one by one, were wrenched open, and the men leant into the great wind; and the doors flapped and crashed madly behind them.

The men were going to see that their boats were firmly secured. The tide was flowing; the gale would drive the sea very high up the beach.

Someone – a woman – had joined Dora at the sea-banks. Sunniva recognized Maisie of Gorse. From time to time Maisie raised her level hand to her brow, gazing westward. She stood there like a rooted stone. The girl of Crag swayed like a flower.

From the window of Don, a mile up the valley from the shore, the bay was all gray and silver scrollings. Inshore, the sea gathered to a fulness and fell, surge after surge, high up the shore; beads of spindrift were blown inland over pasture and oatfield. Here and there, under the blows of the sea, a great stone shifted.

Sunset blazed on the red cliff, suddenly. Then it was as if the sea had thin rinsings of blood.

Maisie went slowly back to her house.

Another crofter staggered out of his house and was thrown by the tempest on to his cabbage-patch. He picked himself up and went at the wind like a stubborn ox.

The tide was still in flood. The waves fell snarling not far from the scattered sterns of the fishing boats.

John Fiord rose to his feet. He went over to the window and took Sunniva by the elbow. 'Sunniva, lass, I have something special to say to thee. Come over now, sit at the fire, listen to me.'

Sunniva took one last look through the window – now a few women, from this croft and that, were struggling shorewards. A woman would pause in mid-step, bent forward, and then, in a flurry and flutter of skirts, be hurled sideways. But always the faces were turned to the sea and the shore.

John Fiord took the girl's hand. 'Sunniva,' he said solemnly (and she looked with preoccupied eyes at his moving lips), 'you are here, you come twice a day to this house and attend to my needs. Eagerly and well it is done. But for you, Sunniva, the schoolmaster would be a poor desolate unkempt creature. You have kept hope alive in me. When she rejected me, that once dear friend in Hamnavoe – how long ago – a year, eighteen months? – I had small wish to live, truly. But the fire was no sooner dead than you rekindled it.'

Sunniva watched his lips, anxiously. She put out her free hand, until she was holding him by both hands, gently and strongly.

The house shuddered under another onset of wind. The china dog stirred on the mantelpiece. Sunniva threw a glance at the window, then her eyes turned back to the face of the man.

'Eager and pleasant your movements about this house, for my benefit, always, Sunniva. With a man's selfishness – but gratefully, too, believe me – I accepted them. Do you remember, my dear, the day that I first came to the schoolhouse? You were the only one in the valley to welcome me. You stood at my door with an armful of flowers. It was a most beautiful thing to do. And now I see – thank God, before it is too late – that everything you do is beautiful beyond words. I think I cannot exist without this grace you have bestowed on me here, in my parents' house.'

Still the wind was rising outside. One violent gust rattled the timbers of the door. A fleck of spindrift clung to a pane, shaking, like some gray sea insect.

Sunniva let go of John Fiord's hand and got to her feet and moved quickly back to the window.

The sea-banks below were lined with people, standing hunch-backed into the tempest. The men had secured their boats and had joined the women above. The sunset had left the crags, but the clouds in the north-west smouldered, and the darkening bay was laced with a deeper red.

From this croft window and that the face of a child looked seaward.

'Sunniva,' said John Fiord, 'that's cruel, to leave me just as I was about to say the most important thing I will ever say to anyone. I think myself to be standing on the verge of a great joy. If I was a poet, I would say beautifully what I have to say. But the passion is there, underneath my stumbling words. And I know that you can feel, more vividly than words can say, my longing.'

He had moved over to the window beside her.

Sunniva's face was pressed hard against the pane. Far out in the bay a shape moved, tossed here and there, dark on the darkness.

'Sunniva,' said John Fiord, 'I am asking you to be my wife.'

Sunniva turned and put him aside, gently. She tugged at the door and eased herself through. The door clashed and shuddered behind her. She hadn't stopped to put on her shawl.

John Fiord was left alone.

One or two last women were fluttering shorewards, flung between the oatfields and the gorged barn, crazy dancers.

Sunniva overtook them; balanced from time to time on a crest of wind, half fallen into a trough and recoil of wind; but her going was stronger than the hen-flurryings of the other women. She overtook them, one after the other.

She stood among the women on the sea-banks: who were beginning already to set up a lamentation.

The men said nothing, but they looked defeated, huddled together, their heads down. There was nothing they could do. Slowly and rhythmically the *Golden Bird* was being broken on the rock.

Sunniva thrust two of the men aside. Clambering among the great round stones, the wind spread her hair about her face and blinded her. She lifted the bright fold from her eyes. Her feet were among the first seethings of sea. She stretched out both hands. An incoming breaker steeped her to the shoulders. She staggered and almost went under.

The girl Dora ran back and fore on the sand like a dog, howling.

The women were screaming above, 'Come back! There's nothing but the boat there! The girl's mad. Where's Lois?'

Lois was the only woman who had stayed at home.

The rock rang like a bell. The engine had fallen out of the *Golden Bird.*

Sunniva's hand was on the yawing hull.

The boat broke in two, and the young fisherman fell out of her. Sunniva caught Matthew in her arms. He clutched at her. A comber went over; it swamped them both; it broke in a long diagonal, snarling, lamenting, hushing, high up the sand.

The woman and the man were still there. Black sea gushed out of them.

Sunniva turned. She dragged him, her fist wound through his black hair, up through the back-surge, hauling and turning and half foundering, on to the stones; and there she left him.

The men were all round the body. 'There's still breath in him! Knock him! Keep the flame going in him, what's left of it!' They knelt, they hurled hot breath one after another into his cold mouth; their fists fell on his chest like hammer blows, rhythmically. Peter of Feaquoy knelt beside Matthew and hurled his breath, again and again, into the wrecked cold mouth.

At last the mouth fluttered.

The women were making low querulations together above, on the sea-banks. The wind had fallen considerably in the last half-hour. A few stars shone out over Caithness. The breakers beat as loud on the shore; but now the tide had begun to ebb.

'Stop that howling,' cried Peter of Feaquoy to the women. 'Go and tell Maisie he's alive. Tell her to put kettles on to boil. His heart could stop yet.'

Matthew groaned. A green slime came from the corner of his mouth.

A star shone in Matthew's eye. The star froze.

'Thunder on him again!' cried one of the men. 'I think we've lost him.'

A light shone from the window of Feaquoy. The face of Lois looked out on the darkling shapes on the shore; that moved here and there about the long still shape on a shelf of rock.

In the window of Gorse, a blind was drawn down slowly.

The Life and Death
of John Voe

One

'And how is poor Jock?' said the woman of Briggs across the burn. 'Is he any better?'

'None better,' said Jock's wife Selina.

The woman of Briggs (Matilda) and Selina filled their pails with burn water and went their ways.

Jock was getting off the Pentland Firth ferry boat, with his sea-chest on his shoulder: after many a thousand sea-miles.

'Why are there so many people in Hamnavoe today?' he wondered. It was a quiet little seaport normally, except when the whalers came back in late summer; and for an hour or two every Wednesday afternoon when the farmers came in to buy and sell their beasts.

It was a tumultuous afternoon, for a Tuesday. Music – brass and drums – came from a hidden square. The town girls and the country girls had put on their finery. There was much teasing from the young men in their black suits. A farm lad with a brick-red face gave a bag of sweets to a pretty sixteen-year old lass. She looked demurely at the flagstones, and put the gift into her basket, which was half-full of coloured paper bags already. The awkward lad stood beside her a minute; then, getting no encouragement, he lost himself in the throng. A troop of town girls pointed at the basket and laughed. The girl who had been honoured blushed, and her lips quivered: was she getting ready for laughter or tears? Jock, half way down the gangplank, couldn't tell, because a foreign-looking man with a hurdy-gurdy came between him and the girls. The monkey on the man's shoulder chattered and spat and showed its teeth.

Other strange fragments of speech – entreaties, proclamations – came to Jock's ears: 'Come, a sixpence and all your future days I will read in your hand: lovers, riches, children' . . . 'Any more for the merry-go-round? Five seats left. Well, off we go!' Another blast of music, and young men and girls flew through the air, round and round in laughing shrieking circles! . . . 'The stuff in this bottle, elixir of life, it will cure most maladies you care to name. You, sir, your cheek is pale. Beware of winter, it brings coughs and declines! Madam, keep this in your cupboard, only a half-crown a bottle, against the evil days when the bread-winner drags his feet, and the bairns begin to peak and pine' . . . Mockery was directed at him from the crowd. Sadly the medicine-man shook his head. A black man stood on a box outside his tent, wrapped in a tiger skin, and licked a glowing poker. A little man danced at his side crying, 'An African prince! Ladies and gentlemen, step inside – I will show you the marvels that this black prince can do. Price, one shilling!' The prince rolled his great eyes round the crowd. Girls shrieked and held on to their partners. There was laughter. 'The poker isn't hot at all! It's painted red, that's what' . . . But undoubtedly the poker had come out of the glowing brazier; and now it came again, sparks flying from it, and the tongue wrapped itself round it.

Jock had been at sea so long he had almost forgotten about the Lammas Fair. Indeed he felt a bit taken aback, slightly insulted, that his homecoming should be on such a day. He had seen plenty of this kind of thing in ports all over the world; much bigger, of course, much more colourful and loud and thronged than this little country fair. But, for the last month, since his discharge in Liverpool, he had cherished the image of himself walking with his sea-chest among the quiet grey houses, and nodding familiarly to this shopkeeper and that housewife. He would have a pot of tea, oatcakes and cheese, in the Temperance Hotel. Then he would hoist his box on his shoulder, happy to be among his own people at last, and set out for his mother's house on the far side of the hill Kringla-fiold. Such was the sweet homecoming he imagined. To have made landfall on a day like this, when a spirit of madness touches townsfolk and country-folk; when instead of shy quiet welcomes from this one and that, those exotic fairground men were urging the folk to all kinds of foolishness and whirlings and tawdry deception – this he had not banked on at all.

The Salvation Army, twelve of them, marched round the corner into view, with banner and sounding brass; and formed a ring at the head of the pier. And the big drum beat.

The door of a pub opened, and a man came out in a loping sidelong lurch, and stumbled, and steadied himself against the wall, and looked with cod eyes at a group of laughing jeering passers-by. A dark bottle was sticking out of his jacket pocket; three small boys, tormentors, were round him, trying to get at his bottle. The drunk took an ill-judged swipe at them with his boot, and almost fell over. The children ran away, half in terror and half in joy . . . The pub door opened again. Three fishermen went inside.

And now it seemed that a sudden spell was being put on the fair. A soaring exquisite thread of melody rose from the heart of the throng. It was so beautiful and pure it made all the other noises cheap and tawdry. The crowd parted. The blind fiddler passed through, wooing his fiddle to him, caressing it, con-spiring with it to put bewitchment on the holiday crowd. The sightless eyes looked at nothing. The varnished bird cried and swooned and triumphed as the bow flashed about the strings.

The music dwindled, it died; the enchantment lasted for half-a-minute maybe. Then the blind fiddler put his cloth cap on the causey, and pennies rattled and rang in the street around it, and fell softly into it. The crowd flowed again about the blind fiddler and hid him from Jock's view.

The music reminded Jock, with a vivid pang, of the girl he had taken out once or twice when the *Bon Voyage* lay in the harbour of Buenos Aires. Juanita was her name, and she was dark as a gypsy, with great black eyes; and in her movements she was sinuous and unpredictable as a ferret. The first meeting, by chance along the sea front, Jock and Juanita had no words in common at all. What merriment it had been, exchanging half-a-dozen phrases! Juanita had laughed to the point of tears at such English words as 'ship' and 'sailor' and 'beautiful' and 'flower' and 'love'. That beautiful Spanish words should have such harsh barbaric equivalents! Let the sailor try them on his clumsy tongue. Jock tried, and the drolleries that emerged from his mouth made her hold her sides, and beg him with a gesture to stop, out of excess merriment! They sat at an open-air café between the statue of a national hero and a fountain, and Jock bought from a lingering flower-girl a poppy for Juanita to put in her hair. And then the girl looked magnificent; Jock, gazing at her, had a catch in his breath. More words of both languages were exchanged, amid laughter and wonderment: 'horses', 'prairie', 'ranch', 'islands', 'sea', 'return', 'kiss'.

It appeared that Juanita had come a week ago to the city with her brother, who hoped to sell a dozen horses at the horsemarket. No, the horses had not been sold yet; Roberto had had offers but none satisfactory. Negotiations were in progress with a dealer; gradually, after hours of enjoyable haggling, the gap in the prices sought and offered was narrowing. The day after tomorrow Roberto was sure of a bargain being struck. And then? And then she would ride back to the house on the prairie with Roberto. On the hacienda she was being missed, for sure. On such an estate as her father's there was much work for a girl to do.

Meantime, in the great city, Juanita was not meant to be out-of-doors by herself, unattended. No: Roberto had, on arrival, taken her at once to the house of their great-aunt Anna Maria, where she was to remain until such time as the horses had been sold. There were things that she could do for the old one, such as listen to her stories and make her, from time to time, a pot of coffee. Alas, the old great-aunt had much deteriorated in the five years since Juanita had last seen her. She had not recognized Juanita at first, and when at last the girl's identity had penetrated the fogs, far from welcoming her, as once she would have done, she appeared cold and resentful. Why had she not been told about this visit? She was too old, too tired, to receive a guest, even a young relative. Well, she might stay for a day or two – no more – but she need expect no entertainment, the great-aunt was tired and slept much. As for going out with Juanita as her chaperon, that was out of the question. Nowadays she never went out, winter or summer, except to the church on a Sunday morning. Now, please, it was her time for rest. There were books and a piano – Juanita must entertain herself as best she could.

On the second morning, Juanita could endure the air of this moribund house no longer. It was Spring. The salt Atlantic air came in at her open casement and intoxicated her. When Roberto had gone, after breakfast, to the horse-market, and the querulous old one had retired to her room, Juanita had gone out by herself: not too far, lest she lose her way in the maze of city streets: merely along the waterfront where the stores of the merchants were, and the skippers and brokers and merchants came and went.

It was a most risky thing to do. If Roberto had chanced to meet her, it was hard to know what he might say and do – a country girl, affluent and well-bred, wandering along a street infested with a thousand sea-ruffians from every nation on earth! The horsemarket was at the other end of the city. She *must* fill her lungs with sea air for an hour, or she would go crazy in that mausoleum of a house. Then suddenly, round a street corner, she all but collided with a blue-eyed handsome young sailor . . .

By now Jock was very much in love with the Argentine girl. There was a sad little silence between them. A petal fell from the poppy and lay on the table between their glasses. Juanita broke the silence. Jock, what of him? Would he stay long in Buenos Aires? Surely he would return, soon, very soon, so that they could spend more such beautiful days together? No?

Jock told her, dully, that in two days time the *Bon Voyage* would sail for Cape Town, then Lisbon, then Liverpool. And that would be the end of a year-long voyage. There, in Liverpool, Jock would be paid off, with a good discharge in his book and a pocketful of sovereigns. From there, somehow, by land or sea he would get home to his grey cold Orkneys. It was melancholy. They were unlikely ever to see each other again. If by some chance, some future trip brought him once more to Argentina, would she not be married, with a jealous husband and two or three vivid children?

At this, Juanita began to weep. Her grief was even more beautiful than her laughter or the music of her speech. Her weeping was not like the slow hard tears of some Orkney lass – it was fluent and open and unrestrained. There, in the middle of the public square, she threw her arms around Jock and summoned him to share in their common bereavement. Jock's face was all bedewed; not with his own tears, for his eyes were dry as opals. He would, normally, have been embarrassed at such an open display. But the boy was in love. He kissed a tear from her cheek; bitter it was, and more intoxicating than a flagon of wine.

There was left to them one day and one evening. Tomorrow, if Jock could get a mate to take watch for him, they would meet again. They would enjoy last hours together, walking on the sea-front perhaps (he would show her *Bon Voyage* among a forest of masts); or going from tavern to café and certainly to the shop where they sold gold and silver rings with good stones set in them; or perhaps just sitting in the public garden between the roses and the prancing statues of heroes, in a serene eloquent silence (for clumsy exchanges, half in Spanish and half in English, were no longer required). And when the shadows lengthened, and the stars came out, and it was night: they would spend every minute of the last night like great gamblers!

'No,' cried Juanita, 'no!' They must never go from each other. Let her think. There must be a way. Jock had been a country boy before he became a sailor – he was acquainted with the earth and things of the earth, no? Wheat fields and cows and horses and dogs. Let her think well. (She furrowed the dark silk of her brows.) Her father was forever engaging men and paying them off, according to what season it was and how in the great ranch things were – rounding up and branding of cattle, sowing of wheat, the time of the foaling of horses and of calving and lambing. Oh, was never tranquility on such a farm: strong hands were required to do that and this, always. Her father: she, Juanita, was the favourite daughter of her father, he would do almost anything to please her. So, if she were to approach her father at some auspicious hour, the day after tomorrow – when he had finished his dinner, say, and was sitting on the veranda smoking a cigar; or when there was singing in the yard and the voices of his five daughters blended well with the deep or falsetto voices of the gauchos (such songs under the stars her father loved very much to hear) – then she would approach her father and take him to one side and whisper a few words into his fond ear such as, 'I have met an honourable boy in the city, he is hard-working and honest, he is a sea-voyager but he is well used to the things that pertain to the land – I should like very much if you would offer him a place here on the hacienda' . . . Her father would say, after half-a-minute's reflection, 'The stranger will have a place on the ranch, if Juanita wishes so' . . . 'And so, Jock, we will live near to each other for many years. We will see each other every day, and every night too' . . . The question of marriage, that might present difficulties, for she had been affianced for two winters, in some sort, to Don Miguel, the coarse avaricious son of the neighbouring rancher – the two fathers having agreed to such an eventual marriage – but they would cross that bridge when they come to it . . .

The girl was suddenly silent in the middle of her great and growing plan. Jock turned to see her, wide-eyed, looking towards the far end of the square. There, lounging against the wall of a Bank, and staring straight at them and their tangled arms, was a young man with a very long thin moustache on his upper lip, and long boots and a gun-belt and a gun.

'My brother, Jorge,' she gasped.

She dropped Jock's hand and rose to her feet. She looked at once back at Jock, and fluttered words at him, 'Tomorrow. We will speak further about this tomorrow. Now I must go.'

Juanita made her way, between horse carriages and dock-side carts, across the wide street to the man who lounged, still unsmiling, against the wall of rough red granite.

Jock saw the brother's lips move. Then he reached forward and hit Juanita – not too hard – across the cheek. But it was enough to break her. She even knelt in front of him, like a dog who expects a second whipping. Across her shuddering shoulders the brother looked again at our sailor. There was no friendship in the look. He bent and with boot and hand urged the girl to her feet. They disappeared round the corner.

A few of her tears were still on Jock's face and hands.

Did Jock forget the Argentine girl, on the long sea-road home? To a large extent he did. Who shall blame him? It was certain that they would never see each other again. She would in due course marry the ill-favoured greedy young Don Miguel, and she would have to go and live with him on his family ranch till old age, among a growing troop of children and grandchildren; and eventually, many years on, she would lie still and gray in her casket with candles about her and a little silver cross between her fingers.

The image of Juanita throbbed vividly in his mind all the passage between Buenos Aires and Cape Town. In Cape Town Jock and a few of his mates flirted with black girls, off and on, until Captain MacKenzie summoned them to his cabin and gave them a fierce tongue-lashing. Did the young fools not know that in this colony there was no mixing of whites and blacks? It was a civil crime – worse, it transgressed the church edicts of those stern Dutch Calvinist settlers. There would be bad trouble if one of them was so much as seen linking arms with a black beauty. Complaints had been made to him, Alistair MacKenzie, by the civil authorities. If the crazy young idiots wanted women, what was wrong with a girl white-skinned like themselves? That was all he had to say . . . As the hangdog faces moved away, the skipper's face relaxed and he put on them a broad merry wink.

Juanita . . . He dreamed on one of the night-watches of what the heroes in the penny romances the sailors read would do. He would sign on the next ship to South America. He would buy or steal a horse, he would go storming by mountain passes and swamps and half-caste villages. Wise old women in lonely huts would sustain the adventurer with dried raw meat and cups of wine. And then one afternoon he would ride stealthily to a white church brimming with incense and the sound of bells; he would tie his faithful horse to the veranda; he would hurl himself like an emissary of fate and seize the white-robed Juanita from her swarthy fiancé, there at the altar rail just as the priest was about to utter the nuptial phrases. And then, almost before the congregation knew what was happening, Jock with his load of radiant innocence and beauty would be up and mounted and off; and somewhere far south in Patagonia some Presbyterian missionary would unite them for ever.

But morning would dawn gray and cold over the Atlantic as *Bon Voyage* held north. The dream dissolved like a lacing of spindrift.

In Lisbon he had almost forgotten Juanita, though many a dark-eyed girl on the pavements reminded him of her, and the music of their speech was like enough Juanita's. He had been brought up in an air of gray commonsense; now, if a girl reminded him of her by a gazelle glance or a dove-like flutter of the hand, he would give her the kind of stony stare that a Hamnavoe shopkeeper gives a persistent debtor.

In Liverpool there were girls with Irish names and Welsh names. But the sailors had small time to make their acquaintance. The unloading took two days; when it was finished they were given their money and their discharge papers. They would have to find their own way home. Here, now, home he was. But whereas he had expected a sober northern landfall, behold he had stumbled into this labyrinth of carnival and foolery: the last station of rejoicing in the country year, apart from Harvest Home, before the hard time of snow and darkness came. The fields were yellow towards harvest, and the island folk danced in the sign of corn.

Juanita was as distant now as the snow of last March.

Jock left his sea-chest in the harbour office. He poured his little torrent of sovereigns from one hand to another, then stowed them safely in the purse in his belt. He set his cheese-cutter cap at a sea-rover's angle on his head.

He sallied out to take his place in the Lammas merriment.

How often, when we think we are bound to have a wonderful time, does the day end in dust and ashes!

Jock began with a dram and a scooner of ale, in the Viking. Having broken a sovereign into a shower of coins, he ordered a dram for a man who had just finished singing a ballad very badly, and a mug of ale for a man who (he remembered) stood at a corner of the bar day in day out with a sad face, who never once bought a drink but whose whiskers always bore a fringe of froth. (It was said that this scrounger had never done a hand's turn of work since his wife had gone off with a whaler a week after their wedding.) Jock paid his tribute to the man's melancholy and patience. (He had had a good fishing boat, the man, and he was said to be good with line and creel, but the boat for years now had been a crooked warped thing among the rocks.) The lazy betrayed one raised sad eyes to Jock's, then buried his face among the ale-froth.

Jock thought to himself, 'If I had brooded on that Juanita like this down-and-out on his good-for-nothing slut of a wife, I might have ended like him' . . . He drowned the sudden thought of her-who-was-gone-from-him-forever with a sip or two of Old Orkney whisky, and a prolonged gargle of Flett's Hamnavoe ale.

A hand smote Jock on the shoulder. It was Albert Stockan that he had sailed with in the the whaler *Eldora* two summers before.

They might have embraced each other, had that kind of greeting between old ship-mates been countenanced in Orkney. They contented themselves with grinning in each other's face for a long time, and a cautious thumping of shoulders and at last of course a dram and another dram.

The corncrake of a singer was on his feet again, but a fisherman's elbow was thrust into his open jaws before he could sound a note; and instead an old navy pensioner with one eye began to play on his melodeon or 'squeeze-box' – it was a sentimental sea ditty, called 'I'll stick to the ship, lads . . .' From hearth-fire to bar counter the drinkers took up the chorus.

Half-a-dozen farm servants came in. It would be hard to say if their faces were red with summer suns or the Lammastide ale of a few taverns.

Albert Stockan, telling another lie about a thing that had happened on the *Eldora*, how a Norsky had swindled him out of thirty shillings playing pontoon one Arctic midnight across a sea-chest (the sun being still above the horizon); this whaler and gambler and fist-fighter Albert Stockan observed over Jock's shoulder the melancholy wife-deserted down-and-outer at the bar, and bade the barman console him with a double rum.

Six Hoy-men came in, one of them being carried by the others; whom they set down carefully on the wide window-seat, drawing his cloth cap down over his face as one might blind a house of mourning.

A far hidden voice cried, 'Here come the Hoy hawks!'

The biggest of the Hoy men set out to look for and pacify the man of insults, but the crowd in the Viking was now too dense for the butt and cleave of his shoulder. He returned; he addressed himself to a little thick glass shaking still with yellowness from the Old Orkney bottle . . . He looked at it

– no, he had had enough – he passed the trembling lamp of drink to him-who-dwelt-forever-in-a-place-of-darkness-and-desertion. 'Maybe, boy,' he said, 'it's the best thing that happened to thee, when she went away with that Icelander.'

A look of anger went over the melancholy one's face – but it passed soon – and he accepted the drink, and drank gloomily.

'Do you mind the time,' said Albert Stockan to Jock, 'you nearly lost us that whale off Lofoten, the time you threw the harpoon at it crooked, and the whale bucked like a thousand-ton bullock and made off, and he would have escaped too, except that first my harpoon nailed him, and slowed him up, so the others had time to nail him good and proper? And nobody spoke to you for the rest of that trip but me, Albert Stockan. Do you mind that, Voe?'

Jock remembered it as if a harpoon had gone into his very skull; for that, even in Stockan's twisted version, had been a shameful episode in his life. He felt like protesting mildly to begin with, 'That isn't the way it happened at all!' Then he felt like throwing his glass of whisky into the liar's head. Then he felt like taking the little detractor by the throat and shaking the lie out of him, the filthy little scum of a slanderer that he was! . . .

At once Jock realized that he was on the verge of getting drunk.

He said, quite quietly, 'I'll see you soon, Albert.'

He drank the lees of his whisky and made for the door. It was easier said than done. There had been a steady influx of customers in the last fifteen minutes. Jock had to ease himself out through men of all shapes and sizes, and one big red-headed woman who was the only women brazen enough to enter a Hamnavoe public house.

The Hoy-men were all round him-that-had-waited-forty-two-years-in-vain-for-his-beloved. 'Thu're not to worry,' one

of the Hoy-men was saying, 'I'm sure I saw thee wife last
weekend in a troop o' seals in the Bring Deep. "Tell Simon,"
says she, "I'll be home afore Yule" . . . Then the seals sank,
and she sank wi' them. It's as sure as I'm standing here.'

He-whose-wife-was-perhaps-a-selkie considered this intelligence gravely. He took a great wash of beer into him. He
wiped his whiskers. Sadly he shook his head.

'A glass o' gin, dear,' shrilled the red-headed slut towards
the bar.

The helpless Hoy-man lay without a stir in the window recess.
Many harpoons of the barley had passed into him that day.

'Shut up with that damn noise, till I hear mesell speakan,'
said an awkward-in-drink quarryman to the little mouse of a
melodeonist who was now pressing and pulling out the
opening notes of a revivalist hymn.

The groundswell of a whaling ballad from the darkest corner
drowned melodeon and fragmented half a dozen narratives and
caused patrons to shout like wolves their orders into the ear of
the barman James; who every five minutes or so for the last half-
hour had gone and shouted at the foot of the stair: 'When are
them two lazy bitches of barmaids coming to help me! I have to
be here, there, everywhere! Right, if they're not coming, accept
my notice as from Friday first!' . . . And now the first of the
barmaids made an appearance, tucking a wisp of brown hair
under her head-band. A roar of welcome broke about her.

> *And from Stromness sailed away, brave boys,*
> *And from Stromness sailed away,*

roared the singers from the corner webbed with shadow.

And now Jock had almost won clear of the ruck.

His eye met the eye of him-that-had-been-a-good-seaworker-
till-the-desertion-of-his-breadbaker-and-shirtwasher. *Never,*

dirged that lorn eye across the drunken loud tumult – *never love and kindness and beauty again. Do not look for them.*

And he raised a mourning glass, yellow and shaking with the corn spirit, in Jock's direction.

Then Jock, sweating and with his stomach whirling withershin inside him, found himself standing on the cobbles of the street. Children with balloons and whirling wood-shaving birds-on-sticks went dancing past him on either side.

'Tut!' cried old Willa from her doorstep. 'Another poor drunken thing of a boy! That landlord! I wish I saw him in the kirkyard.'

Willa's husband was inside, as every day, playing dominoes with the street-sweeper and the lamplighter at the bar counter.

This was a quiet part of Hamnavoe.

The distant noises of the Fair came on the wind.

Fifty yards on was a very populous inn, the Arctic Whaler.

Jock walked on right past it. An extraordinary sound issued from the portal, a weave of joviality, abandonment, recrimination, argument, song-bursts, denials, mirth, rage, and drunken vacuity.

Jock went into the Temperance Hotel for a pot of strong black sweet tea.

Of his twenty sovereigns there were seventeen left, and a handful of what the gambling men called 'snow and mud' – silver and coppers. The gold he stowed again in the belt he wore round his middle, under his shirt.

The noises of the Fair beat all round the sober hostelry where he sat, working out his road home on the palm of his left hand with his right wondering forefinger. Then he laid down his head on the table, between the sugar bowl and the teapot, and went to sleep.

* * *

Where was Jock now? It seemed to him, when he looked around, that he was in some kind of meeting-house or vestry. The place was lit by a single oil lamp, so that the corners and the far door were in shadow. Behind a table sat a figure in a dark robe, and in various benches and chairs about the room sat other men in black robes. He was aware of a presence at his shoulder: a black-robed man stood there, and Jock saw with surprise that it was William Brims, who worked the croft next to his mother. And now William Brims, whom Jock knew for a mild sweet-tempered man, was looking sternly over Jock's shoulder towards the table at the far end where the man who seemed to be the president of this gathering was seated, alone. This president's face was just out of reach of the lamplight, so that Jock got an impression of hollows and shadows only. The flickerings and shadows fell at new angles across the president's face; he had turned his head; he was listening to a man at the side of the hall who was on his feet and speaking in a loud voice. All the black robes were listening, bent forward, one or two fluttering. Jock could only listen, too. Someone or other was being denounced . . . 'Altogether a useless member of society. Brethren, I think I must, by this time, have convinced you of his waywardness and unreliability. Oh no, he wouldn't help his mother and sisters on the croft – that kind of work was not for him. Let me remind you that the good croft of Flinders had been worked by his father and his father's fathers for more than three hundred years. They had enriched those few fields with their sweat and thews and blood, and this youth was the newest link in the chain: on him the spirits of his forefathers, the very spirit of the furrows itself, looked to carry on the work into the fair harvests of the future. Lately the yoke of labour had become lighter in the land – they were their own masters now, there were good roads to the markets at Kirkwall and Hamnavoe, mechanical aids were beginning to appear in the agricultural merchants' shops. No earth-worker henceforth would be stooped and broken with labour by the time he was forty. Men looked to a smiling golden future. Work – always there would be labour in the glebe, hard honest labour – but the fruits of harvest would be three-fold and five-fold and even ten-fold what they had been in the days of our rude ancestors. But this inheritance and this promise: they were not for our hero! Oh no – some kind of restless vagabond blood had gotten into him, nobody knows how. When the time came for him to put his schooldays behind him, he did not turn his face to the croft of his fathers. No, he turned his face to the sea-dazzle, to shifting ebbs and floods; he would be a fisherman, and that only' . . .

Jock had known for some time that he was the subject of this harangue. Some kind of a court was in session, and he was a man arraigned, and he would have to 'thole his assize'.

'Look at him well, my friends!'

Twenty faces from here and there in the court-room turned and squinnied at him. With a slight shock he realized that he knew some of the faces within the circle of the lamp's radiance. They were men of his own parish, whom he recognized; indeed their faces had not changed in the last fifteen years. They were farmers, crofters, the village shop-keeper (his own uncle Wilfred), the minister, the laird's factor, the tailor, the miller, the joiner-boatbuilder-undertaker, the mason . . . Jock looked behind him. William Brims, his keeper, put a single hard grinding look on him, then turned his eyes once more on the shadowy judge.

The prosecutor went on. 'And how long, members of the court, how long does this young bright promising lad help his old grandfather in the fishing boat *Mary Ellen*? One summer and one winter only, a ten-month. The hero is not satisfied with haddocks and lobsters, not he. He must unlock new horizons. Orkney is too small for him – even Scotland and the Iceland waters cannot hold him. It seems that he will try his fortune in a strange land: I refer to the United States of America. Well and good – many an honest Scottish boy has sailed to the New World, and by dint of application and hard work, has made a good living for himself, by speculation or industry. But it seems that the life of our hero is not to be lived according to any accepted pattern. No hard devoted work for him – he will make a fortune, yes, but by a short cut, by one wild dream-like gamble. Mr president, when next we hear of him, he is panning for gold, one among many, in the streams and torrents of California. It is true, some of these outcasts and off-scourings of every country in Europe, a few, had come on glistering veins deep in the mountains. Not the vast majority. Not John Voe. They live, that horde of miners, in crazy dangerous violent townships, erected overnight almost, and doomed to melt back like mushrooms into the soil. Our young Orkneyman does not "strike it rich", as the saying goes.

'The sea – he will go back to the sea, but in a big venturesome ship that trades in the great ports of the world. No doubt, in that strict sea-borne community, he is forced to do some honest labour, winding sheets and scrubbing decks. But no fame, no riches. After a year he is back in Orkney. I am sure his hard-working mother thought: "He is home. My prodigal is home. Now at last I shall get some rest. He is to plough, he will gather into barns at the end of every summer. My boy will be the better of the world-wide experience he has hoarded" . . . If indeed the good woman thought that, she was to be bitterly disappointed by the end of that winter. He showed no inclination, when March came in, to yoke the ox or to wipe the cobwebs from the plough. No: one fine morning, off he slips to the whalers' agent in Hamnavoe. The harbour there is crammed with whaling vessels from Hull and Gravesend and Dundee. The good folk of Hamnavoe, they have a perilous time of it, especially after dark when the dozen ale-houses put up shutters and the drunken harpooners are sent reeling out into the street. Windows broken – chickens and lambs stolen, even a cat or two – young women molested – the burgesses insulted in their own shop doors.

'Our hero enrolls himself in the company of those sea-adventurers: on a whaler called the *Eldora*, master Michael Surfax, esquire.

'I will not weary you with an account of the voyage of the whaler *Eldora*. She did not have a fortunate voyage: she brought no overbrimming freightage of oil and whalebone into the port of Hull. Some mystery surrounds the voyage: the crew, it seems, were reluctant to speak about some details of it; the skipper shut himself behind a cold silence. But it seems that the man in the dock was not a popular man with the crew – far from it. It seems he was a kind of Jonah, an Ahab, or like that ancient mariner who had brought ill-luck on crew and voyage by destroying something beautiful and fortunate and innocent.

'It is not my business to dwell on sailors' superstitions. All we know is: our ill-starred whaling man is transferred, without the sound of pipes or valedictory salutations, to another whaling ship that had perforce to leave the whaling-grounds before her time. It was noticed that his arm was in a sling, and his left hand heavily bandaged.

'I suppose that, by this time, his mother, that good open-handed hard-working woman, had come to expect little amendment or good resolution when he stood once more on her threshold with his new sea-wounds on him. If so, the grace of resignation had been granted her, for after another harvest and winter of idling uselessly by the fire, or by way of variety drinking in the parish ale-house with the more feckless men of the parish, and afterwards with others making nuisances of themselves under the lamplit windows of decent respectable young women (I shall have more to say on that subject presently): I say, when spring came round again it was not to break yet once more the ancient glebe of Flinders that he put his hand – he put his hand to the book of the shipping agent in Hamnavoe – he was enrolled in the crew of the merchant ship *Bon Voyage*, outward bound from Hamnavoe (once stores and water had been taken aboard) for the Americas.

'Mr president of the court, brethren, a month ago John Voe arrived back in Orkney after a voyage of eighteen months. He was apprehended and taken into custody as soon as he stepped ashore, by the officers of this court. At once he made a statement. Oh, our hero Mr Voe is very glib and plausible and mealy-mouthed whenever he finds himself in a corner. I will read you what he said an hour after his arrest. I ask you to refrain from laughter or other expressions of scorn. Here it is, signed by himself: "I freely confess that I have led a wayward and rootless life from the time I left the school, also that I have misconducted myself on sundry occasions by sea and land, and that I have made little profit by goings and comings about the globe. Yet I have gained some store of experience in the different places I have travelled in, and I mean now to settle into a more peaceful mode of life and to work the croft of Flinders that my fathers have worked before me. To help me in this task, now that my mother is getting beyond it, I intend to seek in matrimony a decent respectable hard-working woman, so that by God's help our fields may be fruitful, and be blessed at last with sons diligent at the work of plough and scythe and flail. This work I undertake to perform cheerfully until such time as I am laid with my fathers under the hill; but afterwards there will be a strong son or sons to follow me. And if I look on the sea at all, it will be to catch a few haddocks off-shore, and to raise a few lobster-creels from the quiet rock shelves under Marwick and Yesnaby. The only gold I will toil for henceforth is the gold of harvest corn. I earnestly beg the authorities to believe what I here put my hand to" . . .'

While the prosecutor was reading this document, Jock was aware of little ripples and gusts of merriment in the court. One man – Jock couldn't quite make out his face in the shadows – gave vent to a shout or two of mirth, and then stuffed a spotted red hankie into his mouth. The prosecutor had dimples in his austere cheeks as he read, and had to pause in mid-sentence occasionally. Coy mirthful faces looked round at Jock from time to time, and looked away again. Even his keeper, William Brims, standing behind him, gave a single snort. The skull-angled face of the president of the court relaxed into curves for a time: in a kind of silent kirkyard mirth.

Jock laughed himself, partly to hear that solemn assembly in such mirth, but mostly at the pomposity of the statement (which he never remembered to have made, or signed, in any case.)

For some reason, the jocosity that now possessed the court went on for some time. The prosecutor, suppressing a chuckle from time to time with the back of his hand, went on: 'I ask you to note particularly the part of the statement concerning "a respectable hard-working woman": he intends, he says, to take a respectable hard-working woman in marriage, to help him in the work of the croft, and to provide hard-working sons so that the name Voe might never fail from the fields and folds and furrows of Flinders . . .' (More laughter in court. The judge tapped the table in front of him with a gavel, and the gavel shook a little.)

'This libertine! This reprobate! This dishonourer of the fair name of womankind! Seducer! Freebooter on the dangerous seas of love! I call as a witness Maisie Bain.'

Solemnity returned to the proceedings. The relaxed faces were grave again. The judge wiped a last glister of mirth from the hollow of his eye.

A girl stood at the table almost under the lamp. Jock could see her face clearly. She was the first girl he had ever kissed; once only, and amid blushings and hangings of the head outside the door of the big barn at Harvest Home, under the stars. They would both have been thirteen or fourteen at the time. Afterwards, for a month, he hadn't dared to look at her; though often enough Maisie had given him shy gentle smiles, and even tugged the sleeve of his jersey to make him pay attention.

'Look at that philanderer in the dock,' said the prosecutor. 'Has he been a nuisance to you ever?'

'Many a time,' said Maisie.

'Continue,' said the prosecutor mildly.

'The times I wanted him to be nice to me and he wouldn't,' said Maisie in a hurt voice.

'I always liked you, Maisie,' cried Jock. 'You know that.'

'Silence!' cried the judge, and the timbers of the table trembled under the assault of his gavel. 'The prisoner is not to speak until such time as the court gives him permission.'

The judge permitted himself a thin smile. Members of the court nodded sagely here and there.

'And now, Maisie, tell us, would you ever have gone to the croft Flinders as wife to John Voe?'

'No, indeed,' said Maisie, 'for he was always away at sea, and I'd have been lonely.'

(It seemed to Jock that Maisie was not a day older than the time he had kissed her.)

'You may step down, Maisie,' said the prosecutor. 'I call upon Thomasina Sutherland.'

A middle-aged woman with oven-red cheeks appeared from the shadows. Jock had not given her a thought for years. He remembered, the summer he was fishing with his grandad, the half-dozen times she had been waiting at the shore when the boat came in with its cuithes or crabs. She would be holding out a tray of bannocks with butter and honey in them, oatcakes with butter and white wet cheese, a can of smoking broth. 'Oh, you must both be that cold coming in from the sea! No, no – I want no fish. I thought to myself, the poor boy will be the better of bread and broth' . . . Then she would set the tray of victuals down on a dry rock, and gather up her skirts, and hurry on up the beach.

'That woman!' the old grandfather had said wonderingly, and shaken his head. 'That Thomasina! You must know, boy, she's had three husbands and buried them all. I thought at first, when she came down to the boat with her gifts, it was *me* she was after. God forgive a foolish old man. It's *you* she's after, Jock – a boy with the first hairs on his lip! She'll have no more burying of husbands, Thomasina. You'll still be a young man, Jock, when you fold her thin hands. Folk get crazier and crazier, the older I grow. She's a decent woman, Thomasina, and a well-handed woman, and clean and thrifty, but I wouldn't care for the cast in her eye or the banked-up fire in her face' . . .

Maybe half-a-dozen times in all Thomasina had brought her earth-offerings on a tray down to the fish-cold boat. And all her looks were for the boy. The old grandad could starve or die of cold . . . But she got no looks in return from Jock. He busied himself always with the boat and boxes of fish. Not so much as a word did he console her with. In the end she stopped coming. (Surely, thought Jock in this gloomy court-

room, Thomasina Sutherland had died a widow, three years
back – yet here she was, bold and red and brisk, in the witness-
box.)

'You see this man in the dock: John Voe,' said the prosecutor, quite pleasantly.

'I do,' she cried.

'He stands accused, among other things, of being a nuisance
to women. Now, Mistress Sutherland, was Voe ever a nuisance
to you?'

'He was that,' she said in her loud voice. 'The truth is, he
broke my heart. What could be crueller than that!'

'Did he make wrong promises to you? Did he come knocking at your door at all hours of the night?'

'He wouldn't once break bread with me,' said Thomasina.
'And for that reason I wanted to die. And I did in the end!'

'Thank you, Thomasina,' said the prosecutor. 'You may
step down.'

There followed to the witness stand, one after the other, four
women of different ages that Jock only dimly remembered, at
best. One, Alma Sinclair had kindly come and taken the Flinders
washing home with her one winter when his mother was laid
low with flu, and also she had scrubbed the floor and baked
scones till his mother was on her feet again. 'and he struck me to
the heart, that same Jock, with his coldness,' she cried. (Jock had
never known Alma to shout like that before: she had not by so
much as a glance or a touch given any indication that she cared
for him so deeply. He had thought it strange, certainly, that a
woman from the far side of the hill – a comparative stranger
from two miles away – should have come and succoured them
in that bleak time of illness.) Now she gave Jock a bitter look, and
stepped down, bidden by the judge.

A name 'Andrina Tait' was called that meant nothing to
Jock. Even when the plain-looking lass appeared he searched

about in his mind to set her in her time and place. Andrina whispered and mumbled so that the prosecutor bade her quite sternly to speak up. An image took shape, phrase by phrase, of the laird's big barley field, and the reapers strolling across it with flashing scythes, and the bright swathes falling, and the gleaners bending and gathering and binding. Some of the gleaners were hardly more than children and to them this harvesting was mostly a game; they mingled laughter with the song of a lark that rose and fell and lost itself in the blue all the long afternoon. There were two gleaners in particular, a girl and a boy . . . 'I don't ken what came over me,' faltered Andrina. 'I must have fainted with the heat, but only for a blink. When I came to he was laying me down in the shade of a stook. He went and opened a stone bottle of kirned milk. Yes, and he poured it in a cup and he put the cup to my mouth and tilted it. I think I was never so happy! Soon he made as if to go back to the field. Sir, I'm sorry to say, I made as if I was slipping into a dwam again. Then Jock ran to the burn and he tore off a sleeve of his sark and he soaked it in the water and he came back and tied it about my forehead. I thought I might melt with happiness . . . I'm sorry, sir, for troubling you with a foolish thing like this.'

'You have spoken well,' said the accuser. 'But you must say more, even if it hurts you. You are on oath to tell the truth.'

'I reasoned with myself, why didn't Jock Voe, after my first stroke of weakness, not run and summon my father and my sister Ruth from their harvesting? Why did he take the cure and comforting of me on himself alone? There was but one answer, and that a sweet piercing one – that I could see. It set my heart dancing inside me with happiness.'

'And then?'

'Nothing,' said Andrina after a long silence. 'Not a thing. Nothing in the world. He treated me as if I was a common creature like all the other lasses. I waited and waited. Two midnights when I should have been in bed I stood outside his house, and my heart seemed to be bleeding inside me from a sharp thorn. One night I went so far as to tap on his window, not too loud for fear of waking old Maria his mother. I listened. I heard nothing but snores like a saw going through driftwood.'

'And this heartlessness of young Voe, it has in some sense soured your life ever since?'

'Well, sir, in due course I married Howie Muir, and I like him well enough, and I had four of his bairns that I love in different ways. But I never had a day like that day in the laird's barely field when I was sick. Oh no! Jock Voe has robbed me of a whole treasury of days and years.'

Mrs Andrina Muir – a girl still, it seemed, with a wisp of straw in her black hair – was bidden to stand down.

'Even thus far,' remarked the judge, 'the weight of evidence against the prisoner is grave and onerous indeed. Are there many more broken-hearted Desdemonas or Ophelias to call?'

'Two,' said the procurator. 'Then I rest my case.'

'Let the examination be brief,' said Justice Skull-head. 'Your case my break under a superabundance.'

A name 'Rachel Ingsetter' was called; and Jock had no difficulty in remembering her, for Rachel Ingsetter was known through the length and breadth of the parish, and far beyond, to be the merriest wantonest boldest young hussy that Orkney had heard tell of in living memory. When she was seventeen and a half Rachel Ingsetter had gone off with Hollanders in a Dutch herring boat, and hadn't been heard of again.

And now here she was, as merry as ever, putting laughing looks on every solemn face in the court, until one or two of the faces crinkled in reply. And when she set eyes on Jock she blew him three kisses, making luscious noises with her full red mouth. Then she flung her corn-coloured hair out of her eyes, and she tilted her head back, and her mouth rang like a bell, for joy to be in the company of so many men.

Smack! – down came the judge's gavel. 'Control yourself, woman. This is a court of law, not a music hall!'

The procurator lumbered to his feet. 'I trust, Mistress Ingsetter, you have had a happy sojourn in the Low Countries?'

'It was well enough,' said Rachel. 'I was in Norway, too, and France, and Greenland. I didn't think there were so many fine men in the world, and all so different from one another. But in the end, I missed the Orkney boys. I did. I missed them sorely.'

'The man you see in the dock,' said the accuser, 'John Voe. Did you miss him too?'

Such a voluptuous look she put on Jock then that he was almost as shocked as the other members of the court seemed to be: all except two or three, who regarded the witness with hardly concealed awe and delight.

'I missed him most of all,' said Rachel. 'Night and day I thought about him. Every sea-port we touched, it was always the face of Jock I searched for among the seamen and the dock workers. I must tell you, Mr counsel and all the other misters here present, it was on account of Jock Voe that I left Orkney in the first place. I knew he was somewhere on the seven seas. Do you think for a moment I'd have gone away if Jock was still in the island? I'm not a fool, exactly – I was seasick for a whole month. I got salt scabs all over my face and arms, till I got to look like the ugliest hag you've ever seen. Salt beef, hard biscuits, sour water! I endured them all in the hope of seeing somewhere, in Reykjavik maybe or Calais or St John's, the man I loved. I sought him up and down the oceans. I shouted across the water at passing ships, "Have you a man called Jock Voe aboard?" Never. Nothing. Not a whisper or a shadow. The last thing I muttered, on my sick bed in the attic in Tromso, Norway, was "Jock . . . *Jock Voe* . . ." I was still sighing "Jock Voe" when I came to the place where the ghosts are. And he wasn't there either. And here, at last, he is – I've found him. Bless you, Jock! You're as bonny a man as ever I saw. It does me good to see you standing there, even in a poor bleak place like this, among such company.'

'Rest in peace, Rachel,' Jock managed to stammer. For surely she had pronounced herself dead.

'Let her stand down,' said the judge in a very black voice. Rachel blew Jock another smacker of a kiss, then she turned and was lost among the shadows.

'It should be fairly obvious,' said the procurator, 'that that poor women was led into a life of vagabondage and degradation on account of the spell put upon her by the prisoner.'

There was a nodding of heads here and there; but the handful of court members who had been struck into smiling amazement by the presence of Rachel Ingsetter still sat with tranced looks on their faces.

The judge wrote a few words on the paper in front of him. 'I hardly think it was necessary, Mr procurator, to introduce such a witness. It detracts from the gravity of our proceedings.'

The accuser, rebuked, bowed. He called, 'The senorita Juanita Megaron.'

Jock started as if a thong had lashed him across the face! Juanita of the bleeding poppy – Juanita, the only girl who made the word 'love' a lovely living reality for him, of all the women he had ever met – it was impossible, surely, that Juanita (lost forever) should have come all the way to this sombre Orkney assize. He leaned forward. He could hardly wait for her lissom form to emerge from the shadows. How would she reply, in her half-hundred English words, to the probings of the inquisitor? He sweated, a light sweet dew of expectancy and happiness on his brow and his upper lip.

Nothing stirred in the shadows.

'Juanita Megaron!' called the procurator more loudly.

There was no answer.

'It seems,' remarked the judge, 'that this witness is not in the court. If that is so, I will issue a warrant for her apprehension.'

'Mr president, the witness was duly summoned to appear.'

'She has evidently decided to absent herself. She will be made to answer for it. Mr procurator, I should ask you nevertheless, do you not consider that you have already sufficient evidence to bring home the charge to the accused?'

'The evidence of this person, I am certain, would have been the most telling evidence of all. I was keeping her to this very end, Mr president, as a kind of climax and consummation of this prosecution. For I would, I have no doubt, make it very clear to the court that no one has suffered at the hands of that profligate in the dock, as that poor young South American maiden has suffered, and is suffering still, and will doubtless suffer to her life's end.'

For the first time in that long afternoon, words of the accuser sent a bitter pang through the youth. In all the web of fantasy and illusion that had been spun about him, these were the only true words (or so he hoped: he longed that Juanita should be suffering, as he had again, now, begun to suffer on her account.)

'Oh, Juanita,' he whispered. 'Come. We will have cures for one another.'

But Juanita, summoned a third time peremptorily, did not come.

'Voe,' said the judge, 'a witness against you has failed to turn up. Any evidence she might have given would in any case, in my opinion, be superfluous and unneccessary.'

'I want this witness to appear,' said Jock. 'I demand it!'

'Be that as it may,' said the judge, 'the court will adjourn for ten minutes. When the court resumes, young man, you will be given an opportunity to defend yourself. Make good use of the recess. The court will now rise.'

Then this extraordinary thing happened, that winter fell suddenly in that courtroom. Jock shuddered with the icy draughts that began to move everywhere. The lamp was starved of oil – it began to gulp and flare, and the hectic circle of light grew narrower and narrower.

Jock saw, with horror, that where the gaunt judge had sat a lettered tombstone was set up. He looked wildly about the courtroom; other tombstone flickered here and there. Other members of the court shrivelled – the hale stern men he remembered from his boyhood withered in the space of a few seconds to feeble age and decrepitude. Where well-thatched heads had been, baldness shone and nodded. The most horrid thing of all had happened to the procurator. A skeleton sat at the table where he had been shuffling his papers a minute before: the skeleton slumped: it fell, a long rattling articulation of bones, across the table. His papers were sere and yellow leaves.

Jock was aware that someone was shaking his shoulder violently. His keeper? Jock glanced round. The warder, William Brims, who had stood sternly at his shoulder thus far through the trial, was incapable any more of shaking any man's shoulder. He was, if anything, more withered than the drift of eld that still kept a breath or two sighing through the body of the court. He sat on a step – his hands were shiny and twisted into rheumaticky knots – he struggled for every breath – an overflow of water came from one faded eye. Where was William's fine dark curled beard? A few yellowish-white tufts were stuck here and there about his jaw . . .

Another spasm went through Jock. Someone was shaking him by the shoulders impatiently. His head thudded on wood.

He opened an eye. Mr Peterkin, the proprietor of the Temperance Hotel, was standing over him; a far-from-friendly look on his face. 'Look here, Voe,' he said, 'if I'd known you were as drunk as that you'd never have darkened this door! Look at your tea, man, you've spilled the half of it over you. I wish this Lammas Fair, this day of fools, was over. To think you've come home from sea, and the first thing you do is plunge head-first into this shame and this vanity! Never come here again oozing rum and ale. Now understand that!'

Jock got to his feet, and yawned, and put on his cheese-cutter. His throat was like a little salt-mine.

Where had he left his sea-chest? The shipping office: but it would have closed its doors an hour ago.

Peterkin was the kind of man who quickly forgot his rages.

'Jock, man, I'm glad to see you home again. Only I'm sorry it's such a sorrowful business you've come for. Man, I suppose when a blow like that falls, there's no harm in taking a drink or two. I remember, the night my own mother died, I went to the side door of the Masons Arms for a gill of malt. But there comes a time, Jock, when a man must face the future with a sober heart. Ay, Jock man, it's a sad and a sorry road you'll take to Flinders this night.'

What was the man talking about? Jock had emerged, sweating and heart-wrung, from an assize of shadows, and here was a man of flesh and blood uttering more incomprehension.

In the next ten minutes, Jock learned from the lips of Mr Peterkin that his mother had died a month previously – quite suddenly, a stroke. The neighbour woman had found her lying on the cold stone floor.

What was to be done? The cow, unmilked, was bogling tormentedly in the field. Twenty starving hens had almost eaten the neighbour woman alive! The cat, a lithe piteous darkness, had touched its cold nose to the cold hand that had fed it and comforted it, and then run off and not been seen again.

Neighbour hands had eased the old woman into her grave.

A telegram had been sent to Lloyd's office in London. The *Bon Voyage* was somewhere in the Bay of Biscay.

Once the news of the death had got around, bills began to come in: hatchlings unpaid, a long list of money for groceries due (this from the dead woman's brother-in-law Wilfred Voe who kept the store in the village), a mason's account for a repair to the barn roof.

The factor has brought some common sense to the proceedings. The only son, the sailor, he would never work on the farm, everybody knew that. The three sisters were married to farmers in other islands. The only thing to be done was to sell the run-down croft for what they could get for it: and the stock and the few sticks of furniture: and hold the balance of the sum realized against the sailor's homecoming, whenever that should be.

The croft of Flinders had been sold for fifty pounds at the public roup on the Wednesday of last week.

'She was a good woman,' said Mr Peterkin . . . And after a few seconds he had added, 'Of course you can't go home to Flinders, Jock. A family from Westray have moved in already. There's Westray peat-smoke coming from the chimney. Well, look, Jock, you can stay here for the night. But no drink, Jock! No more drink. I mean that. If you go along that street, somebody's sure to drag you into The Baffin Bay or Gow's Galleon.'

Somewhere, at the other end of the street, the blind fiddler was playing: a soaring sinking heart-piercing elegy.

Jock paid the proprietor for his pot of tea, and drew his cap down over his brows, and went out into the tumultuous town. It was still early evening.

It grieves me to think of the way Jock conducted himself for the remainder of that day. He wandered through a crazy kaleidoscope. Occasionally he called a greeting to some half-familiar face, and increasingly as the evening wore on, to strangers, especially if they were girls and pretty. Sometimes they would dimple and make a response – more often they gave the tipsy sailor a haughty look and turned away.

He found himself among a crowd of children shouting for vengeance on Mr Punch as he reeled from crime to crime – yet the boys and girls laughed too – and what a cheer went up when Punch beat the devil about his horns and sent him howling back to the pit of Hell! . . . A small boy beat Jock on the ribs with excess of delight. Jock gave him a shilling to get himself lemonade and gingerbread.

A man beckoned from the door of The White Horse. Jock, narrowing his eyes, recognized the miller of Birsay. The miller told him, while they stood each other rum, and delicately clashed rims together, what a fine man his father had been – and that, though he didn't know Jock's mother 'that was away', he had heard she was a good enough woman too, in her way. And they had sold the croft while he was on the sea: fancy that – they might have waited a twelvemonth! But solicitors and shopkeepers had their own ways of looking at things – that they did – and anyway, what did a sailor want with a piece of barren hill, mostly muck and dung? Jock was well rid of the place, in his opinion.

Jock listened and drank in silence. That miller would out-speechify a road-full of tinkers, a shore-full of fish-wives. Jock bought him a glass of rum, and went away. Apart from the miller with his throbbing tongue, The White Horse was so full of dry and drinking and drunken men that he was subjected to constant elbowing and thrusting and all manner of nonsense.

In a lull, very faint and far away, a mere thread, the blind fiddler spun his music.

The first flare was being lit, a tangle of hectic lights and shadows, at one corner of the fairground as Jock butted his way out of The White Horse.

Now the young ones in a circle were dancing to a melodeon beside the fountain. A bleak-faced dame in a long gray skirt came and dragged her daughter by the elbow out of the devil's-reel. Good-natured maledictions, sweet cries of commiseration were uttered after the departing mother and daughter. One ploughboy with a red reeking face took the girl by her free arm and tried to coax and drag her back into the dance; for now the bewildered musician had resumed his rant, and the young feet were beating starwards again. And that old grim lady, the mother, she swung her fist and sent the ploughboy reeling against the fountain! His arm went in with a silvery splash.

Jock stood for a while and looked at the circling shrieking girls. He would not be seen in barn or kirk with one of them – not one.

Jock went into The Arctic Whaler. After the cold air outside, the fog of tobacco smoke all but choked him. He had to lean against the doorpost, coughing and wheezing. A man he had never seen before put a glass of whisky in Jock's hand. And that whisky, drunk quickly, put new breath into him.

Once his eyes got used to the tobacco reek and the dim paraffin lamps, Jock's first swift impression was that he had been elected to a parliament of madmen. Nearby a group of sailors and farmers were arguing passionately about Home Rule for Ireland, with wild unfocussed eyes; and over against the bar a frightened-looking youth was being poked about the shoulders and ribs by an old frail-looking man who was supporting himself with a stick. 'Come thu near Jemima, my lass, once more, come within six feet of her, look here, lay so much as a finger on her, you weed, and I'll beat you with this staff of mine into puddings and soup bones – so help me God I will! . . .' The eyes of the threatened seducer rolled round in his head with terror, though he was such a strong-looking youth he could have taken the old man and snapped him across his knee. Another thrust of the gnarled forefinger took him full in the throat and made him sweat and blanch and gulp. Jock, having recently awakened from a dream of torment by old vindictive men, was on the point (a new glass of 'Highland Park' in his fist) of going over and rescuing his contemporary – that cowardly lover, whoever he was – when a countryman with a bottle and glasses stepped between the combatants, and (laughing) rallied them both, and patted them on the shoulders, and put empty glasses in their trembling fingers and filled them to the brim from his bottle. Strange to say, those mortal enemies pledged each other at once; and the old destroyer of young love even cackled into the white face of Jemima's boy, and cried, 'Here's to thee, boy, and long may thu live, and never forget this, thu're welcome to come and see Jemima whenever thu likes, by day or night.'

Another man that Jock had never seen sidled up to him. He said to Jock in a low voice, so that Jock had to put his ear close to the man's mouth to catch his meaning, 'I hate sailors. Don't deny it, you're a sailor. It's no use telling lies to me. You're the scum of the earth, you sailors! You think you can do whatever you like, eh, when you come to port, thieve and rob and fight. I know you. I've seen you in Archangel, and I saw you another time in Oran, and the time I met you in Oran you stole the few shillings I had in my purse – the last money I had – it was in

the Arab bazaar, and I was going to buy a monkey to take
home to my mother. I saw you spending my hard-earned
shillings in a low drink-shop that same night. Don't deny it,
sailor. Because it will do you no good. Do you know what I'm
going to do with you now? – I'm going to cut out your tripes!'
. . . And indeed the sleazy-looking creature was unfolding the
blades of a tobacco knife, and little spirtles of spit came out of
the corners of his mouth. Jock was wondering if he had
sufficient steadiness and accuracy of aim in his seaboot to
kick the knife out of the man's hand: when, behold, the man
was suddenly hanging in the air, his four limbs whirling, and
the huge bald barman carried him head-high to the open door,
and sent him hurling into the darkling chattering music-mad
crowd coming and going on the street. 'Sorry about that,' said
the barman to Jock, rubbing his hands together. 'He's never
been on a boat further than the Holms. Two glasses of thin
beer and he's a pirate or an explorer or a viking.' And the
barman went back through layers of swirling tobacco fog to
his gantry, his glasses, and his musical till.

A mad town! Jock spoke briefly to a quarryman he had sat at
school with; and so two more glasses were drunk. He felt
himself being gathered inexorably into the thickening web of
insensibility. The quarryman shouted, 'Well, Voe, and how
many wives have you got in the ports of Europe, eh?'

Jock said, in a quiet voice, 'I have no wife. I had a girl, once,
but I don't have her any more. I have no house either. They've
sold it. When my purse is empty, I'll take to the roads. There's
many an old tramp that eats turnips and limpets, and sleeps in
a quarry in winter. Do you not remember the old tramp Ezra?
If he saw a woman on the road he would turn and run away
from her over the fields. Ezra had a silver beard.' The
recklessness began to riot in his heart and brain. He laughed.
He unbuckled his money-belt and went up to the counter and

laid ten sovereigns, one after the other, on the counter. 'Barman, give every man in this house a treble whisky. Have one yourself too. When the buccaneer comes back, pay him the shillings I stole out of his purse that night in the bazaar at Oran.'

If a man had suddenly rung a golden bell, no sweeter or more blessed silence could have fallen on that mad-house.

Every word of Jock's quiet voice could be heard distinctly as he said to the gaping barman, 'I will not be drinking any more myself. Goodnight.'

It was quite dark when Jock stood outside, alone, on the thronging street. The darkness was splashed with the flares set here and there about the fairground. The harbour water between the piers gave back the lurid gleams.

There were seven hidden gold sovereigns between himself and destitution. Jock wondered, with a smile, if the shop-keeper in his home parish – his uncle Wilfred – would take him in and maybe give him a job as a storeman or a driver of the grocery van. (His uncle Wilfred and Jock had never got on with each other.)

Where would he sleep tonight?

He was weary of the fairground noises, that was sure. Night had painted the faces of the revellers with hectic shifting red and black shadows. Two men with accordion and bagpipe were making the night hideous with Scottish rants outside the public convenience. Some disaster had overtaken the fruit-and-sweetie stall. A barrel of apples had been knocked over: a riot of small boys were stuffing themselves with the bruised fruit. The stall-holder was shouting, 'Police – the police are coming! I know all your names. You'll be in the court – you'll end in jail, every last one of you!' Some louts came round the corner. They scooped up the stotterng apples and began to pelt the stall-holder with them, till the man had to take refuge under his makeshift counter: from which came whimpers, 'Police . . . I'm ruined!' . . . The little swine! . . .'

Then, from somewhere in the crowd, there was a loud cry, 'Police!' The louts and the children all ran away, except for one small boy who sat on the street, dazed with fruit and chocolate, with apple juice dripping off his chin . . .

A loud announcement from the booth of the Italian knife-thrower Mario Spanducci: a summons, a promise of a feat of extraordinary daring and dexterity soon to commence inside. The megaphone stammered and blared. Mario was once more about to surround the body of a damsel 'of surpassing, of heart-pulsing loveliness' with daggers exquisitely sharp, and each one flaming! Mario would throw them at the girl, one after the other, from a distance of ten yards! . . . 'The like will never be seen again! About to begin. Admittance sixpence, threepence for children!'

Then appeared Mario himself at the flap of the booth, a large man in black breeches and a red satin shirt; he twirled a dagger. There came and stood beside Mario a pale waif of a girl, spangled and with bare arms and legs, who shivered in the night air; and yet she contrived a brave smile. *Dulcinea!* announced the megaphone. 'The girl of the flaming daggers!' A ragged cheer went up from the young men in the crowd – the fishermen and farm-boys – and loud smackings of the lips . . . Jock wondered from what wharf-side of Liverpool or Clydebank the little Dulcinea had been recruited.

There, in the midst of that cataract of Lammas noise, Jock longed suddenly to stop beside some little pool of silence. At the far end of Hamnavoe the street would be empty. There was only one pub – Tommy Isbister's – and on such a night most of Tommy Isbister's patrons would have moved to the clamorous pubs near the heart of the Fair. It was a quiet street.

Old decent folk sat behind drawn curtains, with cats and ferns; the old man with silver spectacles read from the *Orkney Herald* or the *Christian Herald* to an old lady with a mutch on her head. Such a tranquil scene would be taking place in house after house in that quiet south-end part of Hamnavoe.

Jock reasoned that he might have one last drink in Tommy Isbister's – nothing fiery, a long cold schooner of ale – and while he was drinking it he would see what he would do. (No whaling: the Hull and the Dundee whalers wouldn't be calling before April. The local fishing-boats would all be manned.) Well, but there were harvests to be cut all over Orkney soon – many a labourer would be wanted, on this big farm and that . . . After harvest, he would be in the hands of Fate.

So Jock reasoned, as he walked from the mad broken beehive of the fair past the road with the three kirks in it, and the solicitor's and the Bank and the doctor's and a fourth kirk; and past Alexander Graham's, and up one steep street and down another – it surged like a stone wave – and past the dark Post Office and the light-ship pier and the dark custom house, and past the close where John Broon the cobbler lived. He came to the mouth of the vennel where the police station was. From inside the high barred window came plaints and cries, and a broken line or two of song –

> *To lose that gallant whale,*
> *It grieves me ten times more . . .*

The single policeman of Hamnavoe, Long Will, had reaped a fair harvest of law-breakers that day, and there was still an hour or two to go.

Jock was approaching the dark shuttered distillery where Old Orkney whisky was made. Just beyond it was Tommy Isbister's tavern. Jock realized at once that he would not be having a quiet schooner of ale, because Tommy Isbister's was rocking and lurching with noise like a whaling ship in a Lofoten gale. From some of the syllables and accents that came through the lighted smoke-swirling door, Jock judged that it was a crew of discharged whalers indeed who had found their way to this douce decent place.

Another trip, in another such tavern, and he would be drowned and lost beyond recall!

As Jock stood hesitating near the door of the Town Hall, just across from Tommy Isbister's, he became aware of a figure standing in the shadows. It was a girl, with a shawl over her head. The girl was carrying a stone pot on her shoulder. Vessels of that kind had gone out of fashion in Jock's grandmother's time; he dimly remembered to have seen one like it in the corner of the kind old woman's croft. (Nowadays women went with bottles and buckets to well, milk-shop, inn.) The young shawled woman, the stone jar on her shoulder – she reminded Jock of pictures he had seen in an old Bible. And what on earth would she be wanting here, at this time of night, lingering near such a drunken dangerous door? Maybe her father had sent her out for a jar of Tommy's ale to treat his guests; for hundreds of cousins and old acquaintances came into Hamnavoe, by cart and boat, for the Lammas Fair. More likely she had been sent out to get water from Login's Well a hundred yards further on; and now she stood there, afraid to go further, in case some ruffians reeled out of the inn and accosted her . . . Perhaps: but there was something so veiled and mysterious about her! Jock stood in the shadow of the Town Hall. Presently he would declare himself – he would speak to her civilly – he would offer to do the task she had been sent out for: buy a pitcher of ale in the drink-tossed tavern, or see her safely on to Login's Well and its pure waters. (There the great ships of his grandfather's time

had filled their casks: Captain Cook's *Resolution* and *Discovery*,
John Franklin's *Erebus* and *Terror*.) Then, as he watched, the
girl took a hesitant step, and Jock could hear the swilter and
wash and glug of a liquid inside the stone jar. She was not
going to fill it anywhere; she was going to deliver the contents
to someone or other. And who would that be? Then Jock
remembered that there was an old woman called Francina
Watt that made butter and cheese in a little cottage just
beyond Login's Well, up a steep flight of steps. That must
be it – she was a farm girl, she had been sent out with a jar of
milk to deliver to the old cheese-wife. And she was too timid
to dare the smithy-blast of Tommy Isbister's door.

Jock was entranced. Now the girl had set her jar on a flagstone of the street and was sitting on the low wall just above
the noust where the small boats had been hauled up. It was –
apart from the infernal din inside Tommy Isbister's – a still
evening; and Jock, edging round the corner of the Town Hall,
caught other fragrances welling out of the jar: country smells,
the pressed incenses of millwheels and corn-sacks. It was not
milk – it was oat-meal! The girl had been sent out with oat-
meal to the big house of the boat-builder at Ness, whose wife
was well-known for her hospitable cakes and bannocks and
bread.

All this time the sky had been covered in dark clouds that
barely moved, but were silvered at the western edges by the
light of three-quarter moon. It was a beautiful mysterious
light, that etched the girl's profile but kept her features veiled.

The stupid creature! Why did she sit there so hesitant? She
could have been up and past Tommy Isbister's snarling lilting
dangerous portals ten minutes since.

Meantime the noise inside the tavern was getting louder – it
was as flashingly menacing as broken wielded bottles. There
came the sound of Tommy's baton thwacking on half-a-dozen

skulls. And Tommy's wife Nell skirled 'Aloor! Murder!' There followed at once the sound of a broken flagon and surge of fiery waters. Grunts and urgings and threats rose in a sudden chorus. A man came lurching out of the pub and fell on the cobbles and lay sprawled.

Jock moved at once to reassure the frightened girl. As he did so the moon came from behind a cloud and the girl turned to face him, and it was Juanita! The apparition stopped him in his tracks. She stretched out her hands to the jar. The shrieks and yells and sobs inside the pub increased. Jock took one more tranced step forward. This Juanita – he could see now – was blond: a few ringlets of hair had escaped her shawl. This Juanita had blue eyes. But the facial structure was Juanita's exactly; and the bend of the body, and the turn and lift and yearn of the hands, were Juanita, unmistakable.

'Juanita!' he cried.

She shook her head. 'I'm Selina,' she said in a low country accent. 'That's my name – Selina.'

Tommy Isbister's tavern was foundering now! The crew were tumbling and shouldering and thrusting out on to the street. Their eyes flashed in the moonlight. More and more whaling men spilled and reeled out across the street; and 'thwack-thwack' went Tommy Isbister's baton; and 'Murder! Police!' cried Mrs Isbister.

Jock moved forward to save the girl and her loaded jar.

He was too late. He was swept aside. A tumult of feet and rumreeking faces came between him and the girl. He was pummelled and punched.

He cried, 'Tell me the name of your farm, lass!'

'Dottersha', she answered from the far side of the tumult; the word came to his ear sweet and clear.

Dottersha – he remembered, but vaguely, a croft of that name; it had been a name in his father's and his grandfather's mouths, but infrequently. They had had dealings, about a beast or sacks of grain, with the crofter of Dottersha, now and again. He knew, vaguely again, the district where the croft was. It lay on a steep green incline looking out over the parish kirkyard to the hills of Hoy and the unquiet waters where mingled the Pentland Firth and the Atlantic.

Jock had time to see, before he passed out, that the girl was standing on the far side of the tumult. She had no fear of the whaling men at all. The jar was on her shoulder. She was looking at him. Her mouth made the shape 'Come'.

Jock must have lain all night on the sea side of the little wall between the Town Hall and Tommy Isbister's.

When he came to, Nell Isbister was sweeping broken glass against the wall. More than bottles had been broken the previous night. Three of the little panes in the pub window had crazy stars in them.

Long Will, the one and only policeman in Hamnavoe, trod the cobbles gravely between station and tavern. A few more disturbers of the peace had been lodged in Long Will's cells. There were groans and bits of a revivalist hymn. A hidden voice yelled, 'When am I going to get my porridge?' The hungry one was a Hebridean, unmistakeably.

'Mistress Isbister,' said Long Will, 'could you give me a description of the persons who caused a disturbance of the peace in your place last night?'

'They were like devils out of hell,' said Nell Isbister. 'I never saw one of them in my life before, and I hope never to see them again as long as I live.'

'It was a lively day in Hamnavoe,' said Long Will. 'I was kept busy from morning to night. Nothing much will happen between now and Yule.' He licked his pencil. He wrote some words in his notebook.

When the street was quite empty, Jock heard – from far away, from the direction of the fertile wedge between the western sea and the moor where (somewhere) the croft of Dottersha was – the music of the blind fiddler: stilling, soaring, sinking.

Oh, but he felt ill as he rose from his bed of salty stones and shells! – His bones creaked. He felt like a sheaf that had been threshed in a barn.

He took out his purse from inside his shirt and laid his fortune along the stones of the sea wall: seven sovereigns.

'Now,' said Jock, 'this is what I'll do. I'll get my sea-chest from the shipping office. I'll get a bite of breakfast at the Temperance Hotel. Then I'll go and look for Juanita – no, Selina – in the croft above the kirkyard.'

It was a bright morning in late summer. The two little islands in the harbour – the Holms – were indistinct in the early morning fog. A bank of fog was beginning to roll in from the west.

The fiddle had fallen silent.

He passed whaling men, going in groups or singly, going on towards the big pier with gray faces. Long Will had just released them from his hostelry.

But he stayed till early evening in The Arctic Whaler, drinking with the whalers. But not too much. He had a journey to go.

Two

The small girl from the mill. Audrey, came with her milk pail to be filled with Betty the cow's warm milk, and she piped at Selina, as soon as the door opened, 'Grandad wants to know, how is Mr Voe?'

Selina Voe said, 'He has to keep to his bed. He has a lot of pain. Twopence for the milk and a penny change. There's a good lass.'

'Poor Mr Voe,' said Audrey.

Jock had just hurled his harpoon at a whale, and the barb had slithered off the streaming side. The other six harpoons had sunk deep, and adhered. And Tomison at the steering-oar had shouted, his voice shivering across the ice-flecked green water, 'That's six glasses of rum Voe must stand the harpoonists in The White Horse at Hamnavoe!' . . . The whale stirred itself, and they were lost tossed shrieking hunters in new-opened chasms of sea. Six of the seven whale-boats followed, first with a whale stir, then at a whale canter, then at a whale gallop. And then suddenly the whale blundered and stumbled and stilled. Its heart was empty. The sea reddened. There was a huge death fifty leagues north of Cape Farewell.

Captain Surfax of the *Eldora* was delighted.

But it wasn't good enough. A few of the crew, flensing and cutting at the great beast, cast covert looks at Jock Voe.

That man, once more, had come close to being the death of five of them (besides himself).

Who had flung the first harpoon? Voe, he had flung it. Surfax himself had said, 'Voe is the best harpoonist in this sea. I know it. I'm convinced of it. I can tell by the way he holds the harpoon. Just throw your harpoons the way Voe does, and we'll have so many barrels of oil this trip we'll come top-heavy into Hull . . .'

Voe's harpoon had skiddered off the whale like a flat stone off the surface of the sea. And the great threshing the beast made then had all but broken the boats. No: it was no thanks to Voe that here they were, their knives flashing!

Three days before, further west, they had done as Surfax had commanded them, let the Orkneyman lead the assault. The first harpoon had sunk in deep, so deep it must have pierced the quick of the whale's thunderous heart. It had roused itself, it had given a great lash of its fluke, and over had gone the whale-boat *Eric* and seven good men: of whom only three had survived the dragging out and the chest-pumping and kneading that had gone on for more than an hour.

The whale had escaped, with Voe's unlucky harpoon in it. It was dead, most likely. The barb had found its vitals. It was rotting somewhere among the floes.

Surfax had blamed *them* for that. 'If you had followed Voe's harpoon, fast, one after the other, this need never have happened. A whale lost! – what am I to say to the whale masters in Hull? Five men lost – what am I to write to their women back home in Shetland and Sunderland, eh? God give me patience! – a ship of fools.'

And Voe stood higher than before in Captain Surfax's whaler *Eldora*, though he did nothing in any way to curry favour.

It came to this: that by mid-summer the only men in the crew who would talk to Voe were Albert Stockan from Hamnavoe in Orkney, and a Swede called Rollson (only Rollson didn't talk; he made blond signs with his head and hands.)

A man called Macaulay from Harris in the Hebrides said, in his soft voice, 'There is such a thing as an unlucky person in a ship. I have known that. It is not good to have a Jonah on a ship. I am wishing now that this voyage was over, and we were sailing safe and easy through the north isles of Orkney.'

They were eating their biscuits and salt beef when Macaulay said that, and drinking mugs of tea. Jock Voe was sitting against a coil of rope with a steaming mug in his hands. He said nothing.

The whole month of May was barren. On the last day of that month the look-out shouted from the crowsnest – 'Whales! A school of them!'

Captain Michael Surfax, poising his glass, seemed to dance on the bridge. He summoned this one and that to look through the glass. He summoned John Voe. Jock saw the most beautiful sight any whaler can see, a group of whales in the quiet water, a herd, a cluster. They lay like cows at ease in a summer meadow.

'What are you lingering for?' cried the skipper. 'It is not a zoo. This is not an aquarium. Get the boats out and down. Let them not smell you. Go about and about in circles. Who will lead? Who do you think will lead? Voe will lead. There is more whale-knowledge in Voe's little finger than in all the rest of you put together. Quick! Launch! What's wrong with that man? – are his feet stuck in tar? . . . Ah, I have not seen a more beautiful sight! Oh, the port of Hull will be greatly enriched for this day's work. My dear lads, your pockets will jingle – Oh, the Hull lasses will follow the sweet smell of your silver and gold in the month of August, they will that, for this day's doings! . . . Voe, he will order the hunt.'

Voe will order the hunt. The two boats were hardly in the green cold water, with the silver drops coming off the oar-blades, and Voe in the bow of the whale-boat *Murmansk* making a first knowledgeable sweep of his arm to the other boats, when the whales began to move off. At first they went in a gentle dream-like motion, away from the whalers, a drift, a long sea-swoon, with mild sinkings and spoutings.

'After them, Voe!' This from Surfax on the bridge. When he was excited the little man's voice rose to a half-scream. He had made a trumpet of his hands. 'Dig the oars in!'

His yell put panic on the whales. It seemed to wake them from their dream, suddenly. They were up and off, with great plungings and cleavings of the sea, northwards. The thunder of their going echoed among the floes.

It was hopeless to think of going after them, now.

Surfax's voice was like pieces of lead as he summoned the boats back to the *Eldora*.

Surfax shut himself in his cabin for the rest of that day.

The whale-men played pontoon for pennies. Bert Ramsbottom from Filey played his old fiddle in a way to set the teeth on edge. Sandham-Smith, black sheep of a distinguished family, read Thomas Campbell's *Poems* in his hammock. MacSween from Glasgow said to Ramsbottom in a quiet voice. 'Jimmy, you would do me a great favour by not torturing that fiddle.' It did not make for easy companionship when Brendan MacSween spoke quietly like that. Thomas Evans the boy from Anglesey sat writing a letter on his sea-chest. All on board the *Eldora* were busy at something that night, while the sea glimmered like pearl and the floes glittered like crystal and the sun at midnight stood a hands-breadth above the northern horizon, a golden ghost among gently-falling gossamers of sea-mist. Everyone did something alone or in a small group, intently, except Voe. Even his fellow islander Albert Stockan had turned his back on him now, and was trying to teach the negro boy Erastus how to splice a piece of rope.

Rollson the Swede was breathing gently from his hammock: asleep.

From time to time Macaulay would turn from his hand of pontoon and his pile of pennies and glance covertly at Voe: and then whisper a few words to his three card-players.

Another blank week went by. Not a fountain, not one little surging hill broke the horizon.

On the Monday following three whale-men asked to see Captain Surfax. They were admitted into the master's cabin. There was much humming and clearing of throats and shuffling of feet. Surfax looked coldly and speechlessly from face to face.

Macaulay, prompted by a sharp word from the skipper at last, announced that there was much dissatisfaction among the crew. They were far from happy about things as they stood . . .

'It has been a bad season so far,' said Surfax. 'Things will improve. I have known the season to follow such a pattern, more than once, I assure you. After dearth come benison and riches aplenty. I have been a whaling man for thirty-five years.'

'We think it will not improve,' said Macaulay. 'No, captain, we think it will get worse. There will be more whale escapes, more drownings. There is black talk among the men.'

'Black talk!' cried Michael Surfax. 'If there's any black talking to be done aboard this ship, I'll do it! There will be no insubordination. There will be no whispering behind hands. I have broken noses before today. I have taken a knotted rope more than once to this and that thing of a would-be mutineer. I have done so. I am prepared to do worse' . . .

'We don't wish to upset you, captain,' said Ramsbottom.

Surfax's flashes of anger were terrible but quickly over.

He took out his snuff-box and offered each man a pinch in turn. When the volleys of sneezing were over, the three complainants could see (through swimming eyes) that their skipper was smiling.

'Lads,' he said, 'this whaling business, it is totally and wholly dominated by fortune. The wheel of fortune – to men like us that is more important by far than the ship's-wheel, or the tremblings of the compass, or the wheel of the wind that moves here and there, nobody knows how. We can, to a greater or less extent, dominate those other turnings and veerings. We can take steps to deal with them, for shipmen have entered into a kind of compact with them in the course of centuries. A natural-born sailor, he can know and come to grips with the subtle perilous movements of undersea tides. There are a few mariners – very rare and precious they are – who instinctively know the secret movement of whales. They can divine, and judge, and follow, and strike unerringly. I am not one of those favoured mariners. I confess it to you frankly. I am just an honest forthright whaling man, who knows the techniques of his job and does it as best he can. Ninety-nine per cent of whaling skippers are in the same position. That is to say, lads, we may run into a region of good whales and decimate them, in the course of a few days. That *may* happen. On the other hand, an entire season as barren as an iceberg might have to be endured. It is that other wheel that dom-inates an ordinary whaling master, such as myself, entirely – we have no control over it – it is the wheel of fortune, and it turns this way or that, and brings us to gold or to a winter of rags and cold porridge.'

The three complainants looked at each other. They had a frail understanding of what had been said. They were im-pressed by the high-flown eloquence of their skipper almost as much as by his snarlings and fire-spittings.

Two of them accepted more snuff from the inlaid ebony box: not Macaulay.

'Captain,' he said, after a pause, 'there is some ships that have *an unlucky man* aboard. You have read your Bible and the story of Jonah will not be unknown to you, though Jonah to be sure was a man of God. I was interested in what you said about the wheel of luck. It was well said, I will store it up in my mind. We cannot, any of us, turn that wheel either the one way or the other. We must go with it, wherever it takes us. Very good. But there are certain men – very few, thank goodness – who seem to have the power to turn that wheel in a contrary direction. I don't say they do it willingly. By no means. They may be as good shipmates as a man could wish for – on the surface, on the surface only. Deep down, unknown to themselves, there is that in them that compels bad luck upon a ship. The sooner the ship is rid of that person, the better for the skipper and the crew and the voyage. Thank you for your patience, Captain Surfax. That is all I have to say . . . Oh no, I almost forgot. Sandham-Smith read some verses out of a poetry book last night about a sailor and an albatross.'

'You have come here to mention a name,' said Surfax. 'I will have that name now, please.'

Ramsbottom and Stockan shuffled their feet. Macaulay said softly, 'John Voe the Orkneyman.'

Surfax's face paled. He drew a deep breath. He took another pinch of snuff, but the fiery grains went down his throat and he coughed harshly into his handkerchief.

'Voe,' said he. 'John Voe. Let me see' . . . He went over to his desk and opened a heavy ledger. 'Voe, signed on April the fifteenth last at Hamnavoe . . . I am the master of this whaling ship and I am in a position to see very clearly the aptitude and skill of every member of the crew and to make a cold judgement, very soon after sailing, upon the seamanship of each man. I should not be saying such things . . . passing on such con-fidences – to ordinary seamen. No, the reports I make are secrets between myself and my employers in the port of Hull. However, on this occasion I will make an exception. I will read to you what I have written. Here it is. "Since joining the whaling vessel *Eldora* under my command at Hamnavoe, Orkney, the recruit

John Voe, aged twenty-one, has shown himself to be a loyal, cheerful, and hard-working member of the crew. He has, indeed, shown an instinct and a flair for the trade of whaling, in a short time, that I have not known previously in any seaman under my command. I have had no hesitation, soon after we broke into the Arctic Circle, to put Voe in command of one or other of the whale-boats. By his skill and daring he has shown himself entirely worthy of my trust. The season thus far has not yielded us plenteous sea-fruit, but I hope that the latter half will be attended by better fortune. Most of my crew are experienced whalers, and serve well enough in a workaday capacity. I have seen enough in a short space to convince me that Voe ought to be given the opportunity, after he has put one or two voyages behind him, of a higher position of trust in the company's service" . . . That, lads, is what I have written in my log concerning the seaman Voe. I will be communicating it to the shipowners in Hull, in due course.'

His voice dropped and sweetened. He turned a page or two. 'Now, lads, would you really like to hear what I have written about you? I will read it to you if you so wish. First, Hamish Macaulay' . . .

'Thank you, captain,' said Macaulay, 'What is private is private.'

Stockan the other Orkneyman began to snigger. He had been given three bad discharges in the past ten years. He snuffled and snortled and moved his face with glee.

Ramsbottom (who had hardly understood one word of the proceedings) said, 'Thank you very much, captain.'

Macaulay said, 'My grandmother, she had the second-sight. I have a few drops of that blood in my veins. There will be no whales caught by this ship this summer – not one more whale. If we get rid of a certain member of the crew, it could be, captain, that we will have a fair haul.'

That same night, after supper, there was a fist-fight between MacSween and Voe, in the course of which Voe was mauled; before the fighters were dragged from each other, and a kind of seething peace was restored. Captain Surfax must have heard the shouts and the shiftings, but he made no move – as he would have done in normal circumstances – to interfere.

On the sixteenth of July, John Voe, harpooner on board the whaler *Eldora* was transferred to the whaling ship *Sirius* of Dundee, which was about to leave the whaling grounds on account of a sickness that had broken out on board; three of the crew, including the captain, had died; five others lay sick in their hammocks. The *Sirius* had had a poor season also; there was no other course but to return at once. Captain Surfax had a brief discussion with the mate of the *Sirius*, who agreed to allow Voe a passage home, provided he did the work of a crewman.

As the young man stood on the deck of the *Sirius* with his sea-chest on his shoulder, and blue-black swellings about his eyes, Ramsbottom played 'The Lass of Richmond Hill' on his fiddle. The crew cheered, more out of sorrow than vindictiveness or spite.

The wild sun-head of Rollson threw farewells to Jock Voe.

MacSween raised a hand in farewell: he too.

From the bridge, Captain Michael Surfax gave Jock a grave valediction.

It turned out the *Eldora*, and all the other whalers as well, had a poor season. There were few sovereigns to squander that August in the taverns of Hamnavoe, Dundee, and Hull.

Three

Frederika, the old travelling woman, came with the first star. Selina bought a packet of pins and some clothes-pegs and two pairs of bootlaces.

'How long has he been that way?' said Frederika, putting the three pennies into her purse.

'This is the fourth day since he took to his bed,' said Selina. 'Dr Payne didn't say what was wrong with him. Maybe he doesn't know.'

'Dandelion roots,' said old Frederika. 'Dry them and bruise them, then put them on to boil for an hour. Give him the brew to drink, cold. It would be better if you dug up the dandelion roots under the full moon, but he can't wait that long by the look of him. He'd be none the worse if you put a nettle leaf and a dockan leaf under his pillow, and maybe you could boil a piece of dulse from the ebb. A pity the moon's waning but it can't be helped. Do it now, before it gets dark.'

Selina pointed to the bottle of dark stuff on the mantel-piece.

'We're not living in the stone age,' said Selina. 'Dr Payne studied to be a doctor at Aberdeen University. Dr Payne prescribed that medicine up there for him. Do you think you know better than Dr Payne? What'll Dr Payne say when he comes tomorrow and smells seaweed boiling in the pot? Away with you, Frederika. Away with all that nonsense – that's the

Dark Ages. Bless you, Frederika. Call by, any time you're in the parish.'

Frederika went away under a salting of stars.

Jock was getting ready to fight with Tom of the Glebe, on the night of the Dounby Agricultural Show, when all the prize animals had gone back to their byres and stables and fields, and the fiddles were tuning up for the big dance in the Hall.

They were soon to be at fisticuffs because of Rose, the girl from the general merchant's.

Jock and Tom both claimed to be in love with her.

They were to fight in a quiet field, half a mile away from the village and the show-park. Only three or four friends were present. The friends had spent more than an hour trying to placate the rivals, pouring out words of oil and balm; to small avail.

It must have been a comical bout to witness, for both the fighters were more than half drunk with drink taken in the big whisky tent, and afterwards.

'You think,' said Tom, 'you can nod at any lass you like and she'll go to you. You're the important chap that can do anything, now you've signed on to go to America. Rose is *my* lass, she's been my lass since March, and you won't be getting her, mister!'

Jock lunged at Tom and hit him on the arm, and then, unable to check his forward impetus, he fell on his face in the wet grass. Then Tom was on him, and they eddied and rolled here and there like logs in a torrent.

The seconds hauled them to their feet. The shirts of the fighters were soaked with dew and mud and buttercup petals.

Tom, very red in the face now, swung a punch at Jock, who ducked, and Tom tripped over a tussock, whirled round once or twice, and ended up on his back, blinking at the first stars.

Jock should have taken advantage of this situation, but the violence of his efforts had caused the whisky to evaporate and he was ashamed that it should have come to this pass, between two friends.

Meantime Tom, his shirt spattered with dung and daiseis, had been hauled to his feet again.

There was a stir in a bush at the end of the field! Someone was watching them. (The policeman?)

Jock stepped forward with his hand outstretched to offer a truce, and Tom, thinking he was to be punched in the midriff, threw his fist into Jock's face. Blood rushed out, to add poppy petals and rose petals to the already vivid patterns on Jock's white festive shirt.

The bushes stirred, but it was too far away to see who was there, hidden and watching.

The mopping-up of blood sobered the fighters. They look thoroughly ashamed of themselves. But neither was prepared to apologise, not just yet.

'That's enough,' said Sammy Groat the fisherman. 'No more. Not one or the other of you could fight his way out of a paper bag, the state you're in. I declare this fight a draw.'

But Jock and Tom refused to shake hands. They had gone through too much effort and agony for peace to come so suddenly. Tomorrow perhaps . . .

Meantime, blood (having been initially staunched) poured from Jock's nose a second time, in a sudden gush, and the bystanders looked bewildered and a little afraid. What if Jock were to die on their hands: a gray drained corpse?

The bush stirred, and a figure came running through the dewheavy grass. It was Rose.

'Poor Jock,' said Rose, and kissed him, blood and all, and instructed them how to staunch a gushing nose. First, Sammy Groat's cold boat-house key was slid between Jock's shoulders.

Then Jock's head lay in her lap for a good quarter of an hour till the red well was finally sealed.

What happiness! – for a young man who hadn't behaved himself very well that particular day.

But it was Tom, two months later, that stood in the Manse, waiting for Rose the white bride to enter, to the summoning of Mrs Scad at the harmonium.

And Jock stood beside him, the best man, with the ring in his waist-coat pocket: nervously probing every now and then to make quite sure the ring was still there.

That was the week before he sailed on the emigrant ship to America.

Four

Night hung clusters of stars over Orkney. They westered. The banked-up forge of sunrise was in the east. The stars were cinders, soon. They vanished. The forge doors opened in the east. Earth's jewelry, the dew, flashed from innumerable grass-blades.

Selina's blackbird came down to the garden wall. It cocked its head. Would Selina's door never open? Its throat trembled, it sent up gushings of sound, a faltering fountain.

> *Cold cold cold dews!*
> *Sun soon!*
> *The stars were sharp as thorns.*
> *Old one, come with your bowl of oats, come soon.*
> *At your door, look, a small round bird-bowl, black throat,*
>   *offered, trembling.*
> *Summon me!*
> *The rose is older than yon star.*

Selina was late in opening the door that morning.

The blackbird hopped from stone to gooseberry bush.

At last it happened. Selina unlatched the door of Brett to let the morning in. The white cat, Charley, slipped out and trotted softly round the corner, remembering certain young hill rabbits.

The blackbird hopped on to the grass, scattering and shattering a hundred drops of dew
>   *Emerald, opal, diamond!*

The blackbird hopped on to the doorstep. Selina was inside, adding peat to the broken core that had lain a dull red on the hearth all night.

Something was far wrong in the house. Normally, Selina and the blackbird had words with each other, a spate of compliments, cajolery, and gossip. They exchanged news of air and earth. Then Selina would go to the bin for a piece of bannock, and sit down with it beside the table. She would break off a fragment. And then her blackbird would skip, wings half-opened, on to her knee, and begin its darting breakfast.

This had happened every morning for a month.

Something was seriously wrong.

Selina returned to the open door. She looked past the bird into the first flames of day. She didn't seem to see the bird. The bird waited patiently. It dipped past Selina into the house. It turned on the flagstone and hopped on to the box-bed. It put its bead-bright eye on the shut face in the bed; cocked its head; considered the shadow that lay there with crumbling cindery breath.

Selina came back in.

She put her forehead on the mantelpiece now, and stirred the nest of flames with a poker.

Offended, the blackbird hopped from bed to flagstone to doorstop to garden.

It would have to content itself with worms.

The blackbird gave one last look back from the rosebush.

There in the open door stood Selina with a stale bannock in her hand. She broke it quickly and threw the pieces among the grass without a word. Dew soaked into the fragments.

The blackbird eyed them. There was something far wrong this morning. Bread crumbs in Brett were for the fireside: a bowl at the fireside. Not here. From the garden it could pull as many cold worms as it wanted.

Selina dusted her hands and went indoors.

The blackbird tried a piece of dew-soaked bread. It was acceptable. It hopped from fragment to fragment. Yes, the bread was harder and older than usual. A shadow had been kneaded into it.

A mile away, the school bell rang.

The blackbird made of its throat once more a throbbing fountain. *O sweet – sweet morning – all's fresh, all's new and bright, honey-of-dew, this one morning, this one only good morning of summer – May it be well, may it go well with the whole round world – Marvellous morning – O joy – Let the bones go under the hill – The rose is older than yon star –*

Jock was standing with twenty older men from the parish, and a few inquisitive women, in the kale-yard of the croft of Brett. He was so nervous that this upper lip was dewed with light sweat.

Presently the auctioneer arrived for the sale by public roup of the croft of Brett.

'Who'll give me fifty pounds for this fine croft of Brett, with thirty acres arable and twenty-five acres hill and meadow?'

Jock raised a shaking hand.

'Fifty I'm bid,' cried the auctioneer. 'Any advance on fifty?'

James Donald Sinclair, of Smithers, whose many bounteous acres marched with the scant acres of Brett a certain distance up the hill, raised his hand gravely.

'Sixty-five,' chanted the auctioneer. 'Sixty-five I'm bid for this very desirable fertile croft. Come on now, you know it's worth three times the price. Do I see a hand?'

The hand belonged to a clerk from the lawyer's office in Kirkwall. He must be bidding for a client, perhaps one of the townsfolk who wanted a weekend cottage.

'Eighty,' cried the auctioneer. 'Are you all through? Surely not. Just look at this fine croft-house. Strong walls, flag-stone roof and floor. A but-and-ben, wind and watertight. The croft is in good heart. Who am I to tell you that? Just look around you. A Shetland-built boat goes with the croft, of course. That was in the advertisement in the *Orkney Herald.* How many thousands of haddocks and herring and lobsters has that boat drawn from the sea? – I wouldn't like to make a guess. Last August the heifer that won second prize at Dounby came from these fields. Now, men, I assure you, anything under a hundred pounds would be an insult to the good man who laboured hard all his days to make Brett the way it is. Just imagine, if he was alive today, old Cuthbert Tait, and heard your miserable offers, he would drive you off his land, every last man, with his stick.'

The farmers laughed. They liked to listen to the auctioneer when he was in full flight. Jock didn't laugh. The sweat was out on his forehead now. He wiped it with his large red hand-kerchief. Then he carefully folded the hankie and put it back in his pocket, and slowly raised his hand.

'Ninety-five,' cried the auctioneer. 'Ninety-five I'm bid. Now we're on the threshold of common sense. Ninety-five.'

This was Jock's last bid. If another hand was raised, he was out of the game; he was lost, he was sunk.

They were all looking at him. A few of the women were whispering. How on earth had Jock Voe laid his hands on £95? Hadn't he come home from the sea, penniless, at summer's end? And had gotten a poor-paid winter job labouring on the new road. And spent every last ha'penny in the pub on a Friday night.

If they but knew to what depths Jock had sunk in order to raise a hundred pounds! What humiliation! What things he had had to listen to before a bargain was struck!

He had gone, cap in hand, at the weekend, and knocked at the door of his uncle Wilfred who kept the general store down at the crossroads, and who had hoarded money all his life. Every penny was a prisoner, the old folk said concerning Wilfred Voe. Long ago, he had asked three or four women to marry him. What woman would put up with meanness like that? Now Wilfred had long resigned himself to die a bachelor. But, if anything, his appetite for pennies, shillings, half-crowns, and sovereigns increased, the closer the circle of his days narrowed towards darkness and the kirkyard stone.

'Jock,' said uncle Wilfred last Saturday night. 'Am I seeing things? Well, what an honour! When, I wonder, did you last darken this door? Well, come in, come in. But not for too long. Saturday night's my bath night.'

The kitchen was dark and foetid; Wilfred was too mean to employ a cleaning lady, far less a housekeeper. Cobwebs and old grease, and cat-smells.

'Now, Jock, sit down, Jock. I'm very pleased to see you.'

A kettle snorted and spat on top of the range: Wilfred's bathwater.

'And now, Jock, let's not beat about the bush, eh? The boys'll be missing thee up at the pub. The domino players, the draughts champions. A poor place that pub would be without you, Jock. It would never do if old Simonson the hotelier was deprived of Jock's custom. Without Jock, that seller of bad drink would have been in the poor-house years ago'

Jock was speechless. What could he say in the face of such bitter heart-felt talk? How could he ever make his plea?

'I generally have my bath at nine o'clock,' said uncle Wilfred. 'It's a quarter to nine now.'

'I'm to be married next month,' said Jock in hardly more than a whisper.

'Never!' cried Wilfred, in a seeming rapture. 'Oh Jock, you're trying to take the rise of me. Who's the lucky lass, eh? And what will she do for housekeeping money, when Jock gives it all away every weekend to Simonson the inn-keeper? And where, oh where on earth will you live, Jock? What door will you carry your bride through? Eh, answer me that. This is the richest piece of news I've heard in a month of Sundays.'

'The croft of Brett,' said Jock, 'is up for sale by public roup, next Wednesday at half past two.'

'I read that in the *Herald*, right enough,' said Wilfred. 'Poor Cuthbert was trampled by a horse, how long ago? – it must be four months if it's a day. You're not going to tell me, Jock – oh no, it can't be – you're not going to bid for Brett' . . .

'I would like to,' said Jock. 'Since I left the sea and the whaling, I've been wanting to settle down on a croft.'

'Well,' said his uncle, 'and how much do you think Brett 'll go for?'

'I heard,' said Jock, 'a hundred pounds mentioned.'

'Did you, Jock? Is that so? A hundred pounds – that's a small fortune. Not many hundred pounds lying idle in this parish. That's a tidy sum.'

'So I've come here tonight,' said Jock, 'to ask you for the loan of a hundred pounds.'

'Wait a minute, Jock. Wait a minute, till I sit down. I feel weak all of a sudden.'

In the silence Jock could hear the grandfather clock ticking time away solemnly in the corner.

He had been a fool to come.

'Jock, supposing I were to lend you one hundred pounds, can you offer me any security? something solid I could lay hands on if, for example, you defaulted in paying?'

Jock opened and closed his hands. 'Just my strength,' he said, 'and willingness to work hard for my wife and the children that'll come, no doubt.'

'That's no kind of security at all,' said Wilfred. 'Why, you might fall some night coming home from the pub and break your neck. Such things have been. Poor old Cuthbert Tait, he never knew he was going to be turned on and killed by a stallion that morning when he got out of his bed. Think again, Jock. That kettle's nearly boiled dry. It's going to be a late bath tonight, I can see that plainly.'

'I'm sorry to have troubled you,' Jock said, and got to his feet. 'I'll be going now.'

'Wait a minute, Jock – wait a minute,' cried uncle Wilfred and took him lightly by the elbow. 'Just sit down again for five minutes. Surely Mr Simonson and the boys in the pub can hold on for five minutes more.'

Wilfred went over and unlocked his desk. He lit a candle and frowned down on the contents. Finally he lifted something out, closed and re-locked the desk, and brought the little chinking canvas bag over to the table. He threw it on the table: richly it rang.

'In that bag,' said Wilfred, 'there are one hundred sovereigns exactly. Count them, count them – I give you leave to count them, once I've finished my say . . . Well now, a hundred-pound loan, and no security, apart from your strength and the purposefulness of your wife. By the way, you never told me the name of that lucky lass. She'll be kind of lonely at the weekends, of course, when you're drunk all the time up at Simonson's, but she must know what she's taking on. Everybody the length and breadth of Orkney knows about Jock and his carry-on. What is the name of this fearless lass?'

'Selina Black,' whispered Jock.

'Selina!' exclaimed his uncle, and got to his feet. 'Not Selina Black from Dottersha in Stromness parish!'

'Selina Black,' said Jock.

'Well now,' said Wilfred, 'she's a very fine lass, Selina, I'm sure she could have married the schoolteacher or the minister, if she put her mind to it. She could. Instead she's going to marry a poor man who drinks a lot. There are heroines left in the world still.'

'I've stood a lot of insults and kicks-in-the-teeth tonight,' said Jock. 'A hundred pounds is not worth humiliation like that. It shows how desperately I want to buy the croft and settle down in it with Selina. I will borrow the hundred pounds from you at a fair rate of interest.'

'But no security,' said Wilfred. 'Note that, no security. Only your brute strength. That, and the surpassing sweetness of a brave lass.'

'No solid security,' said Jock, rising to his feet. 'I'm sorry to have kept you late from your bath.'

'One moment,' cried Wilfred. He lifted the little sack of sovereigns and urged it into Jock's hand. Jock opened his hand and the hoard chimed on the stone floor.

'Keep your money,' said Jock.

Wilfred laughed. He bent down and lifted the treasure. 'I wouldn't give a hundred pounds to *you*, Jock, supposing you were the last man on earth. I might go to my grave a hundred pounds poorer, but never on account of you, Jock. Tell Selina, that good lass, that the money is for *her*. A loan. We will discuss a fair rate of interest – say ten pounds a year – when I come up to Brett the day after the wedding. For I won't be coming to the wedding – I don't want a bid. I've given enough wedding presents in my time.'

'I'll tell her what you said,' said Jock. This time he accepted the little heavy bag.

'Now, Jock,' said Wilfred. 'I'm putting you on your honour. If one of those hundred sovereigns rings on the counter up at

Simonson's, that's the end. There will be no more dealings with you, on my part.'

'Won't I have to sign a document, or a deed of some sort?' said Jock. 'To make it legal, you know.'

'Yes, Jock, if the loan was for you, I'd have a paper drawn up and signed and witnessed in the lawyer's office in Kirkwall, with red seals and ribbons hanging from it. With Selina it's different. Her word of mouth is good enough. I think ten pounds a year should do . . . Begone. Get away with you. You've ruined my bath tonight. You couldn't wash a mouse in the dregs of this kettle.' (The kettle was putting forth last scalding gasps.)

'I'll tell Selina what you said, and what your terms are,' said Jock, standing in the doorway.

'I hope Brett doesn't go for more than a hundred,' said Wilfred. 'For if it does, Jock, you'll have to build a little hovel for yourselves. Many a bridegroom and bride's had to do that in the past.'

'Goodnight,' said Jock, and closed the door behind him.

Wilfred ran to the door and wrenched it open. 'If ever I hear that you're bad to Selina, I'll ruin you, you drunken waster that you are!'

'Ninety-five,' snapped the Kirkwall auctioneer. 'Ninety-five pounds I'm bid.'

Nothing happened for fully five seconds. Jock's heart was fluttering inside him like a bird in a cage.

'O surely,' said the auctioneer, 'you're not going to let this fine croft, in good heart, go for less than a hundred.'

Jock was at the back of the small crowd. Anxiously he raised his eyes and surveyed the crowd. Not a hand was raised. His heart began to utter a few bird notes inside him: then plummeted, for Sinclair the young farmer of Smithers had raised his hand.

'Thank you,' said the auctioneer. 'One hundred and ten pounds against you. And still it's cheap. If this croft was in Buchan or the Lothians, you'd pay a thousand for it – you would – I swear it.'

Jock was beaten. There was nothing else for it: he would have to go to sea again – maybe to the whaling – till he was an old man. And meantime Selina, waiting in one Hamnavoe room, would lose her dewiness, first wrinkles would come about her eyes and mouth, her chestnut hair would have a thread of gray, then five or six, then many.

Jock turned to go home.

Another hand must have been raised. The auctioneer cried triumphantly. 'One hundred and thirty.'

Jock turned, and saw that the lawyer's clerk from Kirkwall had his pale pen-grooved hand in the air.

Now it would be a fight to the finish between those two: the neighbouring farmer and the person (whoever it was) who was bidding anonymously through the lawyer.

The farmer, red in the face, raised his powerful fist cap-high.

'One hundred and forty-five,' chortled the auctioneer. 'Now you're talking. This is more like the thing.'

The last words were scarcely out when the lawyer's clerk raised a precise hand.

'One hundred and sixty.'

The farmer of Smithers was sweating too, though it was a rather cold afternoon. He scowled round at the man from the office. That a runt like that should be bidding for the stone and clay of Brett, against a man with the same earth as Brett grained into him, who drank the same burn water and shared the same sun and peat-bank from generations back!

It was rage against the arrogance and ruthlessness of bank money that made Sinclair of Smithers raise his fist, head-high; it trembled.

'Thank you,' purred the auctioneer. 'One hundred and seventy-five. I know the men hereabouts have plenty of gold and silver under their beds, locked away.'

'Stop your sarcasm,' said a sullen-looking young farmer. 'Get on with the business.'

The auctioneer turned his head and looked expectantly at the lawyer's clerk. The bidding farmer too looked at the anonymous bidder: who, after consulting his little notebook, raised two fingers.

'Two hundred,' cried the auctioneer. 'Two hundred pounds I'm bid' . . . His head swivelled round to see if the earth-dark hand was raised. No, it wasn't. The farmer James Donald Sinclair of Smithers had had enough. Both his hands were thrust deep in his pockets.

'Are you all through at two hundred pounds for the desirable croft of Brett? It's a bargain still' . . . The little man, his hammer raised, even looked at Jock, as if he might resume the game. Nothing doing. Jock gave him a bleak scowl. Down came the hammer. The game was over. 'Gone at two hundred pounds to Messers A L and W P Crockness, lawyers, Kirkwall.'

The farmers and the inquisitive women began to disperse. The farmer of Smithers ducked through the fence that divided Brett from Smithers: his face was like a thunder cloud. 'I'd have known where I was with you, at least, Voe,' he muttered.

The clucking women were disappointed. It was always better when somebody out of the parish carried off the bidding: then they could speak about him and his forebears for a full week, and wonder (whispering) where he got all that money from.

Yet it would be intriguing, too, to guess whom the solicitors in Kirkwall were bidding for. Some of them were impudent enough to go up and ask the clerk direct. But at that moment the lawyer's clerk was calling after Jock. 'Mr Voe – am I right, you're Mr Voe? – could you spare me a few minutes?'

'What does he want with the likes of Jock Voe?' a woman wondered.

And another: 'Fancy Voe bidding as high as a hundred pounds. Where did *he* get all that money from? A waster like him.'

They tried, the chorus of women, to overhear the conversation of clerk and waster. The more impudent of them cocked their hands to their ears. One even took three steps in their direction.

But the young man from the office had a discreet confessional voice. 'Mr Voe,' he was saying, 'I'm glad you're here. I was rather surprised to see you bidding at the start. What I have to tell you is this – Brett is yours.'

Jock could only shake his head.

'Yours, Mr Voe, lock, stock, and barrel.'

'I don't understand,' Jock stammered.

'We were instructed by a client to bid on your behalf. Not only to bid, but to outbid everyone. In short, to make quite sure that Brett went to you and you alone.'

'Who's behind all this?' said Jock, bewildered.

'I rather hoped you wouldn't ask me that. But since you ask, I'm instructed to tell you.'

He sifted through some papers. 'Your benefactor,' he whispered, 'is Mr Wilfred Voe, general merchant, of this parish.'

'Never!' shouted Jock. 'It's impossible!'

The women had gone in a flock. Hearing Jock's yell, they turned their faces; the most impudent among them turned her feet once more. The day might end with some drama after all. Maybe the waster was in trouble with the law?

'I assure you, it's quite true, Mr Voe. Congratulations. There will be a few papers to sign. Perhaps you could take the coach to Kirkwall sometime before the end of the week. I expect you know where the office is. Now I must be getting back. Yes, indeed, that's my pony and trap down there.'

Jock took Selina with him that same evening when they called at the general merchant's.

The door opened three inches. A meagre gray face looked out at them. 'Selina,' cried Wilfred, and took the inside chain off. 'Come in. Come in. I'm very pleased to see thee, Selina. You look very bonny tonight. Most welcome you are. Sit over there. That's the most comfortable chair. Well well, this is a surprise.'

'The day is full or surprises,' said Jock (who hadn't been invited to sit.) 'I'm sure you can clear up the mystery of the roup sale this afternoon.'

'Was there something wrong?' asked Wilfred.

'Nothing wrong. I bid on the croft till it went to nearly a hundred. After that, I couldn't follow them. It was knocked down at two hundred to a solicitor from Kirkwall.'

'Dear me,' said Wilfred, 'and what would solicitors be wanting with a croft, eh? Selina, are you all right? I'll put on the kettle for a cup of tea. The sight of you, Selina, has brightened my day . . . Two hundred pounds! Well well. Well well. Crofts are getting to be very dear'

'*You* bought the place,' said Jock. 'And the clerk told me afterwards, it was a gift to me.'

'To Selina more than to you, Mr Voe. I'm concerned that Selina, my dear friend, should have a decent start to her marriage . . . Selina, if there'd been a lass like you in this corner of Orkney when I was a young man in my strength, nothing would have stood in the way of me asking you to be Mistress Wilfred Voe.'

'If you're going to charge twenty pounds a year rent,' said Jock, 'I'm sorry – we can't pay it.'

'A gift!' cried Wilfred. 'Surely you know what a gift is. Nobody pays rent on a gift. Brett is a wedding present for you and Selina. Especially to Selina.'

'Thank you very much indeed,' said Jock, his eyes on the floor.

'Toots, man,' said Wilfred. 'You're the only relative I have left. When I die, all my money is going to the Deaf and Dumb Children. I'm giving you your share while I'm still alive. Or rather, I'm giving it to Selina and you, Selina being the major partner . . . Selina, see to it that he doesn't pour Brett down his throat. Keep his nose to the grindstone. There's a time to plough and a time to harvest. He didn't do much about that when his mother, my poor sister-in-law, was alive. See that he observes the seasons in their due courses.'

Selina got to her feet and kissed the sour wrinkled apple of his cheek.

'That kiss was worth more than two hundred pounds,' said Wilfred. 'More. Oh much more. I'm not really *giving* you anything at all. Fill his days with sweetness, Selina . . . See that his shadow never crosses the ale-house door. Keep him from masts and harpoons.'

Jock took the bag of soverigns out of his pocket and set it on the table.

'This wasn't needed after all,' said Jock.

Wilfred picked it up and laid it in Selina's lap.

'This is yours, Selina,' he said. 'You'll need to buy a cow, won't you, and a few sheep, and maybe a pig for the stye. And hens, Selina. I can see you among the hens already. Selina, you'll need a table and chairs, and two china dogs for the mantelpiece. There won't be that much left of the hundred by the time you get Brett well-stocked. I'm giving it to you, Selina, to make quite sure it doesn't go to Simonson the publican . . . Wait, wait.'

He went to the cupboard and took out a dark bottle and three dusty glasses. 'We must drink to Brett, and the generations to come.'

The glasses, held high, trembling with brandy, touched and rang.

'Come and see me any time you like, Selina,' said Wilfred. 'You'll always be welcome. You, Jock, if we meet in the village, I suppose we could nod to each other. But I have nothing more to say to you. We have no other business with each other. Never again, you and me, Jock. If you're bad to Selina I'll come to hear about it, never fear, and I'll take steps to ruin you, man. I have the means . . . Oh, this brandy, it's strong! I've never tasted brandy for twenty years and more . . . Selina, will you be married in white? I don't want an invitation to the wedding – all that drunken dancing! Goodnight, now. Take his arm past Simonson's hotel, Selina. I hope I haven't stoked up any drunken fires inside him with that brandy.'

Jock and Selina stood at the window of Brett, looking in at the bare cold interior.

They did not as yet have the key.

On the road below, three shawled women stood, watching them.

Five

Selina, going to answer a small knock at the door, saw two standing women through the window. Matilda was on the door-step, brazen-faced as ever. Could that tiny butterfly knock have issued from such enormous fists? Down at the kailyard wall stood Sal and Liz. They had their backs turned, they were looking out over the Sound. But, momently, one or other turned her face.

If her fist was delicate, Matilda's mouth was like a trumpet: 'Oh, the poor man, poor Jock! . . . I heard he was very low . . . I doubt, he'll not get over it this time. Nobody lives for ever . . . You poor soul, what'll you do soon, with no breadwinner? . . . Waithe the postman told me. 'Jock's taking gulps of air, the last leapings of the candle.' So Waithe said . . . Now, Selina, you're looking that tired! . . . If ever you need help with him, living or passed on, send word to me, now don't forget . . . Sal and Liz, they're anxious to help, too . . . A great pity, a terrible business . . . it comes to us all.'

'I wouldn't send for you, woman,' said Selina, 'if you were the last person on earth. What do you mean coming here with your brazen tongue! . . . Get away with you, woman. You've disturbed the whole parish. Just look. Turn round and look.'

Indeed the four cows leaning over the fence had, half-way through Matildas lamentation, turned away and gone galloping to the far end of the field. And the blackbird in the window-ledge, come for its crumbs, had shirred its wings and soared into the gooseberry bush, and sat furled and hidden. And the cat had come out of the house and flicked round the corner quick as a tongue. A dog had set up its barking in the next farm.

Sal turned, Liz still looked out over the Sound. Sal was smiling.

Jock Voe of Brett was at the peat-cutting in the month of May, with Selina and Tom Gregg of the Glebe and Tom's wife Rose, and Matilda of Briggs, and little Tessa from the Mill and half-a-dozen children from the other parish out beyond the loch.

Jock cut the peat with a long spade called a tuskar. He sliced through the turf and threw the heavy wet black sod among a scattering of earth-blocks. There the wind and sun would give them a first drying. Afterwards the multitudinous peats would be set up like little dolmens, three by three. Then they would be absolute prey to the blue wind and the yellow sun, at summer's beginning . . . In August they would be as hard and dry as corks. Then the carting home, leading Nod the old horse through the heather ruts and the chunks of granite (relics of a giant-fight when the world was young) . . . On the slope of the hill beside Jock his team laboured to lift into the light ancient compacted shrubs and trees: their fires for next winter.

At noon the peat-cutters called a halt. They moved over to the big basket that Selina and Rose had prepard the evening before: cheese and oat cakes, bannocks, rhubarb jam, two cold chickens, a flask of tea and half-a-dozen bottles of Selina's ale.

The children, who had run an hour since to the far side of the hill, must have smelt the food. Back they came, over the ridge, helter-skelter, chattering and swirling like a swarm of starlings. And they snatched pieces of bannock with rhubarb jam spread on top, and off again with them into the wind, skirling, licking fingers and cheeks. Then a single cry of anguish. The little girl from a farm beyond the loch must have dropped her bannock into the heather, or else that wild boy Sandy Weyland had swept it out of her hand in passing. The bereaved one was quickly comforted by the lass from the Mill. Tessa lifted the jammy bannock out of a patch of scree, wiped a spider and some dust from it and said 'Spiders are lucky, Alice. It'll taste all the better now. Come.' Alice took Tessa's hand and away they rode on the mane of the wind, at times blown backwards and sideways, to catch up with the others . . . Sandy Weyland had sneaked off to play by himself. Soon only the children's voices could be heard, on the far fertile side of the hill.

The peat-cutters had finished their meal. 'Why is it,' said Jock, 'ale never tastes so good at home as it does on this hill? Not even on a winter night late when there's snow outside.'

They laboured all afternoon to give the buried compacted forest back to the sun and wind.

Perhaps the rhythms of the men were not so fluent as in the morning. The ale had put a languor on the arms and shoulders of Tom and Jock. Towards four o'clock they could have lain down and slept among the heather: but the work had to be finished by sunset: and, besides, they didn't want the women's winter-tauntings. 'We near as nothing never had a fire this January at all! The poor things of peat-cutters, they stretched them out half-seas-across on the hill and you never heard such snorings' . . .

Jock sank in his tuskar. What was this, a sudden white curve in the vertical thrust of his cutting? He eased the earth from the whiteness with his tuskar. It was a long thin bone. He eased away more peat: another thin bone, at the end of which was a hand, a small articulated cluster of bones. More scrapings – a rib cage, a thigh bone – and there crowning the column of the vertibrae, and fallen slightly apart, a small skull.

The women, eager to finish the peat-lifting, were annoyed at Jock's summons. They found Jock and Tom examining what was left of a crude clay jar. And 'Look!' cried Rose. A small hoard of flint arrow-heads had been buried at the child's side.

They gaped at all that was left of one of the inhabitants of the parish of four or five thousand years ago.

'A young lord, or a maiden,' said Jock. 'If it had been the likes of me or you, Tom, they wouldn't have buried us with such ceremony. See, he had his arrows to hunt with in the other world, and a jar of something – milk, maybe, or corn or honey for the journey between here and there. It's a small skeleton. I think the pampered creature must have died at the age of ten, or twelve, or thereabouts.'

No more peats were cut that afternoon: though the sun had still an hour's westering in it.

They gathered their tuskars, jackets, and baskets and went down homewards along the sheep-tracks. As they went, they agreed that Tom would tell the teacher and the doctor. They would know what to do about the find. They would get in touch with somebody or other in Edinburgh: the appropriate authority.

Selina and Jock ate their supper at the scrubbed table beside the window. The sun set, in a glory of rose and gold, into the hidden Atlantic. Selina lit the paraffin lamp. They ate, silently, the left-overs from the mid-day meal; there was plenty and to spare. They were both heavy with a weight of work and achievement. It had been a great day's peat cutting.

Jock, putting out his hand for the ale-jug, was aware that someone else was in the room. In the shadows, over by the spinning-wheel, Jock saw a boy – and such a boy as had never been seen in the parish in Jock's minding. The young stranger wore such clothes as an Eskimo or a Laplander would wear. The boy was sorrowing about something: his thin dark face was streaked with tears.

Selina: she was nowhere to be seen. She must have gone out to the henhouse for breakfast eggs . . . The stranger was afraid; there was no doubt about that. He was lost; he had been taken from his home (wherever that was) to an alien place. How could he live without his arrows and his jar of sustenance?

He looked once, timidly, at the burning wick of the lamp; then at the other flames on the hearth. How could the free rooted bird of fire be imprisoned in such cages?

Looking at the boy, Jock felt such an infusion of tenderness and longing as he had not known before: not even on the day Selina had promised to marry him.

Jock gestured: the boy should come and sit down at the table. The boy shook his head, gravely. He had been wrenched out of his own time and thrown into the time of those impious strangers who had made him their prisoner. To eat with them, or to have any communication with them, would be Death – bones scattered, jar broken, arrows flightless forever.

And where was Selina? Selina would be kind to him (never having had, alas, a child of her own.) Jock broke an oatcake on a plate, with butter and a wedge of cheese. He offered the plate to the boy.

The boy shook his head.

There was a great crash, then a bubbling and a squelching!

Selina was at the far end of the table. 'There, you fool, why aren't you eating your supper? You've knocked the ale jug over with your elbow – a hundred pieces! – I'll never be able to mend that. Wake up!'

'It's that hill,' said Jock. 'There's a heaviness comes on a man after a day on that hill' . . .

The boy was not there.

When, an hour later, Selina was breathing softly on the pillow, Jock took the lantern out of the barn, and crossed his field and went up the dark hill, his feet splashed with light.

He gathered the bones together, as many as he could find. He buried the bones in the hill, and the jar and the arrowheads with them. 'Go in peace,' said Jock.

It turned out, Tom had fallen asleep too over his supper – a dark dreamless ocean, rudderless, with slack sails – and when he woke up he hadn't bothered to go and tell the teacher or the doctor . . . Did Jock agree with him, that it might be better to say nothing about the young stone-age hunter? For then all the parish folk, and a few from the town, would come up to the peat-hill at the weekend, gawping and poking about, and trampling their peats to a black mush. And poking their ignorant fingers in the eye sockets.

Jock nodded.

The hill should keep its dead. The ghost should be free on the wind with its winged arrows and jar of mead: to find, after long questing, the door of its last repose.

That weekend, Selina told Jock that there would be a child in the house in winter. There were signs.

Six

Children from the shore district of the parish were on their way to school, their school-bags on their shoulders: a knot of unseemly noise, ravelling and unravelling. One trailed behind, weeping.

'Stop snivelling, you little idiot, Fred,' cried Rosemary.

The tempo of the snivelling increased. Little Fred trailed further behind. His face that had been new washed half-an-hour since, was all slobbered and stained with grief.

Willie kicked every unrooted thing in the road, chiefly stones, but also an empty cigarette packet, a dead mouse, an empty cocoa tin. The cocoa tin made a dreadful noise, again and again: an insane bell.

Jim and Bertie were arguing about the football team to be selected for the game against the boys from the hill district on Saturday first.

'No no,' said Bertie, 'Frank's the man for centre-forward.'

'Frank!' cried Jim, 'I wouldn't have Frank playing in a team against the grannies. Dod's the man. Frank for first reserve.'

'Listen,' said Bert, 'if Frank's not chosen I'm not playing either. So there.'

'That's too bad,' said Jim. 'We'll just have to look for somebody else.'

They trudged on, side by side, little thunder clouds on each brow.

The sniveller had been left far behind. A loop in the road and he was lost to them.

The kicked cocoa tin, again! – it set their teeth on edge.

'Look,' cried Rosemary, pointing to a cloud. 'A kestrel!'

The bird swung, stepping higher, and on up the blue spiral, and up and about, and paused on a topmost stair.

'That isn't a kestrel,' said Mark, who was best in the whole school at Nature Study, 'it's a hen harrier.'

'A kestrel,' said Rosemary quietly. 'I'm saying it's a kestrel. Are you calling me a liar?'

'I'm not calling you anything,' said Mark. 'That bird up there is a hen harrier.'

'A kestrel,' said Rosemary very quietly. 'A kestrel, Mark, say it. Say, a kestrel.'

'Who's the captain of the team, anyway?' said Jim to Bertie.

'You are,' said Bertie, 'and I'm vice-captain.'

'The captain always has the last word,' said Jim. 'The captain's decision is final.'

A very demure little girl, Kirstie, walked by herself, somewhat behind the others. There wasn't a speck of dirt on her anywhere, face or hands or clothes. Her flesh glowed pink and white. She seemed like a Chinese doll new out of its box. She walked along, saying nothing. Her eyes were fixed on the dusty road that daisies and dandelions from the ditch were trying to invade, an immense host crouched and waiting. The dust and the stones held them back.

Clatter – clang – clatter. The hob-nailed boot of Willie lashed out at the tin again. From a perfect cylinder Willie had kicked it into buckled shapelessness.

Thirty yards behind, little Fred followed, dabbing his face in the torn sleeve of his jersey. 'What I'm going to do is, I'm going to tell Miss Graham,' muttered Fred, between sobs, to himself.

They passed a woman standing on the roadside: Liz Aikerness. Liz stood looking up at the croft of Brett. She seemed not to see the scholars as they trooped past, though one or two of them muttered, 'Ay, Liz.'

On they trailed, towards the village and the school half-a-mile away.

'Good morning, Mrs Aikerness,' whispered Kirstie, her lips barely moving.

Rosemary suddenly seized Mark by the arm and twisted it round behind him till he cried out. 'What's the name of that bird up there?' asked Rosemary.

'A hen harrier,' cried Mark. 'Oh, you're hurting me!'

Rosemary gave the arm another twist. 'The bird,' she muttered darkly. 'Give me the name of the bird.'

Mark cried in anguish. 'You're breaking my arm! Please, Rosemary!'

'The bird,' said Rosemary. 'I want the name of the bird.'

Torturer and tortured had come to an unquiet halt in the centre of the road.

The bird in question had vanished out of that airt of sky. Either it had dropped like a stone on a vole or a starling or a field-mouse, and was gorging its fill in the marsh; or it had swung off to seek better hunting on the hill.

Mark cried out again.

'All right,' said Bertie to Jim. 'Have your way. But I won't be playing on Saturday, and if I don't play Sammy and Alan and Roger and Sigurd don't play either. I'm the vice-captain – I have a say, too. What will you do without Alan in the goal, eh?'

'That's traitor's talk,' said Jim.

The kicked tin went before them, an affront to delicate ears. Kirstie's face winced as the cocoa tin went clanging from stone to rut. Then the tin sighed: it had left the road, it had landed in the teeming grass of the ditch.

Fred, far behind now, had stopped weeping. His face had a white resolute look: he would lay his case before Miss Graham. Miss Graham would have something to say to that Rosemary Spence: not for the first time.

'It's a kestrel,' screamed Mark, on furthest ecstasy on the rack. 'It's a kestrel! Oh please, Rosemary!'

They turned, raggedly, a corner. The village was right below them, and the Sound and the hills of Selskay. Sal Norn was milking her cow Dapple in the middle of the field. But she seemed not to be intent on her work, for she was looking at a certain croft high on the hill. Milk zipped and sang into her bucket. Sal went on looking up at Brett croft.

'Remember who's boss in this gang,' said Rosemary. 'Never forget it for one second. What I say goes in this gang.'

Between the captain and the vice-captain of Shoreside Wanderers, a silence seethed. On they walked together.

Willie had lost interest in the tin. He kicked random stones. Every time he kicked the school-bag thwacked on his back. Sometimes a star lived and expired between the tackets of Willie's boot and a stone. Willie decided he would be a Red Indian. 'Yaroo!' he yodelled. 'Yaree. Yaroo.' The hill gave back the echo. Willie pranced in a slow circle, knees high, as if he had feathers in his hair and mocassins on his feet. Yaroo! His hobnailed boot struck a little fleeting galaxy from a stone. Yaree! It was a hideous noise to hear. Even little Kirstie pursed her lips; on her forehead two little vertical furrows momently appeared.

'All right,' said Jim to Bertie. 'Frank can be in the team. But not centre-forward. Left-half. I'll put Frank down for left-half. Sammy must be centre-forward. It's Sammy that scores all our goals. You can't deny that.'

'I agree to Sammy as centre-forward,' said Bertie. 'So, what was all the fuss about?'

Jim and Bertie put arms about each other's shoulders, and walked on, a bit awkwardly, linked together.

Yaroo. Yaree.

'What does teacher's little pet have to say for herself today?' said Rosemary, sidling up to Kirstie. 'Daddy's joy. Teacher's little apple of an eye. Kirstie, answer Rosemary when she speaks to you.'

Kirstie, walking on the grass verge to keep the dust from the gleam on her patent-leather shoes, said nothing.

Fred, trailing far behind, had the white martyr look on him, increasingly.

They could see now the hill children, a score or more, coming helter-skelter down the steep road to the village and the school. 'Yaroo!' one of them answered Willie from half-a-mile away: the cry coming pure and thin. 'Yaroo!'

At the crossroads, Audrey from the Mill joined them. Willie was still at his mouth-din, taking ugly echoes out of the quarry.

'Be quiet!' said Audrey urgently. 'Jock Voe is very ill. Are you so stupid you don't know that? In Brett, up there.'

There indeed it was, the croft, fifty yards up on the side of the hill, silent, its door open to the mild morning air. For two mornings past it had been the most important house in the parish.

Willie looked solemn. They all looked solemn, turning small faces to the important house.

'There's no hope for him this time,' said Audrey with a little artificial sigh. 'He's going to die.'

Now they stood on the road, an untidy group. Willie from in front and Fred from behind joined the group. They looked up at the house where a man would die soon.

As they looked, Selina came to the door and threw oats from a plate to the hens. The brigstones at the door were a sudden tumult of white and red. The cock, a stern overseer, watched his wives scrabbling and clucking, rising and dipping, all about Selina.

'The hens should be quiet,' said Jim. 'It isn't seemly to make a noise like that!'

'Life must go on all the same,' said Bertie piously.

Jim and Bertie were still shackled to each other, Siamese twins.

'My grandad died last winter,' said Willie, and kicked the head off a dandelion.

From the playground a quarter of a mile away, they could hear the mingled battle-cries and lyrics of twenty or thirty children, borne on the gentle summer wind.

They stood in the middle of the road, faces upturned to Brett, in a wondering contemplation.

As they stood, they became aware of a woman standing near the gable end of Brett, unmoving. Matilda's finger was up at her lips, compelling the whole parish to silence.

And then – oh, horrors! – the school bell rang. They could see Miss Graham at the gate of the playground, agitating the bell. The bronze mouth cried and sang. It summoned them to the mysteries of multiplication and history, parsing and poetry.

The boys were up and off before the last pealings of the bell had died into echoes: Jim, Bertie, Fred, Willie, Mark. Helter-skelter they ran, their bags thumping their backs, on and on till the smithy hid them from view.

'This is the first time I've ever been late for school.' said Kirstie demurely, and did not hasten her steps as on she went demurely.

'What'll teacher say to her little milksop today?' said Rosemary. 'Will little milksop cry when teacher gives her the strap for being late?'

Rosemary lifted a foot to run. The last bronze echo was still in the air.

As Rosemary began to run, Kirstie stuck out her foot. Rosemary went spread-eagled into the ditch. Her bag spilled its books. Rosemary shrieked. Her hand was in a clump of nettles.

Quietly Kirstie resumed her journey. She would enter the classroom with not a bronze-gold ringlet displaced. On Kirstie walked, at her usual pace, neither faster nor slower.

Rosemary picked herself up. Her books and jotters were scattered here and there in the grass. Rosemary gathered them up.

Then she set her face homeward, away from school, walking fairly fast. She was crying.

Jock sat at his desk, in the little subscription school, waiting for the word that would launch him into life.

He thought of his granda and his granda's boat *Mary Ellen*, and the ginger cat Nettle and the sea. Today he would be one of that company, for ever and ever.

An old man was sitting outside his tarred hut, eyeing his boat and the sea. It was a beautiful day in July. The Atlantic had ebbed for four hours, leaving a scatter of rockpools and swathes of seaweed. Along the ebb Silas the beachcomber went, probing for wrack.

The thin marmalade cat came out of the hut, licking milk-drops from her whiskers, and blinking in the sunlight. Then she washed her face with her paw. 'A fine morning', said Nettle and sat on the doorstep.

It was such a clear day, the old fisherman could see the mountains of Caithness and Sutherland: Morven and Ben Loyal and their sister summits, a pale dreamy jagged blue line beyond the Pentland Firth.

'Well,' said the old man to the cat, 'and what way are thu this day, Nettle?'

'All right,' said Nettle and yawned. 'I thought you might have gone to the lobsters.'

'We'll go when the tide's slack. Jock said to wait for him. When the tide's slack, I must go and haul the creels that are out there. There's a storm hatching in the west. I know it by my rheumatics. There's other signs too. I don't like it when you can see the mountains of Scotland. When the tide's slack, we must go and haul the creels. They'll be smashed to bits if they're left. I know it.'

The old man slitted his eyes against the sun and probed the horizon. He shook his head. 'I never trust weather like this,' he said. Jock's grandfather had lately taken to say a thing over and over, always in a slightly different way.

Nettle said, crouched on the stone step like a sphinx and looking self-satisfied, 'Fine mackerel we caught on Tuesday. The best I've tasted, fat and oily. Lobsters! – why do we bother with lobsters and partans? Haddocks, I like a good haddock now, either raw or simmered in milk, with a bit of butter.'

'Good money in the lobsters,' said the old man. 'I must catch as many of them blue jewels as I can, before winter. I won't be fishing this time next year. No, Nettle, I feel my age. Next summer, if I'm still alive. I'll be smoking my pipe on the step there beside you. No more boat. No more creels. For ever and ever.'

'What'll we live on?' said Nettle, yawning.

'I have a few shillings in a box under the bed. A sovereign or two.'

'I suppose you'll sell the *Mary Ellen*.'

'I will not sell the *Mary Ellen*. Would a man sell his wife?'

'Nor would a man let his wife lie and rot against a rock,' said Nettle.

'She won't rot. Jock's going to get the *Mary Ellen*, creels and everything. Of course he has a lot to learn. I'm teaching him, I'm giving him tastes of the sea, bit by bit. Slowly he's getting the salt in his blood.'

'I know Jock,' said Nettle. 'Maybe you'll have him for a year or two. Then, mark my words, Jock'll be looking for wider horizons.'

The tide was ebbing still. The sea shrank, laying bare immense tumults of weed, so slippery that now even Silas wouldn't trust himself out there (unless he had known for sure a crate of rum was to be found.) The sea withdrew slowly, with plangent defeated sounds.

Nettle closed her eyes. The old fisherman cut thin slivers of bogey-roll, and kneaded them between his palms. His empty pipe hung slack from toothless gums.

A fishing boat from Hamnavoe went out swiftly on the ebb, then another, then a third. The brown sails flapped idly. Oars were stowed. Only the man at the tiller was vigilant. Far out, the boats turned towards the cliffs of Hoy, and the men began to row. The old man, even with his one deaf ear, could hear the distant voices of the fishermen. 'They're going to set more creels – the idiots,' he said.

'Please,' said Nettle, opening one eye, 'I'm trying to sleep.'

'Sleep – there'll be plenty of time to sleep,' said the old man, puffing gray-blue hanks of smoke. 'Come January, plenty of time. All the time in the world. Nothing but sleep, sleep, sleep. The way it is now, though, I still have to keep an eye on the west. I must still be taking account of sea sounds, that's to say, the few sounds I can still hear. The sea is my old mother. A right Tartar she is! She tells me things – such as, that there'll be a westerly storm before morning . . . Did you hear the school bell, Nettle? My left ear's like a stone.'

Nettle said nothing. Nettle was sunk in a dream of mackerel and milk. Her tail flicked from time to time.

The old man licked his forefinger and held it up. His finger cooled from the west. He nodded. He puffed. He spat on a stone.

Silas must have found something horrid in the ebb. He straightened himself and began to curse and swear. Ever syllable came distinctly to the one good ear beside the pile of creels. The old fisherman shook his head between amusement and disapproval. He disliked coarse language, especially when he was on the brink of setting out in his boat.

There was another half-hour of ebb. Then the Atlantic, after a pause, would begin to herd cold new waters among the islands, glittering wave-flocks.

They would need to hurry, if they were going to catch the last of the ebb.

He got to his feet and looked impatiently in the direction of the hidden school.

The school bell rang. From half-a-mile distant, after the last reverberation came the jubilant voices of children, released from the prison-house into the sun of summer. Today began the long holiday, five weeks of bookless freedom, and five weeks to a child is a century, an aeon, eternity almost.

'So,' said the old fisherman and sat down on the step beside Nettle, and struck a new flame into his pipe.

It came sooner than he expected: a wild shout from the valley behind the beach. 'Granda! Granda! Oh you haven't gone out yet, that's fine!' . . . Down a buttress of rock a boy lowered himself; stumbling, leaping, gesticulating then over the gleaming cold sand. He didn't halt his wild career till he flung himself down on a fish-box, tousled and breathless.

'It's thee, Jock,' said the old man mildly.

'This is the day,' cried the boy. 'This is my very last day at that place! Isn't that grand? Never, never again, Latin and algebra. I'm a fisherman from now on, for ever and ever. The school of the fisherman starts today. Here I am – enrol me.'

'I don't know,' said the old man, 'that I want you. Look at me. Am I rich? Do I eat roast beef off a plate? No, porridge straight out of the pot with a horn spoon. I have one blanket and I lay my sea coat on top of the blanket on the coldest winter nights. I have one dark suit for Sabbath and the Lammas Market. Your mother, she's scraped and she's saved to keep you at that school for five years – or is it six? – so you could keep an account book of the rent you pay to the laird for Flinders and what you pay for seed and gear to the merchants in Hamnavoe. (Now it seems a crofter has to do sums and read a contract.) That poor woman. She has dreams for you beyond the croft. I've seen the wild gleam in her eye now and again, "My Johnny, that gem of a Jock, if he gets enough of the book-learning, he might go to the university in Aberdeen or in Edinburgh, for a lawyer or a doctor or a minister itself" . . . A foolish woman, good-hearted enough, but she takes notions in her head from time to time. What I'm saying, boy, is that you'll be a lot better off in the croft of Flinders than going out west, day in day out, in the *Mary Ellen*. The hill and the barn and the peat-bog, boy, they're always there, good times or ill. But that *Mary Ellen* is hardly stronger than an egg-shell – and look at the profit I have from her after fifty years! Go home and help your mother with Flinders. I don't want you.'

Jock had heard this homily before. He said, 'Now for Hoy and the creels. Are they ready? Oh, good. I'll carry them down to the boat. You finish your pipe.'

'The creels bide where they are,' said the old man, 'till after the storm.'

He pointed with his pipe to the glittering sea beyond the headland.

'What storm? What are you talking about? This is the best bonniest day that ever was.'

'By midnight,' said the old man, 'a man won't be able to stand on this noust against the gale. God help any small boat on the sea then, in all the tumult and spindrift! Creels'll be smashed like matchwood.'

'I can't picture it,' said Jock.

'It takes ten to twenty years to learn them things,' said the grandfather. 'Depending on a man's sea-wit. Some never learn.'

'So, then,' said Jock, 'what's to do?'

'We'll go out on the last of the ebb,' said his grandfather, 'and we'll haul the creels that are there. Let's hope there's three or four lobsters, so I can have my tobacco and dram at the weekend. But we'll set no new creels. Maybe on Monday.'

With a last defeated 'glug-glug' the ebb had reached its furthest stretch.

Silas must have found something good under the cliff now. They heard a victorious yell. He held something up to the sun. The light flashed from it. What could it be – a mirror? a bottle? a sea-streaming plank? Silas bent and stowed the piece of jetsam, whatever it was, in his sack.

Jock gestured impatiently at the *Mary Ellen* and the shining Sound. 'Isn't it time we were off?'

The old man knocked the wet dottle out of his pipe and rose to his feet.

In under five minutes the man and the boy were afloat and rowing south through the slack water.

Nettle slept on, on the doorstone.

Nettle opened one yellow eye. 'Of course there'll be a storm. I knew it by the lashing of my tail. A storm gets into my blood before that sea knows a thing about it. The old man, *he* knows the sea. After Christmas he isn't going to set a foot in the *Mary Ellen*. Nothing but a pipe and a yarn up at the pub. Then the kirkyard. A poor life I'll have then, not a sillock to bite on, unless I steal one here or there. That boy Jock, he won't be contented with the monotonies of fishing – not him. Oh, a year or two, I expect he'll stick at it for a year or two. Then out and away with him: Suez, Buenos Aires, Tokyo, Reykjavik . . . He has the restless look on him already. (I might be better off lodging with Silas – I'll see.) Then this hut will begin to rot, and he'll sell the *Mary Ellen* for a song . . . Ah well.'

Nettle went to sleep again and gave an occasional sweep of the tail.

Now the *Mary Ellen* was a dot southward, where there was a meeting of many waters: Hoy Sound, Pentland Firth, Atlantic Ocean. The dot fluttered – her sail was up – there must be a puff of wind out there.

One by one the other fishing boats returned. Fishermen called from boat to boat: voices thin and clear as bells. By the sound of it, they had hauled some heavy creels. One or two exaggerated their hauls – that is the way of fishermen.

A puff of sea wind ruffled Nettle's fur. The mid-sea changed from silk to sackcloth; and was soon blue flashing silk again.

The Atlantic, rilling and swirling up the beach now, swallowed one by one the lowest rockpools. It fell, idly, among the stones and weed and shells and wrack, over and over.

The Sound was empty of sails.

Smoke rose straight up from the chimney of Silas's hut. Silas was burning driftwood. Simon was about to put on a pot of mussels for his dinner. The plume of smoke shredded out and blew smells of burning salt and tar along the foreshore.

Nettle opened one golden eye. Her tail lashed. She stirred and stood up. She made her back arch; her legs were four rigid pillars. She dug her claws into the wood of the bench savagely, twice. Her fur bristled. Then she flowed in at the door of the old man's shed.

'Here comes the gale,' said Nettle. 'He was a fool to wait for that boy.'

The sea was a darker blue. The advancing waves fell more urgently against the stones, and into the rockpools, and caught up thick tresses of seaweed in the onset. The sea began to make perilous drenching noises, near and far, all along the western coast.

Silas, opening cooked mussels at his table, heard with joy the first prowlings of a gale from the west.

Seven

In the late afternoon Dr Payne arrived from Hamnavoe in his horse-drawn gig.

He opened the door of Brett without knocking. 'The man from the store in the village,' he said. 'He brought me word. Are you all right yourself, woman? You look done in. I've told you a dozen times you should have some woman in to help you.'

'He won't have anybody but me,' said Selina.

'Is he worse? What's been happening, eh, since I was here on Tuesday? Do you notice a change?'

'He's been digging gold in California all morning,' said Selina. 'Gold and horses and playing cards. He speaks a lot about some woman from Argentina. I'm getting to know things about Jock this last week I never knew before. Drink – he's put an ocean of drink down his throat in his time. So it seems. Him that would hardly touch the stuff since we came to Brett – well, maybe a glass at New Year or the Dounby Show. And sometimes he goes after whales for an hour at a time.'

'He's quiet enough now,' said Dr Payne.

'He speaks to his son a lot,' said Selina.

'A son?' said Dr Payne. 'I never knew there was a son.'

'Robert,' said Selina. 'He went to Australia twenty years ago, it must be. Worked on a farm. He hasn't written for twelve years and more. A fine son! He's alive all right. Has a farm of his own and a wife and bairns. In Tasmania. Sandy Traill saw

him, the summer before last. Robert stopped writing a while
ago.'

Dr Payne stepped over to the bed and looked down at Jock.
He tilted his ear for a flutter of breath or a heart tremble. His
fingers sought Jock's cold wrist.

'He'll be quiet for all time now.' he said. 'Jock's by with it.
You've lost your man, woman.'

'I know,' said Selina. 'Thank you for coming.'

On his way back to the gig. Dr Payne passed three women that
lingered at the gate between the flower-garden and the kale-
and-rhubarb patch: Matilda and Sal and Liz.

They waited till Dr Payne's gig disappeared round the bend
of the road.

Then slowly, with serious half-smiling faces, they went up
to the door of Brett.

Jock and Pierre the Frenchman had panned for a week and
they had taken from the torrent not a grain of gold. They left
their paraphernalia with the preacher and hired horses from
the saloon. The wooden town that had grown suddenly five
years ago was withering as quickly. They rode to the seaport
for the weekend. Ships of different nationalities in the harbour: a dozen or more. They got twenty dollars for the pin-
head nuggets in their poke from the broker, after the tedious
business of weighing, assaying, etc.

Now they were sitting at a small table in a saloon near the
harbour front. Jock and Pierre pledged each other in glasses of
some kind of poteen. The liquor was clear but it scalded the
throat. They had not been in this saloon before.

Jock had got to know about half a hundred French words
and Pierre roughly the same number of English words. They
managed quite well on that.

The landlord – a very jovial man – came over to them with a half-filled bottle of poteen. 'I didn't get a chance to speak to you lads, for the crush at the bar,' he said. 'Good lads, all of them. Oh, they have a sing-song now and then near closing time, and some might come to fisticuffs. But fine lads, all of them. I haven't seen your faces before. Did you strike a good vein in the mountain, eh?'

Jock and Pierre shook their heads and smiled.

'A hard life, lads. That gold's all worked out, long since. Would you not like it better sailing the seas? This is a sailors' saloon mostly. Well, you can tell that to look at them. All them fine lads, they have strong salt in their veins. Well now, lads, I'm going to give you a drink on the house, to make you welcome.'

He poured the gray spirit till their glasses were lipping full.

So a piece of the afternoon passed.

'The man's right – why do we bother with gold?' said Jock. 'The gold's played out. We came too late.'

Pierre smiled. 'With gold, beautiful girl, beautiful house, beautiful child. Life is good then. No?'

'King Solomon had to die and leave it at last,' said Jock. 'And how long after that did Sheba wear his diamonds and opals and emeralds?'

'We have laughed,' said Pierre. 'Hard work, yes, for little. But we have laughed very much! I think this is so, laughter is better than gold.'

Sailors came and went in the saloon.

Pierre agreed with Jock that they should pan higher up the stream in the coming week. It was there, higher up, that Andrzej the Pole had gotten to be as rich as a prince ten years back.

The drink was strong, but instead of stoking merry fires in them, it induced a slow torpor and heaviness.

'It's the sea air,' said Jock to Pierre. Pierre spread his hands, smiled, nodded.

Men came and went.

The landlord's hearty welcome rang out, again and again. 'An Irishman,' said Jock. Pierre went to the counter for more drink. 'Pretty girl,' he said to Jock when he returned with the waters of the house. A blonde barmaid was helping the landlord now.

Soon the landlord left the barmaid to attend to the drinkers. He himself was engaged in earnest whispers with a small dark man with a wisp of a black whisker on his lip. Sometimes the landlord would pause and look around him, as if someone might be eavesdropping. Once, Jock thought he was indicating the table where he and Pierre sat. And, sure enough, the gesture and whisper seemed to turn the brown beads of the stranger's eyes on them; before they returned to examine the diagrams that the landlord was sketching with his forefinger on the counter. Their mouths and ears were never more than six inches from each other. The landlord and the Indian-looking man were old acquaintances, obviously.

What a rough merry time the barmaid was having with the sailors and the wharf-men! How they winked at her, with what word-sallies they assaulted her ears, how they touched her on elbow or ear or chin! Sometimes she would laugh, sometimes she was quite curt with them. Once her mouth blazed sudden anger. But mostly she laughed. Her fingers rang the coins betwixt counter and till.

'Two glasses,' said Jock, and put a dollar on the counter. The barmaid's laughing cheeks grew grave; she flashed a look at the landlord (or so it seemed to Jock) and the landlord looked at her and nodded. She filled two glasses from a smaller bottle set far back on the shelf: the liquor trembling in the glasses as gray as sleet. She didn't look at Jock as she put his change on the counter.

Pierre was drowsy when Jock brought the two glasses back to the table.

'Mange,' he said, 'faut manger.'

'We'll drink this,' said Jock. 'Then we'll look for a steak-house. And we'd better find some place to sleep before it gets too dark.'

A fight broke out in the far corner of the saloon, a Swede and a Lascar. Then was seen what an efficient landlord he was. He vaulted the counter, he grabbed the fighters by their scruffs, and he ran them out howling like dogs, into the dark lane that led down to the waterfront, the masts and ware-houses.

The landlord came back dusting his hands, chuckling like a boy. Jock was impressed; the Swede had been broad and solid, fifteen or sixteen stones.

The little man, the landlord's confidant, had slipped out. Now the landlord and barmaid served drinks and rattled coins together, busily. The drinking men were not so teasing and gallant to the barmaid now that the landlord ruled behind the counter. A wink or a grin – that was all they felt inclined to risk now. The barmaid never raised her eyes above the patrons' hands.

Pierre tilted his head back and emptied his glass at one go.

'Next week,' he said, smiling at Jock, 'we strike rich. No trouble . . .' When Pierre got to his feet, Jock could see how drunk he was. He swayed, he had to hold on to the table. 'Come back soon,' Pierre said, his mouth slack. Off he staggered towards the jakes that was in the lane outside, holding on to a table here and there as he went.

The landlord followed Pierre with his eyes all the way out. In the doorway, Pierre lurched against a Baltic skipper, but the man gave him a friendly pat and smile, and turned him in the true direction.

Jock sipped his drink. His hand fumbled, putting the glass down; the glass rocked and steadied; and then he knew he was almost as drunk as Pierre.

The sea air, outside, might sober them. Jock very much hoped so. No steak-house, no lodging-house, would be willing to have two so obviously incapable men.

Jock shook his head violently. The bar spun round and round. When it stilled, he saw that the barmaid was looking at him, with slow shakings of her head. The landlord was eyeing him speculatively. And the little man, the landlord's confidant, had returned to his place. He was looking at Jock, too, and nodding his head. Jock looked at them, one after the other, blankly. The faces merged, blurred, fell apart again. When Jock had them in some kind of focus, they were engaged on other business. The landlord's forefinger was making diagrams on the counter once more.

Why had Pierre not returned?

The two hired horses – where had they left the horses? Pierre knew. Pierre had led them into the ostler's yard, the time that Jock was still bargaining with the broker. Jock vaguely remembered that he and Pierre intended to see to the horses' welfare after they had eaten. Jock took another sip.

He was aware of a crude scent, a woman's musk, close to his nostrils. 'Don't drink any more of that,' the barmaid urged him in a whisper. 'No more. Leave it. Get out as fast as you can.'

'Where's Pierre?' he mumbled to her.

She shook her head, and turned and went back to collecting glasses at the tables. Jock, looking up, saw to his surprise that the tables were nearly deserted. A few last patrons were crowding out through the door. The landlord stood at the side of the door like a shepherd, laughing, nodding.

Still there was no sign of Pierre.

Jock heaved himself upright, was overshadowed, was thrust down into his seat again by powerful hands. The landlord was looking down at him, his face all merry solicitude. At his back stood the little dark man, the landlord's friend; who stepped forward abruptly and felt Jock's shoulders and eased Jock's jaw open and looked at his teeth and down his throat.

'This one will do well enough,' he said. 'In good condition. Well, good enough, fifty dollars. The Frenchie, on the slight side, might not stand up to it. Thirty, thirty-five dollars for the Frenchie.'

'Must go,' said Jock. 'Must find Pierre. Horses. A bed for the night.'

'Your friend, he's being well looked after,' said the landlord. 'A bed. Don't worry about that. There's a wide bed and a deep sleep for you this night.'

There was a kind of paralysis in Jock's legs and arms. Even his mouth was stiff.

'You haven't downed your fine drink,' said the landlord. 'There's the loveliest poppies in it were ever crushed. Finish it, my friend.' He in his turn prised Jock's mouth wide, and he lifted the glass and flung what remained of the gray stuff down Jock's throat.

The last thing Jock remembered, the bronze-haired bar-maid was collecting empty glasses from the empty table where he and Pierre had sat.

There were only the four of them in the saloon.

The black wave gathered from the pit of his stomach, it seemed, and rose into his throat and head, and, breaking, drowned all his senses.

Jock came to himself in a sailing-ship. He was aware first of the pulse and wash of the sea. He was lying between-decks; he had been gathered into a voyage, he didn't know how or where. As for his body, it seemed as if a wedge had been driven into his skull. He sat up and retched. Nothing came but a thread of acid, a brown juice. He groaned. His innards seemed to be made of foetid smouldering rags.

Bare feet pattered down from above. A pleasant voice said, 'So, come to yourself, have you, at last? Take it easy. No hurry. They won't put you to work before tomorrow. The skipper's a decent enough man. You'll be all right.'

'The horses,' said Jock. 'Must see to the horses. And Pierre – where's Pierre?'

'That was some "mickey finn" they passed you,' said the young seaman, and sat down companionably on a chest near Jock. 'You've been out for two days. Pierre? Your friend? I don't know anything about him, shipmate . . . I'll bring you a glass of water and an oat biscuit. Don't move.'

After Jock had stomached the oatcake and the mug of water, Larry (the Australian sailor) told him they were in the Pacific, out of San Francisco, Melbourne bound. After Melbourne, Calcutta, Cape Town, Santa Cruz, Brest, Glasgow. Cargo of clocks, oil barrels, steel girders.

Eight

He moved to the tryst, the boy from the ships, a man fated

Dottersha: the name of her farm. That one word the girl had given the night before, on the street between the Town Hall and Isbister's Inn. Then a surge and maul and thrust of whalers with bottles had swept them apart

He walked away from the harbour with its ship and the darkling Lammas horses, the negro with the hot iron, the flares, the blind fiddler

He lingered on the sheep-path that crosses the hill (Was this the way?)

The fiddle at the Fair was, now, a fading star

The hill began to wrap itself in a shawl of haar. Coldness touched his mouth

The hill with its stones and graves spoke

> *Beyond the breath and fleeting dust of her,*
> *never think, man, to find a jewel*
>   *Beyond the quick wild honey, think love to*
> *be a long winter*

Desire sang on a branch of his blood, 'The rose is older than yon star'

They sabbathed, shawl by shawl, the sisterhood of the hill: three soft shrunken mouths
   Farm-house and kirk and inn and smithy and boat-house –
lintels wither, the rooftree falls, the good folk are skulls among
stone withering pages. Turn back
   'New horsemen, other ships'

Water from the well, it falls between her fingers, returns to ocean
and clouds
   'Opal. Emerald. Diamond'

And the thousand-year saga of the islanders, it is sour breath,
stillness, a dead dream at the last
   'There's a jar buried somewhere, in this hill. The first poem is in it'

Sea dirges on the reef below, hidden. Hidden the sunset-drinking corn-drowned lark

Blind and silent, the lover drifted on the moor between two voices

            Ah, a house on the moor! –
            the ghost of a house!

            Over the lintel was carved
            HOUSE OF WOMEN
            Not a woman stirred, outside
            or in

            He knocked. No one answered.
            He pushed open the door.

It was dark and cold inside
the house

He opened a cupboard. In the
cupboard was a small clay
jar with markings on it

He tasted the stuff in the jar:
honey! His flesh glowed with lost
suns and blossoms. He sipped again

Now the window was black
as tar

He stopped. He discovered with
blind hands the shape of a bed.
He covered himself with coarse
weave

Sleep! He slept

The man woke. The window
was gray. He took down the jar
to taste more honey

The single jar stood on the shelf –
the shape of it had changed, and it
was of coarser clay

He opened it. It was crammed
with salt

(The man heard, somewhere in
the house, a small cry)

He went through the rooms
of the house in search of a
child. The house was empty still

He returned to the room with
the cupboard and jar. He said,
Young one, whoever you are, you
won't starve because of me –
There will be fish for the salting

He came to a room where
the hearth was cold and the
lamp empty

On a stone of one wall was
carved the shape of a fish

He looked at the rune so long
that it seemed to pass into him
and become part of him

In another room, hidden, a
girl was singing

The man said, Lost and
darkling creature, I have to
bring you oil and driftwood
always

The song guttered out. It
stopped. It faltered into
low cries of pain

The man wandered again
through the rooms of the house

He saw his reflection in a
pane. Furrows in the face,
a mesh of gray through his
black beard

A poor house, he said.
There should be a bowl on the
sill, daffodils or roses or
heather, to say what time of
year it is – yes – and to spill
some beauty into a bleak place.
This jar is all, it seems

He took the jar from the shelf.
An earth smell came out of it –
it was half full of flailed corn.
His hands that held the jar were
twisted with many summers of work and pain

Through the corridors of the
house a contented cry came. It
must (he thought) be a woman over
new loaves and ale, well pleased,
arms and face fire-flushed

Lost one in this house, he
said, *there will always be*
cornstalks – there is nothing
more I can do for myself or
for you

He scratched an ear-of-corn
on a stone beside the stone
with the carved fish

He lay down on the bed.
He was as weary as if he
had toiled, sunrise to
sunset, in a harvest field

He lay under a thick blanket:
green the warp, yellow the
weft

His dream was about the
one jar that flowed always
from shape to shape, and was
ripeness, keeping, care, sorrow,
delight, kiss of comfort. Then
in his dream the jar fell from
his weak hands and broke on the
stone floor

The man woke. He knew now
that he was old

A thin-spun silver trailed over
the blanket. His hands were like
shreds of net, or winter roots

Seven women of different
ages stood about his bed. They
all, from first to last, had the
same fleeting look: the lost
girl at the Lammas fair

One by one, beginning with
the youngest, they bent over
and kissed him

The mid-most woman smelt
of roses and sunlight. Her
mouth had the wild honey
taste

The oldest one dropped
tears on his face

Then the seven women
covered their faces and
went out of the room

He slept on into the starred
ebb of winter

He opened his eyes

A young man was standing
in the open door. He carried
a jar on his shoulder

The young man turned
once and greeted him – then
in the heart of that winter
he went out into the
harvest-hoarding sun

John Voe said, *That is
my son. He is carrying
away the dust of my
death*